THE LIFE AND SOUL OF THE PARTY

In a year of parties and celebrations, friends get together to have a good time ... Meet Melissa and Paul: Five years after they split up he's still looking for love in all the wrong places while she wants the one thing she can't have: Paul. Meet Chris and Vicky: They're so in tune they brush their teeth in time with each other. So what is Chris doing risking it all for a meaningless affair? Meet Cooper and Laura: He wants to settle down, she wants to take a grown-up gap year — but can their relationship really survive a year apart?

MIKE GAYLE

THE LIFE
AND SOUL
OF THE PARTY

Complete and Unabridged

CHARNWOOD
Leicester

Fir[st published in Great Britain in 2]008 by
Hodder & Stoughton

by [arrangement with Hodder & Stou]ghton
[A division of Hodder Headline]
London

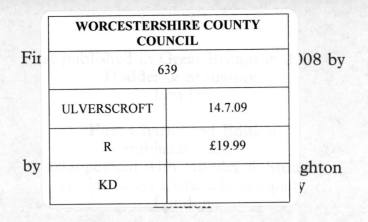

The moral right of the author has been asserted

All characters in this publication are fictitious and any resemblance to real persons, living or dead, is purely coincidental.

British Library CIP Data

Gayle, Mike.
  The life and soul of the party
  1. Couples- -Fiction.
  2. Parties- -Fiction.
  3. Large type books.
  I. Title
  823.9′2-dc22

  ISBN 978–1–84782–688–6

Published by
F. A. Thorpe (Publishing)
Anstey, Leicestershire

Set by Words & Graphics Ltd.
Anstey, Leicestershire
Printed and bound in Great Britain by
T. J. International Ltd., Padstow, Cornwall

This book is printed on acid-free paper

To the girls. For everything.

Melissa and Billy's House-Warming Party

September 2006

Melissa

It was a Friday just after midday, and Billy and I were lying in bed occupied in two very different activities. Billy had booked the day off work to help out with the arrangements for tonight's party and was sound asleep, while I, grateful to still be on the summer break from university, lay next to him frantically making a list of all the things we needed to do. So far the list covered everything from remembering to invite our new neighbours right through to a note about defrosting the mini chocolate éclairs. There were other things on the list too: about bottle openers and corkscrews; buying bags of ice and moving furniture; double-checking the master RSVP list and borrowing Vicky's curling tongs. But it was the first item that made me the happiest: 'Tell Billy I love him the minute he wakes up.'

Leaving Billy snoring gently into his pillow I made my way to the bathroom, took a shower and then got dressed for the day. Emerging half an hour later I was surprised to see that Billy was now awake and reading my copy of *Grazia*.

'Hello, gorgeous,' said Billy looking up from the magazine. He stretched and yawned. 'I haven't missed anything, have I?'

'And what would you do if you had?'

'Nothing much. It's not like it's worth crying over spilt milk is it?' He held out his arms towards me. 'So come on then, Ms Vickery, where's my morning kiss?'

I walked over to the bed and gave him a long, slow kiss, then picked up my notepad from the bedside table.

'I love you, you know,' I said tearing off the top two pages and handing them to Billy, 'look, it's even on my list.'

Billy looked down at the pages. 'That's not very flattering, is it? You need to remind yourself that you love me?'

'No, I have to remind myself to *tell* you. That's different.'

Billy speed-read the list. 'So what are the things that have got an asterisk next to them?'

'Those are the things that you're doing while I nip out to the supermarket.'

'Is it always going to be like this living with you? Will I wake up every day from a restful sleep only to be handed a twenty-item To Do List? What am I? Your personal slave?'

I nodded, straight faced. 'It was all there in the contract. Or didn't you bother reading the small print?'

Billy lunged towards me and we had this weird kind of play fight where Billy allowed me to pin him down before flipping me over, pinning me down in return and torturing me with the threat of breathing in my ear — the one thing he knows that I can't stand. Inevitably this sort of play fighting led to kissing but just as he attempted to relieve me of my T-shirt I came to my senses.

4

'Look,' I said, laughing as I slapped away his hands, 'the shopping for tonight isn't going to buy itself, you know,' and I was up and out of the bedroom before he'd even managed to get off the bed.

'I love you,' I called back up the stairs, as I opened the front door. 'Call me if you need anything.'

It was cold and raining — weather more suited to late November than mid-August. Sad that we wouldn't be able to make the most of the garden for the party, I put up my umbrella and set off.

The rain was easing by the time I reached the big Somerfield on Wilbraham Road. Putting my umbrella away I rummaged in my purse for a pound coin for the trolley. For some reason the coin wouldn't go into the slot properly and I was struggling to force it in when my phone rang from inside my bag. I assumed it would be Billy reminding me to add some essential item to my shopping list so I was sort of surprised when I saw Chris's name flashing up on the screen on my mobile.

Thinking that Chris was just calling to tease or torture me as was usual, before he could say a word I barked into the phone: 'You'd better not be calling to tell me you're not coming tonight!' He didn't laugh.

There was a long silence and then he said: 'Listen, Mel, I've got some really bad news.'

'What's happened? It's not Vicky, is it? Nothing's happened to the baby, has it?'

'It's nothing like that. It's Paul. I've just taken a call from Hannah's mum. Paul was on his way to the Midlands for a conference and was involved in a crash on the south-bound carriageway of the M6. Six people died and Paul was one of them. He's gone, Mel. I can't believe it but he's gone.'

As Chris broke down in tears on the other end of the line I felt myself buckling. My whole body started to shake as a throbbing ball of tightness began to grow inside my stomach. I tried to fight it, to keep it in, but then a noise I barely recognised as human left my lips. As I hit the floor I could feel blood seeping through the knees of my jeans. All around me there was commotion, panicked voices asking me if I was all right as complete strangers helped me to my feet. But no matter how hard I tried to shape the words, the only thing that came out of me was the noise. Over and over and over again as if it was never going to stop.

Nine Months Earlier

Ed and Sharon's New Year's Eve Party

December 2005

Melissa

Hi, my name's Melissa . . . Melissa Vickery and this . . . well, this is sort of my story . . . actually that's wrong. It's not 'my' story at all. It's our story. The story of me and my friends: Vicky and Chris; Chris's brother Cooper and his girlfriend Laura; Hannah (a girl who got sucked into the mess we called our lives through no fault of her own); Billy (a boy who got sucked into the mess we called our lives through no fault of *his* own) and of course it's the story of Paul, our friend who's no longer with us.

What else is this story about? Well, I think at its heart it's about love and getting older; it's about the year in our lives where we all made a lot of mistakes and the things we did to try to make them right again; more generally it's about that feeling . . . that feeling that you get sometimes when you feel as though you're completely and utterly lost — when you feel as if everyone around has the answer to the meaning of life, apart from you; it's about those times when we make the right decisions . . . and the times when we make the wrong ones too; it's about the people in our lives who, though they don't share our blood or bear our surnames, we think of as family; it's about those rare glorious moments that sometimes spring into your life out of nowhere that you wish could last for ever. It's about those moments of unbearable sadness ... those moments of heartbreaking clarity ... when you realise just how little time we all really have and how much you regret failing to take the opportunity to tell the people closest to you how much you love them and how much they mean to you. But mostly, this is a story about parties, about those special times when groups of friends, and friends of friends, get together for no other reason than to have a good time.

* * *

New Year's Eve 2005. It was just after six and I was in my bedroom in the flat that I shared with Creepy Susie, my flatmate/landlady. I call Susie 'creepy' because that's exactly what she was. Despite being ten years my senior, Susie had a creepily large collection of teddy bears and a creepy boyfriend called Steve, who somehow always managed to be lingering outside the bathroom whenever I emerged from the shower. On top of all that, I was pretty sure she snooped around my room when I was out which I'm pretty sure is the very definition of creepy.

The only reason I put up with Susie's creepiness was because, as a thirty-four-year-old mature student with no boyfriend and no money, I had no choice in the matter whatsoever. Anyway, having lived in enough nightmare houseshares in the fifteen years I'd been in

Manchester, to know that, as bad as Susie was, there were a lot of people out there who could be a good deal creepier.

* * *

My plan for the night ahead was simple: along with my friends Vicky, Chris, Cooper and Laura, I was heading to Ed and Sharon's house for their annual New Year's Eve party. As a rule I hated New Year's Eve and couldn't think of many things I'd rather do less than celebrate the arrival of yet another twelve months heralding more debt, more university assignments and a greater sense of being left behind by my peers, but I had no alternative. The only thing I hate more than New Year's Eve itself is the thought of spending it alone.

Looking down at the bed in front of me I tried to make my mind up about the various potential party outfits I had laid out there. There was a black floaty top and jeans; a green dress I'd bought last summer in the sales teamed with opaque black tights and boots; and a dark blue dress that I was ninety-nine per cent sure I could no longer fit into and green shoes with a bit of a heel. I tried to imagine myself in the clothes without having to go through the trial and effort of actually putting them on but the longer I pored over them, the more I came to realise that nothing I had chosen was quite right. All the clothes seemed just a little bit too showy for a house party . . . which might have been okay for Vicky and Laura — who could pull off 'showy' without looking ridiculous — but for me it would look for all the world as though I was someone trying too hard.

Returning the rejected clothes to the wardrobe, I noticed, lying crumpled across a pair of black pumps that I hadn't worn in years, a black long-sleeved top that had fallen off its hanger. I picked it up, slipped off my dressing-gown and tried it on. Although it was creased it just sort of felt right so I searched around some more and found a green knitted cardigan I'd bought in Oxfam a couple of months earlier; it went perfectly with the top and, inspired, I made a final trip to the wardrobe and rejected all manner of trousers and skirts and even trouser/skirt combos before closing the door in defeat. That was when I spotted the jeans that I'd been wearing all day. They were lying on the floor by the door. I straightened them out, slipped them on and checked myself in the mirror. I couldn't believe it. They looked great. The whole outfit was coming together very nicely indeed. Now all that I needed was the right footwear. After some moments of deep deliberation I opted for my Converse baseball boots which I eventually found by the radiator underneath the window swamped by a large mountain of ironing.

My baseball boots were almost as frayed and worn-out looking as my jeans. They were a faded brick-red colour and so heavily scuffed that I couldn't even wear them in the rain because the seam on the right one had a tear in it as I had discovered to my dismay one wet morning. Still,

12

grateful that it wasn't actually raining I slipped them on, tied the laces and surveyed my new outfit in the mirror one last time. It was depressing. I looked like a student — which wasn't exactly the look I was going for — but at least I didn't look as though I was trying too hard.

I tied my hair back in a ponytail and began searching around my room for my make-up bag which I eventually located underneath a stack of magazines by the side of my bed. Rooting around inside it for an eyeliner that hadn't spoiled, I tipped the whole lot out on to the bed in frustration and was about to scream when my mobile phone rang.

'Hey, babe, it's me.'

It was my friend Vicky.

'Hey, you,' I replied. 'How are things?'

'I've just put William to bed and told him Mum's babysitting him tonight and he went off on one as though I was leaving him in the care of the big bad wolf. I wouldn't mind but I know his gran will spoil him to death like she always does.'

Of all my friends here in Manchester I'd known Vicky the longest. We met during the first year that I'd spent studying Business and Economics at UMIST before I was kicked off my course for being completely and utterly hopeless. Vicky and I had both lived in the same halls of residence and I'd been drawn to her because, unlike most of the other eighteen year olds I met during freshers' week, Vicky didn't act like she was trying to cram several years' worth of repressed teenage rebellion into seven days of debauchery. In fact, she didn't act like she was eighteen at all. She seemed older and wiser somehow and even though she'd only been in the city for the same length of time as me she seemed to know the clubs and bars around Manchester like the back of her hand. So, rather than following the student hordes to grotty pubs and clubs playing the same music you heard everywhere in Manchester, thanks to Vicky we ended up in clubs in the depths of rough housing estates, warehouse parties in industrial estates on the edge of the city centre and the kinds of bars you had no chance of finding without being in the know. In short, back then, she had been an education in how to be cool. Fifteen years on, she was married to Chris, mother to William, my four-year-old godson, and hadn't set foot in a nightclub since the late nineties, but to me she would always be the girl who was too cool for school.

'Anyway,' continued Vicky. 'About the plans for tonight. Chris and Cooper earlier have decided we're all meeting at eight in The Old Oak.'

'Why eight? I thought that was when the party started?'

'It is,' she sighed, 'but you know what the boys are like. Apparently it's far too emasculating to arrive at a party at the time actually written on the invitation. Anyway, how does that sound?'

'Fine by me.' I paused to consider in what tone of voice best to ask the question on my lips, and decided to go with casual indifference. 'What about Paul and Hannah? Are they coming or not?'

'I don't know,' replied Vicky. 'Chris left a message on Paul's mobile but he hasn't got back to him yet. I'm sure he'll turn up though, don't you think? There's never been a New Year's Eve that we haven't all spent together. And somehow I can't imagine Hannah is going to change all that.' Vicky paused. 'You are okay about him coming, aren't you?'

'Of course I am,' I replied. 'I'll see you later, then, yeah?'

'Yeah,' replied Vicky. 'I'll see you later.'

Vicky

After I put the phone down I had a clear picture of Melissa sitting alone in her tiny bedroom thinking about Paul and Hannah, worrying where her life was going and why, of the two of them, it was Paul who was happy and not her. And as much as I loved Paul as a friend, I couldn't help feeling angry with him on Melissa's behalf. It was awful the way things had ended between them. Absolutely awful. And even though five years had passed since they split up, for all the moving forward Melissa had done, it might as well have been yesterday.

I was there when Melissa and Paul first met. We were both twenty-three, living in that post-student nether world where you're no longer in full-time education but you don't exactly feel like a full-time member of the workforce either. Mel and I were living in a house-share in Longsight and spent most of our time buying clothes and music and, above all, chasing boys. One night in November a bunch of us met up for a drink in Chorlton with the plan of moving on to a club night in Hulme afterwards. Just after last orders in the Jockey, one of the girls we were with heard from a friend of hers about a party going on round the corner from the pub and so we decided we'd give it a try; if it was any good we could at least save ourselves money on the cab fare getting over to Hulme.

I'd never seen so many people crammed into such a small space. Though it was only a small terrace it felt as though the entire population of the pub had come along to the party too. I wanted to leave straight away and probably would have done had I not managed to lose Melissa within moments of arriving. Half an hour later I eventually found her out in the garden talking to a couple of guys in the freezing cold.

'Vicks, this is Paul and Chris,' she said with a grin. 'They lured me out here with the promise of a hidden stash of booze.'

'She's lying,' protested Paul. 'It was her banging on about 'hidden booze' that lured us out here!'

Paul and Chris seemed cool and funny without being pompous and annoying and, best of all, they were good looking enough to make me want to join in with the conversation. I could tell straight away that Melissa was doing her best to try to impress Paul, which was fine by me. His friend Chris — tall and handsome, thoughtful without being morose — was more my type anyway, and I was happy to focus all my attention on him.

Around three in the morning, with the party showing no signs of flagging, the four of us decided to leave and headed towards Chorlton Park for a change of scene. We climbed over the gate and sat on the kids' swings, knocking back lukewarm Red Stripe that we'd liberated from a kitchen sink full of melted ice at the party, and putting the world to rights with the kind of heated political debates that you can only have when you're drunk, in your early twenties and have never held down a full-time job. Eventually we calmed down and started talking about the future.

'So, where do you see yourself in ten years' time?' asked Paul, directing his question at Melissa.

Melissa shrugged. 'Why do you ask?'

'Curiosity.'

Melissa thought the question over. 'Ten years from now I'll be . . . ' she paused and looked at me, ' . . . what? Thirty-three? That sounds like a lifetime away.'

'So, what will you be doing 'a lifetime' from now?' prompted Paul.

Melissa took a swig from the can in her hand. 'Okay, okay. Ten years from now I'd like to be . . . right here.'

'What, in Chorlton Park?'

'No! But in Manchester at least . . . and by then I'll have gone back to university and finished a degree in something more interesting than Business and Economics like — I don't know — Art History. I always loved the academic part of my Art 'A' level more than the sitting around drawing stuff. I like knowing the stories behind paintings, the reasons why artists create the things they do.'

'So what would you be doing for a job?'

'I don't know. Something worthwhile, I hope. Maybe something for a charity. And I'd be living in one of those sweet little terraces on Beech Road.'

'On your own?'

Melissa laughed. 'No, with my bloke.'

'And what's he like, this bloke?'

'He's nice and caring and funny. Likes animals and is good to his mother.' She paused, then added: 'And he never ever forgets my birthday.'

'Sounds like a made-up bloke to me.' Paul grinned at Chris.

'Nope,' replied Melissa. 'He's out there somewhere. And do you know what? One day I'll find him.'

The interesting thing was that although two relationships started at that party they both went in completely different directions. Whereas Chris and I were rock solid from day one, moving in together after nine months and getting married a few years later, Melissa and Paul were always volatile. In the early days it seemed like every other week they would have one argument or another only to make up by the end of the night. After a year or two they appeared to calm down and for a long while things were good between them. I remember them laughing. I remember them being happy. I can even remember thinking to myself when they moved in together (partly out of love but mostly out of convenience) that this was it. They would settle down into the kind of comfortable groove that Chris and I were already in. Finally there would be no more fights, no more arguments, and no more conflict. I even thought that one day the two of them might get married and have kids.

Quite when they began to fall apart I was never really sure but Melissa always claimed that it was somewhere around the time that Paul turned thirty. It started with small rows about nothing, which eventually progressed into bigger rows about everything. Paul would get annoyed at Melissa and then Melissa would get annoyed right back, thereby guaranteeing that every petty quibble ended in full-scale war. As bad as it was, though, I never guessed that Paul would want to get out of the relationship because by this time they came as a pair. You never got one without the other. And I found that comforting because I understood it. That was exactly how things would always be with Chris and me.

I think I assumed that these arguments were just a 'phase' or a 'bad patch' or 'one of those things' that all couples go through only to come out the other side stronger. I'd lost count of the times when friends of ours would appear to be on the verge of splitting up only to announce a few weeks later that they were getting married or having kids or leaving their jobs to go travelling. I didn't realise that Paul was so genuinely unhappy with the way things were between him and Melissa. And I certainly hadn't guessed that he was capable of speeding up the demise of their relationship with a catalyst so lazily constructed that I still find it hard to forgive him.

It happened like this. Out in town one night with Chris and Chris's brother Cooper and some other mates, Paul got talking to a girl in a club and went home with her. What he didn't know though was that one of her housemates, Sara, was a friend of our friend Laura, who had even actually met Paul once out with Melissa. And although Paul hadn't recognised her next morning as she left to go to work, Sara had recognised him straight away and told Laura everything. Laura checked the story with Cooper (who lied) and asked me to check the story with Chris (who told a different lie). This validated matters enough for Laura and me to present our evidence directly to Melissa.

Melissa was devastated; it cut her to the bone. She challenged Paul the moment he got in from work and the second he admitted it she packed her bags and came to stay with me and Chris.

For most people that would have been the end of the story but not for Melissa. Because she was still in love with him, she just couldn't seem to let go of what they had. Paul must have felt the same way because about six weeks after the split Melissa had a long talk with Paul and announced that despite all that had happened they were going to try and stay friends. I assumed that this was just a way of saying that they would carry on sleeping together but it wasn't that at all. Melissa really did want them to be friends and nothing more. And even though in the months that followed she stayed over at his house on numerous occasions, sometimes even sharing the same bed, nothing ever happened between them. According to Melissa all they ever did was talk with an honesty and openness that they had never been able to achieve when they had been together. With the single-mindedness of a scientist on the verge of making a medical breakthrough, Melissa made it her mission to use these conversations to analyse why things hadn't worked out for them. Taking Paul's confessions and half-mumbled revelations, she did her best to make sense of them and then one evening, not far from the first anniversary of the Big Split, she made a pronouncement to Paul that seemed to take even her by surprise. She said: 'You think you don't want what other people want. You think that all you want is to be alone. But it's not true. The day will come when you'll be so sick of being alone that you won't know what to do. And when that happens come and find me and we'll pick up right where we left off.'

When I heard what she'd said to him I got so angry that I lost it completely. I told her to her face how pathetic she was being to let Paul walk all over her and that the last thing she needed was to promise to hang around for him to get his act together. I told her straight. Paul didn't deserve her. He wasn't going to miraculously turn into some kind of Prince Charming overnight. And if she was under some misguided notion that she was going to be the woman who was going to fix whatever was broken inside Paul and make him want to settle down then she was wrong. The best thing she could do would be to move on to someone else as soon as possible instead of hanging around for him like somekind of lapdog. Melissa's response? She just got up, walked out and didn't speak to me for the best part of a month.

Billy

It was just after seven, I was on the phone with Freya and my New Year's Eve was not off to a good start at all.

'So, what are you up to tonight?' I asked.

'Gina and Danni have got me tickets for some club in town,' said Freya. 'Apparently it's going to be really good.'

'What sort of thing?'

'Don't know.'

'Dancey or indie?'

'Indie.'

'Which club?'

'I don't know.'

There was a long pause.

'What about you then?' she asked. 'Are you hitting the town with the gruesome twosome?'

She meant my housemates Seb and Brian.

'Yeah,' I lied.

'Anywhere good?'

'Some club in town.'

'Indie or dancey?'

'Dancey, I think.'

Another long pause.

'Well, have a good New Year, yeah?' she said. 'I'll be thinking of you come midnight.'

My heart still skipped a beat even though I knew that Freya would not be thinking about me at all come midnight. When the bongs arrived she would be thinking about whichever tight-trouser-wearing, big-haired, 'Look at me I'm in a band' loser that she'd selected as her next victim. 'And I'll be thinking of you too,' I replied, realising just how much I didn't want this call to end. 'Are you going to make any resolutions?'

'No,' said Freya firmly. 'I'm not into all that. You?'

'I'm making a few.'

'Like what?'

'You know, the usual.'

There was a short silence, which was undoubtedly Freya considering digging a little deeper before deciding against it. 'Well, good luck with all that then. And we'll catch up soon, yeah? Go for a drink or something, yeah?'

'Definitely. Let's catch up soon.'

I put my phone down on the empty computer-printer box that doubled as my bedside table, picked up the remote for my CD player, pressed play. As 'A River Ain't Too Much To Love' filled my ears I lay down on my bed, closed my eyes and wondered whether Bill Callahan had ever had problems with 'the ladies' when he was twenty-four like me.

I'd never been entirely convinced that what I'd felt for Freya had been love (after all how could it be real love if she didn't love me back?) but even so, what I felt now was torture.

I'd first got to know her when she took a job at the Duck and Drake at a period of my life when Brian, Seb and I virtually lived there. A lot of our mates used to go there and as we too became regulars we got to know most of the staff. So when I turned up one Saturday night and saw Freya standing behind the bar, it took me by surprise: she was absolutely amazing. She had shoulder-length black hair that, along with the way she dressed, made her look as if she had just stepped out of a time machine from 1963. She had that whole doe-eyed, sexy indie-chick thing going on and the most beautiful face I had ever seen.

I guessed from the way she dressed that she was into music and so over the course of a couple of conversations, as I got my round in, I'd drop in the names of a few bands that I thought she might like and when those worked, I dropped in a few more, then a few more. After about a month of name dropping bands like crazy she told me that a band we'd both been raving about recently were playing at Night and Day and asked me if I fancied coming along. I couldn't believe it. A date. With Freya. This kind of luck was unheard of in my life. I was over the moon.

Though we'd arranged to meet at Dry on Oldham Street at eight, Freya didn't turn up until minutes to nine.

'I'm really sorry I'm so late.'

'It's fine.'

'No, it's not. You see, the thing is . . . ' she

stopped, a bit tearful, 'the thing is . . . I've just had a massive row with Justin.'

'Who's Justin?'

'My boyfriend.'

The news that she wasn't single knocked me sideways, even though it made perfect sense that a girl like Freya would have guys throwing themselves at her left, right and centre.

On the way to Night and Day, Freya gave me a potted history of her and her boyfriend, right up to and including the fight that they had just had. I listened attentively and gave her advice on how to sort out the problem, even though this guy sounded an awful lot like some of the idiots who had been on my course at university — all rock-star poses and daft haircuts without a shred of personality between them.

At about ten o'clock, when the headline band came on stage, Freya suggested that we move towards the front and before I could say a word she grabbed me by the hand and led me right to the front of the stage. And from the band's opening song to their closing encore she didn't let go of my hand.

At the end of the night we filed out of the venue and headed to a fast-food place for curry and chips, which we ate sitting on a bench next to the bus stop before getting the bus back to Withington. Later, as we parted to go our separate ways, she told me she'd had a great time and that she would call me in the morning. The call never came.

The next I saw of her was about a week later, when I turned up at the Drake with Seb and

Brian to find her behind the bar.

'I'm sorry. I didn't call you, did I? It's just that ... well ... Justin and I sort of got back together.'

'Great,' I replied, with as much enthusiasm as I could muster. 'I'm really, really pleased for you.'

'Good, because in a way it was all down to you.'

'Really?'

'I followed your advice to the letter and before I knew it we were having this massive heart to heart and we realised that we were just both really wary of getting hurt. Ever since that night things have just been perfect.'

It didn't last though. Like most devastatingly pretty girls, Freya had spectacularly bad taste in men and soon Justin was superseded by a whole litany of poseurs who could smell her father-issues and lack of self-esteem from a mile away. And although the names changed (Oscar, Tom, Jamie and Lucien) the pattern remained the same. They'd fancy her, she'd fancy them, they'd get off together at some crappy indie club in town, then a few weeks later she'd find them snogging some other girl in the same club; or she'd find out they already had a girlfriend; or they would simply stop calling altogether. Distraught, she would turn to me for comfort and support. And while I'd be hugging her and telling her how it'd all be all right in the end, she'd be telling me how special I was and how different I was from the other guys. And all the time I'd be thinking to myself 'If I can just hang on a bit longer maybe she'll finally see just how mad about her I really am.'

Anyway, to cut a long story short, a few nights before Christmas Eve, following the demise of yet another short-lived hook-up with a skinny, scruffy, waste of skin and bone called Luke, Freya dropped round at mine to claim both consolation and a free bottle of wine. We joked about how love was a game for losers and made plans for a perfect New Year's Eve.

'How about I come to yours?' she said. 'We can order a takeaway.'

'And drink as much as our livers can take!' I added.

'And then when we're well and truly wrecked,' said Freya, really getting into the rhythm of things, 'we can watch *Eternal Sunshine of the Spotless Mind* for the millionth time.'

At this particular moment we were the closest we had been in all the time I'd known her and so I decided that six months of unrequited love was more than enough for anyone and attempted to convert a good-night embrace into something more. Honestly, I couldn't have misjudged the situation more if I'd tried. The second my lips touched hers Freya pulled away and was all 'I'm really flattered, Billy, but I don't really see you like 'that',' and although I wished I had some kind of comeback, I didn't say a thing because I was too busy willing the earth to open up and swallow me whole.

★ ★ ★

With five hours to go before midnight I still had no idea what I was going to do with my New Year's Eve. I called Seb and Brian to see if there were any tickets left for the club night they were going to but apparently the whole thing had sold out months ago and tickets were now changing hands for ten times their face value. I didn't really fancy the idea of bankrupting myself just so that I didn't have to see the New Year in watching *Jools Holland* so I told them to have a good time and decided to put on yet more melancholy music, turn off the lights, climb back into bed and allow myself the indulgence of feeling totally and utterly depressed. After a few minutes realising that I wasn't exactly being a man about all this I got out of bed, picked up my mobile and called my older sister Nadine.

Chatting to her about life in general for a bit to give her the illusion that I wasn't after anything (covering topics as diverse as our parents, the love life of my middle sister Amy, and Nadine's impending thirty-fifth birthday) I finally jumped in with two feet and asked her the big question.

'So, sis, what are you up to tonight?'

'I'm off to a party.'

'You're thirty-five!' I exclaimed. 'Do people your age still have parties?'

Nadine laughed. 'You're such a cheeky little sod sometimes.'

'Ah,' I replied. 'But you love me for it, don't you? So this party, is it local?'

'It's in Chorlton. My friends Ed and Sharon. Why?'

'Well, I'm sort of at a loose end and I was

28

wondering if I could come with you.'

'You'd hate it,' she said quickly. 'I'm not saying it'll be a bunch of people standing around talking house prices and swapping notes from the Habitat catalogue but that's not far off, Billy. There won't be any drugs, raids by the police or young girls throwing up in the bathroom.'

Looking around my sad bedroom, I allowed my eyes to come to rest on the portable TV on top of the chest of drawers in the corner. Jools Holland could wait. A boring party full of boring people my sister's age it may be, but at least it was somewhere to go.

'It sounds perfect,' I replied. 'Give me ten minutes to sort myself out and I'll be ready.'

Melissa

It was just after eight when I arrived at the Old Grey. The pub — a favourite with the older crowd in Chorlton — was packed out as it would be just before last orders on a Saturday night. Vicky and Laura were at a table near the jukebox, hemmed in on all sides by large groups of what Laura liked to call 'people like us' but who could equally be labelled 'slightly worn at the edges, Big Issue-buying, left-leaning, thirty-something graduates who still feel like students even if they aren't'. Searching around the bar for an empty stool, I eventually located one and made my way over to my friends.

'So where are the boys?'

'At the bar,' replied Laura. 'Although they

seem to be taking forever about it.'

I looked at Vicky. 'And still no word of Paul and Hannah?'

Vicky shook her head. 'Not yet but I'm sure they'll be here soon.'

I think it must have been obvious that I couldn't work out whether I was relieved or not because Laura reached across the table and touched my hand. 'What do you want to drink, babe?'

'I'm fine for the minute,' I replied. 'Maybe a bit later.'

'Don't be silly. Getting drinks is what boys do best.' Laura pulled out her mobile and dialled. 'Coop, it's me. Melissa's here now, can you get her a drink?'

Cooper and Chris, waiting patiently to be served at the bar, smiled and waved at us.

'What are you drinking?'

'I'll have a Becks if that's all right?'

Laura rolled her eyes as though my politeness was trying her patience. 'Melissa wants a bottle of Becks and a packet of prawn cocktail crisps and be quick about it!'

I poked her in the elbow with my finger. 'You tell him right now that I don't want any crisps . . . least of all prawn cocktail.'

'You might not . . . but I certainly do. I'm starving.'

Vicky looked perplexed. 'I thought you were on that Courtney Cox diet? Are prawn cocktail crisps part of the menu?'

'Tomorrow,' grinned Laura. 'The diet starts tomorrow.'

Laura and I had been friends for as long as she had been going out with Cooper, which give or take a few months was about six years. Cooper had met her when he'd first moved to Manchester after splitting up with his girlfriend. I hadn't been too sure about Laura at first; she seemed much more of a boys' girl than a girls' girl, thriving on any male attention that was available. And although she'd probably be the first to admit that this was true, she was also a lot of other things besides and it was these that made me warm to her over time. For starters, she could be really funny when she wanted to be which I consider a good sign; beautiful people like Laura rarely bother cultivating a sense of humour. She was also burdened with more than her fair share of insecurities (she hated her nose, was a borderline bulimic through her teenage years and constantly put herself down for not being smart enough). And so once I discovered her human side, I found it much easier to like her and, with the minimum of adjustment, space was made to include Laura in the tight bond that existed between Vicky and me.

While we waited for our drinks we exchanged stories about our various days.

'Well, my highlight,' Vicky began, 'was watching Chris trying to teach William how to fly the kite we got for him for Christmas. It would've been hilarious if it hadn't been so cold. Chris was running around like a demon trying to get the thing in the air and William kept asking if it was time to go home because he was freezing to death.'

'Well, given that I only got out of bed about four hours ago,' began Laura, 'I'm guessing this is probably the highlight of my day.'

Vicky could hardly believe it. 'Four hours ago?'

Laura nodded sheepishly. 'I went out with a few of my old work friends from Albright High last night and it turned into a bit of a late one. I didn't get in until three.'

'How about you, Mel?' asked Vicky. 'What have you been up to today?'

'Nothing much,' I sighed, 'I read about ten pages of that Monica Ali book that you lent me, watched a double episode of *Deal or No Deal* and finished off the entire top layer of the selection of chocolate biscuits that my evil stick-thin sister Mia gave me for Christmas. Not exactly the most fruitful of days but I'm not complaining.'

Vicky laughed. 'I'd kill to spend the afternoon watching Noel Edmunds and eating biscuits.'

'You're welcome to my life any time you want it. Really, just say the word and it's yours. You have my life and I'll move into yours and raise William as my own.'

'You do realise you'll have to sleep with Chris, then, don't you?'

I pulled a face and replied: 'Ours would be a chaste marriage.'

'So anyway,' said Laura grinning, 'moving on from that distasteful picture, how are we all feeling in general about the year ahead? Optimistic?'

'As you all know,' I began, 'I hate New Year's

Eve *and* thinking about the future, so it would be fair to say that I'm pretty pessimistic about it all.'

Vicky disagreed. 'I love the idea of being handed a clean slate every year and setting myself a whole new set of goals.'

'There speaks Wonder Woman,' I replied. 'So what's your goal for this New Year then, Vicky? Something involving those cookbooks of yours. Maybe it's time you finally applied to appear on *Ready Steady Cook.* You'd be ace on that.'

'Cheeky cow! No *Ready Steady Cook* for me.'

'Well then, you should have another baby,' suggested Laura. 'You and Chris make great babies, it's a proven fact. William is quite possibly my favourite human being on the entire planet.'

'Well, I'm afraid you're not his.' Vicky gave me a wink. 'Before we came out tonight it was Auntie Mel this and Auntie Mel that. I think he's got a massive crush on you, Mel.'

'Fine by me,' I replied. 'What is he, four? I'm more than willing to hang on another twenty-six years for the right one.'

'That is so wrong on about a million different levels,' groaned Vicky.

'So, are you going to have another baby then?' Laura was probing.

Vicky shook her head. 'I've only ever wanted one.'

'Looks like you and Cooper will have to take up the slack then,' I said to Laura.

'Cooper would have kids at the drop of a hat if I let him,' she said despairingly. 'Your William's such a walking advert for procreation that I've lost count of the times Coop's dropped subtle-as-a-brick hints like, 'How great would it be to have one of those around the house?' and I'm like, 'Are you insane? I can barely look after myself let alone another human being.''

'So you don't ever want kids then?' asked Vicky.

'There's too much I haven't done for me to even think about any of that. In fact if there's one resolution I do want to make this year, it's to go travelling. I want to see a bit more of the world. I want to spend time in a place where it isn't always raining. I want to live a little. Do you know what I mean?'

I nodded. 'You and Cooper should definitely do it. Grown-up gap years are all the rage for the discerning thirty-something.'

'Tell that to my boyfriend. If it wasn't for the fact that he's making us save up a stupid deposit for a stupid house I'd do it in a heartbeat.'

Vicky sighed. 'You know you really shouldn't give him such a hard time. Cooper's just doing what Cooper does. He wants the best for you both.'

Laura shrugged and fingered the label of the beer bottle in front of her. 'I don't know, maybe he does. But why does he have to be so boring about it?'

'Look.' Vicky tried to lift the mood around the table. 'Let's not get depressed. It's New Year's Eve and we're all together so let's just enjoy ourselves.'

34

Chris

It was just after nine by the time we left the Old Grey and made our way to Sharon and Ed's. On the way I tried Paul's mobile a couple of times but kept getting his voicemail. This was one hundred per cent typical of Paul. He never returned people's calls if he could help it and when you had a go at him he'd just look at you as if you were acting like some kind of girl making a big deal out of nothing and say: 'I'd let you know if I wasn't coming, wouldn't I?'

Whilst hitting redial I thought about how long Paul and I had been friends. We first met through mates of mates one summer night outside The Black Horse in the days before they knocked down Shambles Square and moved it over the road. I was in the second year of my law degree and I'd just finished my exams — a whole bunch of us had been sitting drinking on the benches outside the pub since late afternoon. Heading up to the bar to get a round in I'd ended up standing next to Paul. We were both quite drunk by this point in the evening and out of nowhere Paul turned round and told me a joke about a nun and a polar bear that was so ridiculously puerile that even thinking about it now can still put a smile on my face.

We got chatting and he told me a bit about himself. He was in the second year of a Social Studies degree at MMU and though he'd been born in Stockport he had moved around the country quite a bit with his parents before ending up back where he started at the age of fifteen. That was pretty much it for biography because after that all we talked about was football and motor-racing before the conversation as a whole disintegrated into the typical mix of music and films, clothes and trainers, in fact all the usual stuff employed by certain types of men to separate the wheat from the chaff.

Despite us both proving our credentials with talk of obscure Italian horror films, the back catalogue of the Stones and several shared sitcom favourites, we didn't have a great deal to do with each other after that night-out, apart from the odd nod of the head or short conversation whenever we bumped into each other (usually either coming in or out of Piccadilly Records). It wasn't anything personal. I doubt that either of us gave it any consideration at all, but if we had it would have been something along the lines of if we were meant to be friends then it would happen whether or not we did anything about it.

A few months later, on an unseasonably mild afternoon at the beginning of our final term we once again found ourselves sitting outside The Black Horse with the same group of mutual friends. But this time by the end of the night we ended up making plans to go for a drink, and go and see bands together, and somehow we both followed through with these haphazard arrangements and gradually became the best of friends.

I tried his number one last time. It still switched to his voicemail. Giving up, I returned my phone to my pocket and caught up with the others.

Melissa

There were already quite a few people lingering outside Ed and Sharon's tiny terraced house by the time we arrived. Some had just arrived and were congregating by the door saying hello to each other, while others were enjoying the first of many 'last' cigarettes before they resolved, once again, to give up for ever at midnight — something I could appreciate as an ex-smoker myself. I recognised two of the smokers outside as Fraser and Helen, who I'd first met when Vicky and I moved into a shared house with them in our early twenties. The boys claimed it was too cold to stand outside talking so they headed straight indoors taking Vicky and Laura with them. As I hadn't seen Fraser and Helen since they went travelling over a year and half ago, I told the others I'd see them inside and stood chatting for a while. I was dying to hear their travelling stories and although they were a bit self-conscious at first, wary of coming across like those irritating people who constantly evangelise about the wonders of seeing the world they relaxed when I assured them I was genuinely pleased that they appeared to have had such a great time. They seemed so much happier with their lives in general and with each other specifically that it made me hopeful about my own future too.

Leaving Fraser and Helen finishing their cigarettes I entered the house. The hallway was crammed wall to wall with party-goers who — even though I didn't know most of them

— all appeared to be the same vintage as me which was reassuring: at least if I got drunk and ended up dancing I would feel my peers' sympathy rather than their embarrassment.

In my search for Vicky and the others, I ended up bumping into an inordinate number of people that I hadn't seen in ages and it made me think about a newspaper survey I once read that said each person in the UK on average knows at least one hundred and twenty people. I remember thinking at the time how a hundred and twenty people seemed like a lot, but standing here at this party, suddenly it didn't seem like such an outrageous figure after all. Some were friends, some were friends of friends of friends, but I knew that if I started a conversation with any of them within minutes we'd discover that we had people or places in common. I'm guessing in university towns and cities from Edinburgh to Southampton and from Cambridge to Cardiff there were pockets of people like us — refugees who'd arrived with the intention of finishing off our education but never found the wherewithal to make it back home again.

I eventually found Vicky and Laura but, conscious of the fact that I hadn't got a drink in my hands and that my plan for the evening was to drink myself silly, I made an excuse about needing a drink of water, and headed for the kitchen.

Ed and Sharon's kitchen, was, like the rest of the house, packed with people but I eventually spotted all the booze lined up on the kitchen counter next to the sink. I'd asked Vicky to give

Sharon and Ed my contribution — a bottle of Sancerre that had cost me nearly a tenner — when we first arrived and I was dying to try it. Scanning the various bottles and cans in search of it I eventually found it, minus its cork and empty, poking out of a green recycling box on the floor. Resigning myself to the situation I selected a sophisticated-looking oak-aged Chardonnay with a posh label to open as remuneration, even though there was already an open bottle of Sainsbury's own-label Chardonnay right in front of me.

Cringing at how I was letting myself down by three-quarter filling a plastic pint glass with wine (I couldn't find any others) that to make matters worse I had no proper claim on, a male voice from behind me said: 'All right, fella, what are you looking so guilty about?'

I spun round almost spilling the wine all over me only to find Chris and Cooper standing behind me grinning like idiots. 'Okay, okay,' I replied. 'You caught me in the act. Someone drank the whole of that bottle of wine I brought with me. I didn't even get a sip.'

'So now you're wreaking your revenge by searching out the most expensive bottle you can find and chucking the lot into a pint glass?' Chris laughed. 'What are you? Some kind of student waster?'

'You're such a git to me sometimes.'

Chris put his arm around me. 'You know I only do it because I love you.'

Chris and Cooper were more like older brothers than friends. The pair of them often teased me mercilessly (their jokes focusing mainly on the notion they had that I was a bit flaky, lacked ambition and was hopeless with men) but the flipside of this kind of abuse is that as their honorary 'little sister' it was their duty to protect me. Over the years that I'd known them both I'd lost count of the times that one or the other had walked me home in the rain, picked me up from the airport, put up shelves in my bedroom, even sorted out dodgy guys in bars giving me hassle.

Obviously I'd known Chris longer than Cooper. In fact it was hard to believe that Chris had ever existed apart from the unit I'd come to know and love as 'Chris and Vicky'. In many ways he was the complete opposite of Paul. Whereas life with Paul was like being on a rollercoaster with highs that thrilled every nerve ending and lows that took you to the depths of despair, Chris was a lot more even and steady. You always knew exactly where you stood with him and how he would react in any given situation. He just seemed to give off this aura of authority, so much so that whenever any of us had a 'real world' problem, like when I was being hassled by a debt-collection agency over an unpaid mobile phone bill a few years ago, I didn't take my problem to Paul, or Cooper, I took it straight to Chris, and he sorted the whole thing out with a few phone calls.

Chris picked up a bottle of champagne from behind my back and held it aloft. 'Still,' he said giving me a wink, 'if you're going to do this revenge thing at all, at least do it properly.'

40

'You can't do that!' I said, outraged as Chris pulled off the foil and began attacking the twisty metal surrounding the cork. 'What if Ed and Sharon are saving it for midnight?'

'It's okay, Mel,' Cooper chipped in. 'No need to get your knickers all bunched up, mate. Laura and I brought it with us. We've had it sitting in our fridge for ages. Me and Laura don't really like the stuff so we brought it along tonight, but you can consider it your belated Christmas present if you like.'

Before I could protest Chris popped the cork. Everyone in the kitchen looked at us with disdain as though we were acting like a bunch of yobs, which I suppose in a way we were.

Chris took a swig from the bottle and then handed it to me. 'Happy New year, Mel.'

'I really shouldn't be doing this,' I said taking the bottle from his hand. 'You two are always leading me into bad ways.'

'Us? Never.'

I took a swig. 'So, are either of you going to make any New Year's resolutions?'

Chris shook his head. 'Don't believe in them. I mean, what's the point?'

'They're only supposed to be a bit of fun.'

Chris didn't look convinced. 'Okay, so what's yours?'

'I've got a list as long as my arm . . . I'm taking up jogging . . . I'm going to start cycling into uni . . . I'm going to cut down on takeaways . . . and read more books . . . watch less TV . . . and . . . do you want me to carry on?'

Chris did a mock cringe. 'Please don't.'

I turned to Cooper. 'What about you? Unlike your useless brother here you must have a few.'

'No resolutions as such, just some plans.'

'Like what?'

'To buy a house. I'm sick of renting. It's money down the drain. Laura and I should have enough saved for a deposit by the middle of the year as long as house prices don't carry on going through the roof.'

I thought about Laura's comments back at the Old Oak about wanting to go travelling and sensed trouble on the horizon but said nothing.

'Still, getting a house of your own isn't the be all and end all, is it?'

Chris laughed. 'I think you're making Mel feel bad about the fact that she's wasting valuable time playing at being a student again rather than getting on the property ladder.'

I punched Chris in the shoulder as hard as I could. 'It's unbelievable how much of a tosser you can be sometimes.'

Cooper grinned. 'Just ignore him, he's not worth the effort.' He looked at me sheepishly. 'I suppose you're right: getting a house isn't the be all and end all but it's a step forward, isn't it? And that's all I want really — a couple of steps forward.'

There was something about the look on Cooper's face, like a child desperately trying to hide a secret that made me curious.

'What other 'steps forward' are you thinking about?'

Cooper just smiled enigmatically.

'You're not . . . ?'

'What?'

'Going to ask Laura to marry you, are you?'

'Yeah, right. Do I look like a mug?'

'What do you mean? I think you and Laura make a brilliant couple. Plus, it's been ages since I've been to a good wedding. You should do it.'

Cooper rolled his eyes. 'Well, much as I'd like to help you out by throwing a good party, Mel, I'm afraid that won't be happening any time soon. But I'll be sure to let you know if I change my mind, okay?'

I looked at Chris in the hope that he might back me up but he just shrugged and offered me the champagne again. I glanced up at the clock on the wall. It was twenty minutes past ten and there was still no sign of Paul and Hannah.

'So where's his Lordship then?' I asked, directing the question at both Chris and Cooper. 'He is still coming, isn't he?'

Chris shrugged. 'That's what he told me but you know what he's like, your guess is as good as mine.'

'Maybe Hannah didn't fancy the idea of spending the biggest night of the year with a bunch of her boyfriend's friends who don't really like her,' suggested Cooper. 'I don't think I'd be here if I was her. After all, she's not you, is she?'

It was all I could do to stop myself from throwing my arms around Coop and kissing him. 'Thanks for the solidarity, Coop, but she's Paul's girlfriend so we should be nice to her. He's always been nice to the guys I've seen in the past.'

'Maybe to your face,' said Chris solemnly.

43

'Why, what has he said?'

Chris shook his head. 'Look, I'm saying nothing. But take it from me, he's never been anywhere near as happy as he makes out when you're seeing someone.'

Although this was news to me it didn't exactly make me feel any better.

'Doesn't matter anyway,' I replied. 'The truth is I like her, and I can definitely see what Paul sees in her.'

Cooper laughed. 'Well, that's hardly rocket science, she's very easy on the eye.'

'I mean beyond all that superficial stuff,' I replied. 'I was talking to her the last time she was round at Chris and Vicky's and she was telling me about some of the stuff she's doing on her MA. I didn't have a clue what she was talking about — it was like she was talking in a different language. She's so clever it's frightening.'

Chris put an arm round my shoulder as though he was drawing me close in order to impart an important piece of wisdom which of course he was, because one of the downsides of being Chris and Cooper's 'little sister' was that every once in a while I had to endure their unsolicited advice about my private life.

'Considering what a Hannah-fan you are,' observed Chris, 'I bet you'd have a face on you that could turn milk if she walked in with Paul right now.'

I pretended to look for the champagne but could feel myself starting to flush.

'Listen, Mel,' he continued. 'I know this might sound a bit harsh and for the life of me I don't mean it that way but seeing as we're about to begin a new year, why don't you do yourself a massive favour and just move on? Hanging on to Paul like this is doing you no good at all.'

Even though Chris wasn't being all that serious I could feel tears pricking at the back of my eyes before he had even finished.

'If it was that easy,' I replied, 'don't you think that I'd have done it by now?'

'Of course you can do it,' replied Chris, oblivious to the look of disbelief emanating from Cooper's face. 'You just have to want it badly enough, that's all. Look, all I'm saying is that you and Paul are mates and that's great but I think that now he's finally moved on, maybe you should too.'

Chris

I have no idea who'd died and made me Minister of Home Truths but whoever it was I wish they hadn't bothered. Melissa looked crushed when I finished delivering my big piece of advice and all I could think was: 'Why didn't I keep my big mouth shut?'

'Maybe you're right,' she said after a long silence. 'Maybe I am wasting my time here with Paul. Maybe I should just go home right now.'

I could tell that Melissa was absolutely serious about leaving and could already picture the scene Vicky would make when she found out it was my fault that her best friend was spending New Year's Eve on her own.

'You can't go, Mel. First off it's just wrong, second, you shouldn't listen to anything I've got to say about anything, because what do I know? And finally, if you go home early and Vicky finds out that you've gone because of me she will go insane.'

'She would, wouldn't she?' said Melissa, the beginnings of a smile on her face. 'She'd make your life a misery for days.'

'Days? Try weeks.'

Melissa sighed. 'Look, Chris, I know you meant well and that you're probably right about me and Paul, it's just . . . you know . . . some things are easier said than done, aren't they? You can't really think I want to be like this, can you? You can't really think that I enjoy waking up on my own only to end the day in bed alone too. You have no idea how lucky you are having Vicky and William. No idea at all.'

'I really am sorry, mate. I haven't a clue about anything. You just do what you've got to do and from now on I'll keep my mouth shut.'

'Okay, you're forgiven. But if you start with any of that 'Melissa's a flaky Southern layabout stuff' again I will grass you up in a second.' She picked up her plastic cup of wine. 'Right, boys, I'm off to find some proper people to talk to, okay?'

'No hard feelings, mate?'

Melissa smiled. 'Of course not. We're fine. I'll see you later?'

'Yeah. Later.'

I watched Melissa leave the kitchen then turned to Cooper and sighed. 'I really should learn to keep my big mouth shut, shouldn't I? It's not like it takes a genius to work out that Melissa doesn't want to hear the truth about her and Paul.'

'And certainly not tonight of all nights,' added Cooper. 'New Year's Eve always puts people in a weird frame of mind.'

I raised an eyebrow, relieved at the opportunity to talk about something else. 'Like you? What was all that stuff going on with your face when Mel was talking about you and Laura getting hitched? For a second I thought that you might be — '

'I am.'

'You are what?'

'Going to ask her. Not tonight. But this New Year, definitely.'

'You're joking?'

He shook his head. 'No, I'm absolutely serious. I was thinking of asking her on her birthday in April. That way it'll give me enough time to save up for the ring without raiding our savings.'

'You do know you can't just get any old rubbish for an engagement ring and hope that she'll be so flattered that she won't notice it's gold plated?'

Cooper grinned. 'That's why I'm planning to give it to her over a candle-lit dinner.'

I shook my head and picked up the bottle of champagne. 'Well, best of luck to you, bruv. I hope it all goes well when you do the deed.'

'Cheers.' Cooper took the bottle from me. He took a swig and winced. 'Nope,' he said resignedly, 'still can't stand this stuff.'

Melissa

Determined to think about something other than Paul, I ended up circulating the party on my own for about an hour, dipping in and out of conversations. Most of the people I spoke to were friends that I'd first met in pubs and clubs during my early twenties and now, a decade on, only met up with at the occasional party or summer barbecue. Of course most of them were settled now, coupled up with kids or tethered down by massive mortgages, but there was a small yet resilient battalion still fighting the good fight as though the last ten years hadn't happened. It was these friends in particular that I was always pleased to see. It was great to hear that people like Cathy and Brendan were still in bands, that Dean and Lewis were still actively pursuing their dream of becoming full-time artists and even that Alistair and Baxter were still running the same city-centre indie club nights that they had been involved with when I'd first got to know them as a nineteen-year-old student. It felt good seeing all these people in one place at the same time. It felt good knowing that they were all getting on with their lives. It made me feel as though I was part of something larger than myself.

In the middle of a conversation with Carl and Louisa, whose big news was that Louisa was pregnant, I decided that I needed another drink to keep me going. I made my excuses and tried to make my way out of the room but every few steps someone I hadn't seen in ages emerged from the wings with an air kiss and a desperate need to catch up. Manjeet and Aaron were moving down to London, Joel and Rowena had just bought a house over in Withington and Tina (formerly of Tina and Alan and currently of Tina and Susan) had left teaching and was now trying to write a novel. Beginning to feel as if I was coming down with a massive case of information overload, I managed with a struggle to reach the door to the hallway but before I could make it out of the room I felt a tap on my shoulder and turned round. Standing in front of me was a tall young-looking guy wearing a pinstriped jacket with a green T-shirt that had yellow writing on it. I didn't recognise him but the way he was looking at me — as though we were old friends — convinced me that I must have met him at some long-forgotten party. I was about to kiss him on the cheek and ask how he was doing before politely making my excuses and escaping to the kitchen, when he did something really odd. Raising his foot in the air so that I could see that he was wearing brick-red baseball boots just like my own he said: 'Snap.'

Billy

It had taken me over two hours, three cans of Carlsberg, and all the courage I possessed in order to approach the girl in the red Converse.

I'd spotted her the moment she entered the living room some time after nine. I'd been bored out of my mind making small talk with my sister's mates when boom, there she was. She seemed different from the other women at the party. Prettier. More thoughtful. Older than me but without making me feel like it would require a huge leap of the imagination to picture us being together. That, along with the style of her hair, the cardigan she was wearing, her frayed jeans and the fact that she seemed the total opposite of Freya made me think that if I was going to pull at this party then this girl would be it.

Normally I would never have dreamed of trying to chat up a girl like that in a million years especially with a line that boiled down to little more than: 'Wow, look at us, we've got the same footwear.' And what made it worse of course was the fact that it was so obviously just a cheesy chat-up line. I might have been better off just saying: 'Do you think that at some point this evening you might be drunk enough to consider getting off with a complete stranger?' At least then I might have gained a few points for sheer brazenness.

Still, since the girl in the Converse was unknown to my sister and her immediate friends (I'd already checked out that avenue), if I was ever going to have a hope of talking to her I had no choice but to try something on my own. Looking over at the three remaining cans of Carlsberg I'd brought with me and placed on the mantle, I decided that if Dutch courage was what I needed, then I'd have to settle for Danish courage as that was all I had to hand. I pulled one can out of its plastic carrier, opened it and began drinking, giving myself an eleven o'clock deadline to make my move.

Melissa

You can imagine how weird this was. There I was trying to escape the room when this guy just appears from nowhere, taps me on the shoulder and, dangling his foot in front of me, says: 'Snap.'

I was confused to say the least.

I decided to humour him. 'Great minds, eh?'

'I was thinking the same thing.'

With nothing springing to mind that might help me recognise this guy, I played for time and gestured to his chest with my empty plastic cup. 'What does your T-shirt say?'

He pulled his jacket open so I could read the words of his T-shirt — a cryptic fake film review that said: An athlete, a criminal, a brain, a princess and a basketcase bond in detention at a Chicago High School (1985).

'*The Breakfast Club*,' I said grinning. 'I love that film.'

'Me too,' he replied. 'What's your favourite bit?'

'Though I love it I can barely remember it — I haven't seen it in ages. How about you?'

'The bit when they're all dancing . . . and pretty much any scene with Ally Sheedy in it.'

I smiled. 'So you're a Sheedy man?'

'All the way.'

I remembered how at school you could always divide boys into the ones who considered themselves to be tortured poets (and therefore

51

fancied Ally Sheedy) and the boys who were just boys (and therefore fancied Molly Ringwald). I had to smile at the thought that this guy fancied himself as a tortured poet.

'This is really awful of me,' I said after a few moments, 'but I seem to have completely forgotten your name.'

'That's because we've never met before,' he said looking slightly uncomfortable. 'Can I be straight with you? I only came over because . . . well . . . you seemed nice and it's New Year's Eve . . . and we'll all be singing Auld Lang Syne in a bit . . . so I just thought I'd come over and say hello.' He offered me his hand and I think he was about to tell his name but then he stopped and looked over my shoulder. I turned round too to see what he was looking at and there, standing right behind me, all alone, was Paul.

Billy

Even without knowing anything about either of them I could tell straight away that these two had history. The second Melissa saw Paul her whole being lit up like a switch inside her had been flipped. Seeing them together like that made me think how Freya was the only person I could think of who could make me feel the way this girl was feeling.

'We all thought you weren't coming,' said Melissa.

'I'm just a bit late, that's all,' he replied.

Melissa bit her lip. 'Where's Hannah? Getting a drink?'

He shook his head. 'No, she . . . er . . . she couldn't make it.'

Melissa looked concerned. 'Nothing wrong, is there?'

'No, nothing's wrong,' replied Paul. 'She's fine.' He paused. 'So what have I missed?'

Melissa smiled. 'Nothing much really, Laura wants to go travelling and Cooper wants to save up for a deposit for a house and it's all going to end in disaster; and Chris and Vicky are, well, you know . . . *Chris and Vicky* and I . . . I . . . '

I could tell that Melissa had just recalled the fact that prior to Paul's arrival she had been in the middle of a conversation with me and now I was dangling, like some kind of spare part, wishing one of them would put me out of my misery.

Melissa looked at me apologetically.

'Paul, this is . . . '

'Billy,' I replied. 'My name's Billy.'

'That's it. Billy,' said Melissa. 'This is Billy. And Billy, this is Paul. He and I are old friends.'

'Very old friends,' added Paul. 'How long has it been? Ten or eleven years?'

'Twelve,' replied Melissa. 'Twelve long years.'

Melissa

Half past midnight. Thirty minutes into a brand-new year. And Paul and I, having shouted, cheered and done the Auld Lang Syne thing with everyone else at midnight, were outside in Ed and Sharon's back garden sitting on their damp patio furniture with a freshly purloined bottle of

53

wine watching an explosion of fireworks in the night sky. I could feel the damp of the table soaking right through my jeans to my underwear but I didn't care. There was something different about Paul tonight. I could sense it.

'Genius idea of yours,' I said as yet another firework popped and sparkled in the sky. 'Leave the comfort of a nice warm house and sit outside in the rain.'

Paul shrugged. 'You could've said no.'

'And miss out on all this? Never.'

Paul took a sip of wine and handed the bottle to me. I put it to my lips, took a long, deep gulp and swallowed. It felt good to drink wine like this. An instant reminder of the days when finer graces genuinely didn't matter.

'I haven't drunk straight from the bottle like this since the year we all went to Glastonbury. And for some reason I've done it twice tonight.'

Paul smiled. 'I remember that year at Glastonbury. That was the year we bought those bottles of homemade wine from that hippie guy near the main stage and Cooper refused to drink it in case it was laced with weed killer. Do you remember? Like a hippie hasn't got better things to do with his time than poison a bunch of middle-class layabouts.'

'I remember the hippie . . . and I sort of remember handing him the cash but other than pushing the corks into the bottle with my keys, I don't remember much about that night at all.' I paused and laughed. 'Still, somehow I just get a sense that it might have been one of the best nights of my life.'

'Easily up there in the top ten.'

I glanced at Paul. He looked thoughtful and pensive.

'So are you going to tell me what's going on?'

'What do you want to know?'

'Well, where's Hannah for starters?'

'I'm guessing she's at home. I don't know for sure. We split up just before Christmas.'

There it was. Paul and Hannah had split up. They were over. It didn't seem to make any sense given how happy they had been last time I had seen them together, all loved up and fawning over each other.

'How did she take it?' I asked carefully.

'How do you know it was me?'

'Come on, Paul,' I laughed. 'This is me you're talking to.'

'She'll be fine,' he said obliquely. 'It wasn't like I was the love of her life.'

'And you'd know that how exactly?'

'You think I was?'

I shook my head. 'I doubt you'll ever be the love of anyone's life. It would be tantamount to making a public admission that you didn't have much of a life to begin with. I have to admit I'm surprised though. I actually would've put money on you and Hannah going the distance.'

'Even though she's so young?'

'She's twenty-three. That's not so young.'

'Do you think?'

I sighed. 'It looks like it was more your problem than hers.'

Paul pulled at the label on the wine, eventually tearing off a small strip. 'I wasn't right for her.

And I think she knew it.'

'Ah, so it was Hannah's fault you split up? You were doing her dirty work for her? Come on, surely not even you believe that?'

Paul didn't reply and I didn't say anything to ease the tension because I was thinking about Hannah and how I knew exactly how she would be feeling and what would be going through her mind.

We sat in silence. Paul proceeded to tap his left foot in time to some imaginary soundtrack in his head which made me want to sit as still as I could just to be awkward. It was only when Ed and Sharon's back door opened spilling light and music into the garden that we both jolted back to life but then relaxed when we saw that it was Vicky.

'Everything okay?' she called out.

'Yeah, we're all good,' replied Paul.

'I'm just letting you know that Chris and I will probably be getting off soon.'

'We'll be in soon,' I replied. 'Don't go without saying goodbye, okay?'

Vicky closed the door, plunging us both back into the darkness and silence. Paul coughed and then looked at me. 'Do you know Chris and Vicky will have been married ten years this coming year? A kid. A proper home. A proper life. All in ten years.'

I nodded, wondering where he was going with this train of thought.

'I suppose it's just got me thinking,' he continued, 'You know — about wasted time.'

I put on a rubbish American accent in the

hope of lightening the mood: 'You're preaching to the choir.'

I went to take another swig of wine but misjudged the manoeuvre, missed my mouth altogether and spilled some down my chin. I wiped my face with the sleeve of my cardigan and looked over at Paul to see that he was watching me with a look in his eyes that I couldn't quite work out.

'Have I still got wine on my face?'

Paul shook his head.

'Then what?'

'You wouldn't believe me if I told you.'

'Try me.'

He stood up, turned to face me and held my hands. 'You think you don't want what other people want,' he began. 'You think that all you want is to be alone. But it's not true. The day will come when you'll be so sick of being alone that you won't know what to do. And when it happens come and find me and we'll pick up right where we left off.'

I pulled my hands away from him. 'Do you think that's funny?' I barked. 'Is that what I am? Just some kind of pathetic joke?'

'Of course not, Mel,' he said urgently. 'If you would just listen for a second I'm trying to tell you that you were right.' He grabbed my hands again. 'You asked me earlier why I'd split up with Hannah and here's your answer: I split up with Hannah because of you. I did feel for Hannah. It's true. I liked her a lot. But the thing I couldn't escape was that she wasn't you.'

'I don't understand,' I replied. 'I don't

understand what you're saying at all.'

'Well understand this,' he said, kissing me as a firework roared up into the sky and filled the air with a rainbow of tiny stars. 'Understand that right here and now I'm asking you to pick up where we left off.'

One Month Later

Charlotte and Cameron's House-Warming Party

January 2006

Melissa

It was just after five on the last Saturday in January and I was standing at the bus stop outside the university library. It had been raining solidly all day and now that it was dark the streets seemed deserted. As a sudden gust of wind blew a sheet of rain against the shelter I huddled myself further into the corner for protection, closed my eyes and wished that I was somewhere else.

My day so far had already proved nothing more than an utter waste of time. I'd been given an essay title before Christmas, three thousand words on: *The Meaning of the Metaphysical in Seventeenth-Century Art*. Given that I frequently found it difficult to understand a single word that my lecturer said past the point that she opened her mouth to say good morning, I'd relegated the essay to the lower reaches of my To Do list in the hope that, if left long enough, it might somehow write itself. I ignored it for so long in fact that I forgot about it completely until the Friday morning when my lecturer reminded us that it was due in first thing Monday morning. With two shifts of my part-time job at Blue-Bar to complete and Charlotte and Cameron's house-warming party

61

to focus on, I'd begun to wonder when exactly I was going to find the time to breathe, let alone write an essay. Determined to get as much of it done as possible before time ran out altogether, I'd optimistically set my alarm for six in the morning in the hope of getting a head start on the day. What I failed to take into consideration was how quickly six o'clock in the morning came round when, following an evening of drinking and talking, you only allow yourself to give in to sleep at two.

The moment my clock radio lurched into life, dragging me from the deepest of deep sleeps to a confused state of consciousness, was one I'd rather forget. Everything hurt. My ears, my brain, my limbs. And I wanted it to stop. So pushing my bedside table away from the wall, I'd reached down to the socket and in one swift movement yanked the plug out. Taking a few moments to savour the merciful silence, I rolled over on to my side, sleepily kissed Paul's ear, and allowed myself to fall gently back to sleep.

The next sound that I heard was the front door slamming shut as Creepy Susie left to go to work at the bank. Turning to face my clock radio I was horrified to see that the digital display was completely blank. That was when it all came back to me. I reached for my watch, hoping that it might be eight, or even nine at the very latest and was horrified to see that it was nearly midday. In that instant my entire future life flashed before my eyes: the essay wouldn't get done, I would fail my course and be doomed to work at Blue-Bar forever.

Cursing my decision to re-enter higher education as a so-called 'mature' student, I'd flung myself into the shower, grabbed some clean underwear, recycled the clothes that I'd been wearing the night before and, grabbing a piece of toast and a bottle of water, left Paul unconscious underneath my duvet.

By the time I reached the university library, not only were all the tables in the Art History department taken by my fellow last-minute-essay-writing course members but, of the sixteen text books on the reading list, only one was still on the reference shelves. And I strongly suspected that the only reason for this was because some juvenile joker had deftly sketched a penis in marker pen on the front cover that featured a reproduction of a Rubens' portrait of Marchesa Brigida Spinola Doria.

I spent most of the afternoon in the library during which time I managed to sketch out a rough essay plan and make ten pages of notes. By the time I decided to call it a day I was completely demoralised by both the concept of education and what I perceived to be a distinct inability to carry out my life as a fully formed adult.

As I left the library and walked out into the dark and the rain the only thing that kept me going was the fact that in a short while I'd forget all about the rain and the cold, my unwritten essay and my shifts at Blue-Bar. I tried to concentrate on the simple images of happiness: kicking off my shoes and climbing into bed; reading the weekend's newspaper from cover to cover and falling asleep; but the thought that gave me the warmest glow was seeing Paul again.

★ ★ ★

Of course I'd had my shaky moments since we'd got back together but as far as I was concerned the past weeks had been nothing short of perfect. The best start to a new year I'd ever had. After Ed and Sharon's party, Paul and I had walked back to his place hand-in-hand, neither one of us able to believe that after all this time apart — five whole years — we were finally back together again. And though I had a thousand and one questions in my head about where things were going, I didn't ask a single one. I shouted down every last shred of fear and doubt, determined to act first and ask questions later. Yes, things were complicated. But that didn't seem to matter any more.

When I woke up on New Year's Day lying in Paul's arms I told myself that even if it all ended in the next few seconds, to have experienced that single morning moment, to have felt the delight of knowing the thing you hope for most in life could come true, all of it would have been worth the pain that would inevitably follow.

And it was inevitable.

All the evidence said so. Paul had only just split up with Hannah and I was obviously part of the rebound. The stuff about wanting what Chris and Vicky had got smacked too much of Paul's binary logic: one second everything is off then he flicks a switch in his head and turns everything back on again. How was I supposed to follow a line of thinking that was more dependent on individual gut reaction than rational thought? Before Paul had even woken up I'd convinced myself that this would all seem like a monumental mistake to him.

I got up and dressed without waking him and was almost at his front gate when I heard him call my name. I tried to explain that I didn't blame him for what had happened but I just couldn't seem to get the words out. And that was the moment that Paul chose to tell me that he loved me for the very first time since we split up. I was torn. When you love someone as much as I loved Paul, you have a constant battle between the sane self-preserving you who is outraged at having been treated so badly and the vulnerable besotted you who wants to fall right back in love and jump into the past with both feet. This besotted you wins out eventually because it just feels so good, so sweet to let it.

But at the same time as I felt this love, rather than being happy I was angry and hurt. I told him that his words were 'just words' and I reminded him of the fact that he had broken my heart, of the fact that there had been times when I thought I would never recover from what he did to me. I reminded him of the fact that in the five years we were apart I'd never moved on from him, preferring to wait patiently for him like (Vicky's words sprung to mind) 'some sort of lap dog' when I should have found some self-respect and moved on. And finally I told him that I was angry and I was hurt and that I wasn't sure if I'd ever be able to forgive him for what he'd done.

There was a long silence. And as I stood there looking at Paul, wondering which way things were going to go, I realised that I just wasn't angry any more.

Hannah

It was early evening and I was sitting in my tiny flat in Prestwich. For the fifth time in the last hour I reached inside my bag, took out my Nokia, scrolled through the address book until I got to Paul's number and paused with my thumb hovering above the call button. At the last moment my nerve failed me. I put my phone down on the coffee table in front of me, closed my eyes and thought about Paul.

Paul and I first met at the party my cousin Sophie threw for her husband Stephen's fortieth birthday. As a surprise Sophie had hired one of the screens at the Cornerhouse for the evening and invited forty of Stephen's friends and family to watch his favourite film, *Reservoir Dogs*. Just to make sure that everyone got into the spirit of the evening, the invitation had stated in embossed scarlet print that the dress code was: Black suit, white shirt, black tie and sunglasses (hand gun: optional).

It had been a real spectacle arriving at the venue to see all of Stephen's friends queued up in the rain outside the cinema as if they were waiting to get into a convention for contract killers. Everyone who had been invited to the

66

party really made an effort to look the part. Apart from one: Paul. On the morning of the party he had forgotten to take his suit with him into work and would've ended up missing the film altogether if he'd gone back home and so, dressed in T-shirt and jeans, he'd stood out like the proverbial sore thumb.

After the screening I'd been milling around on my own when Stephen called me over and introduced us. Paul and I initially made polite small talk during which I learned his name and the fact that he and Stephen knew each through working for the city's social services' vulnerable adult team but then Stephen, having already drunk far too much, entered into a massive monologue about the perils of turning forty. Before he could get into full flow he was interrupted by Sophie demanding that he circulate, so Paul and I were left on our own.

We remained together for the rest of the night. Although we were enjoying each other's company I remember wondering whether this was simply because, like him, I was one of the few single people at the party and we'd realised that the evening was going to be a lot less stressful if we worked as a team. However, when a pretty red-haired woman who was clearly very pleased to see Paul came over to say hello, and I offered him the opportunity to go his own way, he dismissed her with a subtle but ruthless efficiency that made me think perhaps we were thinking on the same wavelength.

At the end of the evening Paul asked me if I was interested in sharing a taxi home even though Chorlton and Prestwich weren't exactly in the same direction. Although I didn't want our evening together to end, a voice inside me told me to take things slowly and so I explained that I had to be up early in the morning for work. He nodded and suggested that we go out some time but rather than just leaving it at that he actually got out his work diary and suggested some dates on the spot.

We met up again on the Tuesday of the following week. He took me to the opening of a new show at a city art gallery that one of his friends was involved in and we spent all night talking and making jokes, barely looking at any of the paintings. At one point during the night he asked me point blank how old I was and for a second I considered lying because even though age wasn't an issue for me — my last boyfriend had been a good deal older than me — it made me think that perhaps it was an issue for Paul. In the end I told him straight out that I was twenty-three and then he asked me if I knew how old he was and I told him that I'd guessed from some of the things that he'd said that he was in his mid-thirties. I asked if my age was going to be a problem (which was odd considering that we hadn't even kissed) and he said no, it was for my benefit, not his. When I asked him to explain he just said, 'It's just that the older you get the more baggage you collect and I've got more than my fair share.' I would've asked him more but then his friend who was involved in the show came over and the moment was lost.

The following weekend we went to a Spanish restaurant on Deansgate for lunchtime tapas and we had the best time ever. All we did was talk and talk like there was no tomorrow. In fact we talked so much that it was early evening by the time we left and as we stood watching the traffic pass by it felt completely natural to kiss him — as if we had known each other for years rather than days. As we walked back along Deansgate hand-in-hand pausing only to indulge in our mutual compulsion to kiss I remember saying to myself, in a way that I'm ashamed to admit, given how I'd promised that I would take things slowly, 'I think this is it. I really think I might fall in love with you.'

After a beginning as sweet and romantic as ours I think I can be forgiven for being taken by surprise by the way things ended. I hadn't seen it coming at all. Why would I? We'd been together nearly nine months, I'd thought things were going fine and we were supposed to be going to his work's Christmas party.

My flatmates had gone out for the night and I was waiting for Paul to pick me up when he called my mobile. I thought he was calling to say he was on his way or stuck in traffic, never guessing for a second that something was wrong. Before he could say a word I started asking about the party and who was going to be there and what time he thought we would leave, but he just cut me dead and said: 'I think we should stop seeing each other.'

Since then, I'd seen Paul only once, and that was to get some things of mine that I'd left at his house — amongst them a silver necklace that my mother had bought me for my twenty-first-birthday. I'd planned to leave my request on his home answerphone when I knew he'd be at work and was completely thrown when after three rings or so my call was answered by Melissa.

Paul and I had rowed about his friendship with Melissa on several occasions when we were together. It wasn't just that she was his ex-girlfriend that bothered me or that she was his age, or even that they were so close. What really bothered me was the fact that even though it had been nearly five years since they had split up, she was obviously still in love with Paul. What was worse was that Paul knew it too. Though he never said anything directly about his feelings towards her I could just tell that he felt some sort of obligation towards her that was completely non-negotiable. So why did I put up with it? Why didn't I just walk away? I don't know. I really wish I knew for sure. But if I had to hazard a guess it would come down to this: I loved Paul and the thought of losing him because of his friendship with Melissa genuinely terrified me.

Determined not to give her the pleasure of knowing she'd unsettled me, and without going into any pleasantries at all, I told Melissa what I was after and asked if she would pass the message on to Paul when he returned home. Half an hour later Paul returned my call, brusque and to the point and so, mirroring his manners, I said that I didn't care about the other things but I wanted my necklace back immediately. And so we arranged to meet after work in town on the Monday of the following week.

I stood under the awning outside the HMV store on Market Street watching hordes of sales shoppers making their way through the rain. Paul was over ten minutes late, allegedly because of a meeting that over-ran. He was different from how he had been on the phone. He even tried to make small talk but I was too angry to respond. He took the necklace out of his jacket pocket and handed me a small black hold-all with the rest of my belongings.

'I'm really sorry,' he said. 'About everything. You didn't deserve this. None of this was your fault.'

I didn't reply. I just took my things from him and walked away.

That was weeks ago now and I'd neither seen nor heard from him since.

Opening my eyes I looked at the digital display on the DVD player under the TV. It was getting late and I could feel a sense of despair rising in me at the thought that time was running out. Glancing from the clock on the video to the phone on the table and back again, I decided to try him again later and called my sister Jessica instead.

Melissa

It was just after nine-thirty and Paul and I were standing outside Charlotte and Cameron's

71

imposing three-storey Edwardian house in Didsbury, finding it hard to believe that we actually knew people who owned houses as big as this.

'This is amazing,' I said as we stood staring up at it. 'Everything from the front door through to the huge sash windows seems like it's been built on a larger scale than normal houses. It's like a palace for giants.' I sighed. 'I'm in love with this place and I haven't even been inside it yet.'

Paul grinned. 'Maybe I'll buy you one, one day . . . if you're good.'

'What with? Brass buttons?'

Paul squeezed my hand. 'I have my ways.'

Despite having been back together just under a month, we hadn't told anyone about us yet although I reckoned that Vicky had her suspicions. She had grilled me several times about New Year's Eve and had seemed less than convinced by my answers. Tonight, at Charlotte and Cameron's, we were finally going to go public.

'So, are you ready for this, or what?' I asked.

'You're making too big a deal about it,' said Paul. 'No one will care one way or the other that we're back together.'

'Just you wait and see,' I said knowingly.

I rang the doorbell and waited and after a few moments Charlotte came to the door and welcomed us both in, with Cameron right behind her. I hadn't seen them since last summer at Cooper and Laura's barbecue so I was really pleased to be there.

'It's great to see you, Charlie.' I kissed her on

the cheek. 'You look so well and your house is amazing.'

Before Charlotte and I could have a proper catch-up the doorbell rang again and so while Paul and Cameron started exchanging opinions on City's recent form I stood on my own admiring the Minton tiled floor, the framed prints (a couple of Miros, an Andy Warhol and a Modigliani) and the rectangular mirror above the arty-looking radiator and found myself wondering whether one day Paul and I could ever have a place of our own just as nice as this.

★ ★ ★

As more people arrived, Paul and I eventually gravitated from the hallway to the back room before making our way to the kitchen, greeting people as we went. In the kitchen we finally found our friends huddled in conversation in front of Charlotte and Cameron's huge American-style fridge. No one commented on the fact that Paul and I had arrived together: the boys automatically shared out a four-pack of Stella refusing Laura's offer of a glass because 'it would ruin the drinking experience as a whole'. Laura rolled her eyes, while I inwardly chastised myself for finding Coop's comment even faintly amusing. Vicky grabbed a half-full bottle of rosé from the kitchen counter and shared it out between herself, me and Laura.

'This place is beautiful,' said Vicky deliberately taking in the whole room. 'How much do you reckon they paid for it?'

Charlotte and Cameron's kitchen was like something out of a magazine. All the units were in gloss white and all the appliances were made from stainless steel and were so spotless they must have been brand new.

'I shudder to think,' replied Laura. 'Just the thought of getting a mortgage makes me feel sick.'

I looked over at Paul to see if now was the right time to break our big news. He gave me the nod and so I called for everyone's attention.

'I know this is going to sound a bit weird,' I began, 'and that it will probably all end in tears, but I just want you all to know that Paul and I . . . well, we've sort of got back together.'

Unable to hide his look of disbelief, Chris turned to Paul for confirmation.

'Look,' said Paul, 'it's no big deal, all right? We've been back together since New Year's Eve and things are going great and I for one think that's pretty much all you need to know.'

'You've obviously both lost your minds!' Chris was wide-eyed. 'Let's put this to a vote, shall we? Raise your hand in the air if you agree with Mr Rogers here when he says that he and Melissa getting back together is — and I quote — 'no big deal'?'

Vicky and Laura shook their heads in a disapproving manner but neither of them put their hands in the air.

'And who agrees with me,' continued Chris, 'when I say that them getting back together is probably the biggest deal of this century so far?'

Chris and Cooper waved their hands in the air

like overly excited school boys.

'Then, it's just as well that neither of us gives a toss one way or the other what any of you lot think,' said Paul, grinning. 'Now, unless we're going to sit here all night dissecting the repercussions of what is essentially none of your business, might I suggest that we get on with drinking beer and talking nonsense?'

Grateful that the underlying tension of the moment was over everyone laughed and moved on to other topics.

'I'm sorry about that,' said Laura after a few moments.

'It's okay,' I replied.

Vicky gave me a hug. 'You must get sick of people like us doom-mongering about anything to do with you and Paul.'

I laughed. 'I do get a bit sick of it but it's not like I blame you all. Even I'm a little bit freaked by everything that's happened.'

Vicky nodded. 'But things are going well?'

'Couldn't be better. Things are different.'

'Different how?'

'It's hard to say exactly. It's more him that's changed than me. It's like . . . I don't know . . . he's finally grown up.' I paused. 'I know how this looks. You think it's like watching the first five minutes of a disaster film where you're just waiting for something to go wrong. I know why you feel like that. If I hadn't seen the way he is now, or heard first-hand the things that he has been saying to me, well I'd be waiting for it all to go wrong too. I mean he's not exactly what you'd call a safe bet. He's Paul. The original scourge of womankind. If the tables were turned I wouldn't think twice about advising the two of you to run for the hills. But like I said, he's changed. And I like what I see now. I like it more than ever.'

Vicky smiled warmly. 'Then I'm thrilled for you.'

'Me too,' said Laura.

'Really?'

'Absolutely.'

Hearing my friends say this made me feel genuinely relieved. Things were going to be good this time. Us getting back together wasn't going to be the disaster everyone thought. This really would be my happy ever after.

Chris

It was just after eleven and I was outside having a cigarette and sharing my opinion on the big news with Vicky. Since Paul and Melissa had dropped their bombshell we had all been grinning like idiots, wishing them well and reassuring them everything really would be okay.

'It just makes me feel a bit weird,' I explained. 'The idea of the two of them getting back together . . . I don't know . . . it's not going to work, is it? Paul's not right for her and she's not right for him and the whole thing is just going to blow up in their faces.'

Vicky nodded. 'I know what you mean. Sometimes I look at our friends' lives, not just Melissa and Paul's, and I can't help but think that — '

76

' — you're glad you're not them?'

'No,' said Vicky quickly. 'That's an awful thing to say. I love them to bits.'

'I'm not saying you don't.'

'Good.'

'It's just that I feel a bit mean for saying it, that's all.'

'You haven't actually said anything yet. Maybe you should start with Cooper and Laura. They're always good for a laugh.'

'I don't understand what they're doing,' continued Vicky. 'They've been together ages and he's absolutely mad about her and yet I always get the feeling that Laura's not all that bothered.'

'You haven't told her that he's going to propose, have you?'

'No, of course not. But I've got a horrible feeling that she's going to turn him down. I just wish that if she wasn't serious about him she'd let him go so he could find someone who would really appreciate him.'

I laughed. 'Maybe you should put yourself forward as a candidate.'

'Trust you to twist things around like that! Don't get me wrong, I love Laura, but I worry that they're not right for each other. And I worry that they're going to miss out on what they really want by being with each other.'

'They'll be fine. Once you get to our age you don't split up unless things are really, really bad. None of us can face the idea of going back to the beginning because we've all travelled too far to where we are to make it worth the effort.'

Vicky shot me another disapproving look. 'So you're saying they'll stay together out of laziness?'

'I wouldn't call it laziness exactly. Maybe realism would be a better word.'

'Realism?'

'Or pragmatism. Anything that basically means accepting the first truth of being in your thirties: that you can't always get what you want but that what you've got is always going to be better than nothing.'

'Is that why we've lasted as long as we have? Pragmatism?'

'No.'

'Then why are we still together?'

'How am I supposed to answer that without giving you the ammunition to make my life a misery? No thanks. I'll keep schtum.'

'You can have a free pass,' said Vicky. 'Say what you like without fear of me having a go.'

'Like that free pass you gave me when you asked me if I thought you were turning into your mother?' I shook my head. 'Never again.'

'A real free pass this time. No retribution whatsoever.'

'No, thanks,' I replied having mulled over her proposition for all of half a second. 'I think we're on safer ground talking about Melissa and Paul.'

Hannah

By the time I ended my marathon phone conversation with my sister it was just after eleven. And of the many things that she said to me the one thing that she was adamant about was that I was making a big mistake even thinking about calling Paul tonight. Time and time again she kept coming back to it until she almost convinced me that she was right. Calling Paul wasn't just a bad idea. It was the worst idea that I had ever had. But as I started getting ready for bed, taking off my make-up and brushing my teeth, I found myself taking one last look at my mobile lying on the table in the hallway to see if I'd missed any calls and before I'd even fully realised what I was doing I had dialled his number.

'Hello?'

I could hear music and talking in the background as though he was at a party or out at a bar somewhere in town.

'It's me, Hannah,' I said thinking how odd it was hearing his voice after being apart these past few weeks. 'I really need to talk to you.'

There was a long silence — the sound of someone clearly caught off guard.

'It's really late,' he said eventually. 'Can't it wait?'

'No, it can't,' I replied. 'I need to talk to you right now. I wouldn't ask if it didn't mean a lot to me, Paul. You know that.' I could feel myself starting to cry. 'Please, I'm asking just this one thing. This one thing and then I swear on my life you'll never have to do this again.'

'If it's so important,' he sighed, 'why don't you just tell me now and get it over with?'

'I can't,' I explained. 'I need to see you in person.'

'Look, Hannah,' he began, 'I'm really sorry but I think you ought to know that I'm seeing someone, okay? So if this is about you and me getting back together it's not going to happen.'

This was hardly big news. I couldn't imagine Paul staying on his own for long. I briefly wondered who it might be but it was too miserable a thought.

'It's not about getting back together, I promise you. Look, if you give me twenty minutes to get ready and drive over to wherever you are we can talk and you can go right back to your friends, okay? I just need a few minutes of your time. I'm begging you, please.'

There was one last long silence.

'Five minutes,' he said. 'Five minutes and then I'm gone.'

Vicky

It was nearly half past eleven and Charlotte and I were standing in the hallway reminiscing about our time at Northbridge Primary when Cameron came up and asked where the spare tea towels were as someone had spilt red wine on the sofa. At the mention of the words 'red wine' in conjunction with 'sofa' Charlotte sprung to life as if she was a doctor on *ER* and ordered Cameron to look for soda water while she disappeared to assess the damage.

Now seemed as good a time as any to go to the loo and I joined the queue outside the bathroom upstairs, thinking about my earlier conversation with Chris. As close as Melissa and I were, sometimes I couldn't even begin to understand how she coped with everything going on in her life. The lack of money, flat-sharing with strangers, and especially her latest saga with Paul. All fine and part of life in general when you're in your twenties but enough to make me feel sick with tension at the thought of doing it at our time of life.

Not many people know this, but in my entire adult life (starting from the age of seventeen with my very first boyfriend) I'd never actually been single. Not even for a day. When I had first admitted this to Chris he thought I was joking so I gave him a detailed breakdown of my entire relationship CV right on the spot: eight years, three boyfriends, no gaps (but with some minimal overlapping caused by my extricating myself from the guy I was sort of seeing — Alex Deedman — in order to go out with boyfriend number three — Chris Cooper). Though I'd tried to explain to him that my lack of singleness hadn't been a deliberate strategy, I was afraid Chris would assume my actions made me a cliché of feminine neediness. I'd even contemplated redrawing my CV with a few invented periods of singleness scattered in for good luck but hated the thought of lying to him, even about something so small.

Emerging from the loo some time later I headed downstairs in search of Chris. On my way to the front living room I spotted Chris's friend Tony. He was holding the hand of a pretty girl with dark brown wavy hair that came down past her shoulders. Looking at her face for a moment I thought I saw a flash of recognition on her face, even though I was sure we hadn't met before.

'Long time no see. Have you just turned up?'

Tony flashed me his trademark big grin. 'We weren't going to come 'cos Polly wasn't feeling great, but then I got to thinking how I hadn't seen some of this crowd in ages and so with a bit of cajoling she valiantly made the effort. How are you, anyway? You're looking good. Where's the old man tonight?'

'Your guess is as good as mine.' I smiled at Tony's friend.

Tony suddenly came to life. 'Sorry, Vicks,' he apologised. He turned to Polly. 'You remember Chris, don't you? He was the one cooking at Cooper's barbecue last summer.'

'I think I know the one you're on about,' said Polly amiably. 'The one who told the Elephant Man story?'

'Yeah,' replied Tony. 'That's the one. Well, this is Vicky, my mate Chris's wife. And this,' continued Tony gesturing to the girl, 'is Polly Matthews, my girlfriend, best mate and,' cheesily, 'the light of my life.'

Chris

Tony and I were friends from back in our early twenties when we'd lived in a houseshare in Rusholme during my final year at university. One Saturday afternoon Tony had got it into his head to get his nose pierced. Rather than getting it

82

done properly however, he opted to get it done on the cheap by a goth girl he fancied two doors down from us who owned her own home-piercing kit. Within hours of putting the stud in his nose the whole side of his face swelled up to the size of a football, thereby earning him the nickname 'Elephant Man Tony'.

Tony was one of those people to whom this type of thing was always happening and I delighted in telling the stories of his misfortunes to pretty much anyone who would listen, even more so when the person in question was female. So when Tony introduced me to his new girlfriend, Polly, at Cooper and Laura's barbecue last summer it was almost inevitable that the 'Elephant Man' story would get an airing.

'I can't believe you went through all that pain just for a girl,' said Polly, laughing as I finished the story.

'That's not the half of it,' replied Tony. 'I didn't even get a look in with the goth girl. She ended up going out with Chris's mate Paul about a fortnight after that. Turns out she was into guys with normal-shaped heads.'

For a moment or two I felt bad for making Tony look so hopeless in front of his new lady friend and so to balance things out at bit I shared a few stories with Polly that showed him in a slightly better light. Eventually even Tony grew tired of being the centre of attention so he moved on to an altogether different conversation with Cooper, leaving me to entertain Polly (who didn't know anyone else at the party) on my own.

We talked for nearly an hour about pretty

much anything at all that came to mind. I kept telling her that she shouldn't feel trapped and even advised her to find someone more exciting to talk to. She replied she had no intention of going anywhere now that she was in with a man who was cooking the burgers.

The conversation only came to a close when I realised that I'd cooked all of the food that was in my charge and people started to call me over to join them and eat.

'Look,' I said, 'I'd better go. It was really nice talking to you.'

'You too,' she replied. 'Maybe I'll see you later.'

'Yeah,' I replied. 'That would be nice.'

I didn't really think anything more about the encounter. Yes, I'll admit that I was aware of how attractive she was (it was hard not to given that she had more than a touch of the Natalie Imbruglias about her — the dark hair, the tanned skin, the big Bambi-like eyes) but at that point in time that was it. To me she was just a mate's girlfriend, and that was all. I had no intention of anything else happening, not even on a subconscious level. I was a married man. I had a wife and a kid. And as far as I was concerned that was the end of the story.

Around one in the morning, as people were beginning to go home, I'd disappeared inside the house to use the toilet: my bladder was bursting after having over-indulged on the crates of Stella that Cooper and I had brought back from a recent duty-free trip to Calais. As I came out of the loo into the darkness of the upstairs hallway I was surprised to see Polly standing to one side as though she had been waiting for me.

'I just wanted to thank you for making my evening so entertaining,' she said. 'I would've been lost without you.'

'No problem. It's always nice to wheel out Tony's Elephant Man story to someone new. You and Tony should come round for dinner at ours some time.'

'That would be lovely,' she replied. 'I'll get Tony to sort something out.' She reached out her arms as though she was going to hug me goodbye and although I thought it was a little over familiar given that she was my mate's girlfriend and I'd only known her five seconds I decided to go with the flow and open my arms to embrace her.

The moment our bodies were pressed against each other, I quickly became aware that this was no ordinary platonic embrace. This was something else. And I was standing on one side of a line which, were I to cross it, would inevitably lead to trouble. But rather than take a step backwards and place myself in a position of safety, I took a step forwards, putting myself well within the danger zone. I felt as if I couldn't help myself. She was young, pretty and for some reason known only to herself she wanted me. I just didn't think I was in any sort of position to refuse. I bent my head down and leaned in towards Polly's open lip-glossed lips. I had no idea how long we kissed for, minutes, seconds, none of it really mattered now that I was on the wrong side of the line. I was kissing someone who wasn't Vicky and in doing so I was betraying not only my wife but also a good friend of mine and, rather than feeling guilty, I felt thoroughly exhilarated. And when I broke off from the kiss it wasn't because I was scared of being caught (even though I was) or because I'd come to my senses (as I definitely hadn't) but rather because in that single kiss I'd got everything that my ego required: confirmation that I still had what it took to pull girls who looked like Polly.

I chalked the whole episode down to a drunken lapse in judgement. She was young, she was pretty, and it had been an awfully long time since someone like that had even noticed I was alive, let alone considered me worthy of attention. With me feeling this way and Polly looking the way she did, and most importantly of all, with Vicky at home looking after William, the best way forward was to never talk or think about Polly ever again and so I opted to put it all behind me and focus on the future. Things were good between me and Vicky, William was getting more wonderful with every passing day and barring the occasional lapse in control when I found myself reliving that moment with Polly, I was convinced that I'd moved on. Then one moment when I was least expecting it, as if from nowhere she popped back into my life and things were never the same again.

Melissa

It was getting late, I was tired and the warm fuzzy feeling I'd achieved through an evening's drinking was beginning to wear off to be replaced by a knot in my stomach about the essay that I had to hand in on Monday. Making my excuses to a group of Charlotte and Cameron's friends I'd been talking to for a while, I went to seek out Paul (last seen talking to some of Cameron's rugby-playing friends) for a kiss and a cuddle.

I spotted Paul through the crowd of bodies. He was standing by the open front door with his mobile to his ear. I waved to get his attention but he didn't see me so I lingered in the hallway waiting for him to finish his call. Bored, restless and experiencing the weird sensation of missing someone who was less than twenty feet away from me I took out my phone and typed out 'I love you!' in a text message and then pressed send. Even as I returned my phone to my bag I was regretting my actions.

With no way of retrieving the text, the next best course of action seemed to be to send another message saying something self-deprecating along the lines of: 'Please ignore: drunk while text messaging', but at that moment Paul ended his call so I decided I'd tell him myself.

By the time I reached the front door though, he was nowhere to be seen. I scanned the smokers lined up outside Charlotte and Cameron's bay window to see if, after eight years as a non-smoker, he had been tempted to have a crafty one for old times' sake, but he wasn't there either. Now I was really confused. It was only when my attention turned towards the road as a car drove past blaring loud music that I caught a glimpse of Paul's green parka heading in the direction of Wilbraham Road. I tried to tell myself there were a million and one legitimate reasons why he could have left the party without telling me. I tried to tell myself that everything would be okay. But the more I tried to calm myself down the more I could feel myself reverting to my natural fall-back position of doubt and fear. So, without even bothering to head back inside and get my coat I followed him.

It felt weird trailing Paul in the darkness like I was some kind of poor excuse for a private detective. Weird and ridiculous and wrong. After all, what was I doing with him if I didn't have it in me to trust him? The longer I followed him the more obvious it became that he wasn't doing anything out of the ordinary or sinister and gradually I persuaded myself there would be some kind of straightforward explanation. Maybe it was a prank that one of the boys was pulling. Or he was heading to a late-night off-licence to get more drink. Or he was taking a short walk to clear his head. Or even that he was going to get a surprise for me and by doing what I was doing, not only was I ruining the surprise but also showing him first hand that I didn't believe that he had really changed. I was almost ready to turn back when he suddenly came to an abrupt halt near the bus stop less than a hundred feet away from me. From his body language I could tell that he was nervous, and when a woman got out of a car parked on the opposite side of the road it looked as though he was preparing for a confrontation.

The woman and Paul began talking, their

breath rising into the air and mingling overhead. I wanted to get nearer and so continued up the road but the closer I got, the fewer places there were to hide.

As soon as I stepped out of the shadows I recognised the woman immediately. There was no mistaking her. The slim figure. The shoulder-length hair. The grey coat that I'd admired the first time Paul had introduced us. Paul was still seeing Hannah. Or maybe he was going to start seeing her again. That made more sense. The way they were acting seemed like the beginning of something rather than the end. Perhaps he had called her. Told her that he'd changed his mind about me. Maybe he'd even told her that he still loved her.

I had no idea what I was going to say but I didn't doubt for a second what kind of force I'd use to say it. I just couldn't believe Paul would do something like this to me again. Worse than that, I couldn't believe that I was still falling for his lies.

'What's going on?' I yelled once I was within earshot. Paul and Hannah turned to look at me. Paul's eyes widened in surprise but then he just closed them, his head hanging down like a worn-out boxer against the ropes. I was crying, which hadn't been part of my plan at all. 'Tell me what's going on,' I demanded. 'Tell me what's going on right now or I swear I'll make you regret the day you met me.'

Paul opened his eyes. 'It's not what you think,' he said. 'I swear on my life it's not what you think.'

'Then what is it?' I replied. 'Stop scaring me,

89

Paul! What's going on here? Just tell me the truth.'

'I've fucked up, Mel,' he said quietly. 'I've really fucked things up this time.'

A feeling of dread overcame me. I didn't even want to blink in case I missed some microscopic change in his demeanour that might telegraph in advance what I was about to discover.

'She's pregnant,' he said, looking away. 'Hannah's pregnant with my baby.'

Chris

I was leaning against the wall at the front of Charlotte and Cameron's house, halfway through my cigarette and already contemplating having another when I heard the front door open and someone come outside. When I saw that the someone was Polly I looked away but could sense that she had come outside specifically to find me.

'I saw you come out here a while ago.'

I nodded but said nothing.

'Come on, Chris, I really did try my best to get out of tonight. I promise you I did. I told Tony I was feeling ill but he insisted we come.'

'Don't worry, it's not your fault. It's the price you pay for having people in common.'

There was a long silence.

'How are you?'

'I'm okay. You?'

'I've been better.'

There was a hesitancy in her voice as if she had something further to say and I looked straight at her for the first time.

90

'What's up?'

'Nothing,' she replied. 'It's just . . . it's just . . . '

'It's just what?'

'I just met your wife. I didn't mean to. Tony started talking to her. I didn't know how to escape.'

Something deep inside my chest snapped. The two worlds that I had put such effort into keeping separate had collided and were spilling over into each other.

'It really was an accident,' said Polly.

This information didn't make things any easier.

'She seems really nice,' added Polly.

'That's because she is.'

I threw my cigarette on the ground and stubbed it out with my heel.

'Where does Tony think you are?'

'Getting my phone from the car.'

'Is anyone watching us?'

Polly turned and looked up at the house. 'No.'

'Still, though . . . '

'You know this is difficult for me too.'

'It's difficult for everyone.'

Polly gently grazed my hand with her fingertips.

'I love you, you know. I'm not expecting you to say it back. I just wanted you to know. I'd better go. Maybe I'll see you inside later.'

'Yeah,' I replied. 'Maybe later.'

Melissa

'She's pregnant?' I couldn't believe what I was hearing. 'She can't be. It's not true. Tell me it's not true.'

Paul reached for my hands.

'It's true, Mel. I wish it wasn't. But it's all true.'

'But how?' I cried. 'How can it be?'

He looked over at Hannah. 'She called me while I was at the party. She said she needed to see me right away. She sounded upset. I didn't want to come at all. But I felt like I owed her. I thought I could find out what she wanted and be back at the party before you'd even noticed I'd gone.'

I found the courage to look directly at Hannah. The moment our eyes met she looked away. There was over a decade between the two of us. A whole decade. When I was her age I was having the time of my life. Going to parties, bars and clubs with Paul, Vicky and Chris, with nothing more pressing on my mind than the ever-constant search for the next party. And yet here was Hannah, supposedly with her entire life ahead of her, embroiled in a ridiculous love triangle with a pair of jaded idiots old enough to be her significantly older siblings. For a few moments I almost felt sorry for her, but then I recalled my life was falling apart and that if anyone deserved sympathy right now, it was me.

Chris

It all happened just under two months earlier.

I work in legal recruitment. And that year my boss decided that rather than take us all out for a meal, like he usually did, he would book tables at the Midland Hotel for a joint office Christmas party along with several other companies.

Standing at the bar in the main ballroom, waiting to buy a round of drinks for the team that I managed, I felt a tap on my shoulder and turned to see Polly standing in front of me.

'You don't recognise me, do you?' said Polly.

'Of course I do,' I replied. 'You're . . . what's-her-name aren't you?'

Polly laughed. 'Now I *know* you don't remember me.'

'You're Polly Matthews,' I replied, 'you're twenty-eight, you work for a marketing consultancy specialising in food branding, you were born in Lincoln, you went to university in York and your middle name is Louise.'

It was all stuff that she had told me that night we'd first met and of course by referencing these facts I was also referencing in as roundabout a manner as I could manage the fact that we had kissed.

'So you *were* listening?' She asked.

'Just to the interesting bits,' I replied.

She told me that she was here at the hotel with her company and that her colleagues had been drinking since just after lunchtime; although she had only joined them around five, she had more than made up for lost time.

'Well, you look sober enough to me.'

'Believe me, I'm not.'

Just as we'd reached the end of the conversation, the DJ played an old Take That song and the whole ballroom erupted in collective euphoria.

'Relight My Fire,' she said, almost squealing with delight, 'I love this song. You have to come

93

and dance with me.'

'I don't dance,' I replied.

'And I don't care,' replied Polly. She grabbed my hand and led me to the dance floor.

We ended up dancing for over an hour: camping it up to boy bands, disco tunes and cheesy Eighties nostalgia — channelling the flamboyance of the music as an excuse to initiate physical contact: hand to hand, hands to waist then lower back, hips together swaying in time to the music. When an unfamiliar dance song came on and the dance floor emptied Polly led me out of the ballroom. We kissed in the foyer and only stopped when someone from Polly's office passed by. Nervous and jumpy at nearly being caught out we made our way separately to the cloakroom to get our things and leave. Outside a waiting taxi, we were momentarily baffled by the driver's question about where we wanted to go. For the first time that evening I took the lead and called out the hotel near Piccadilly station where we sometimes put up important clients. The only room they had left was a junior suite which cost a fortune, but I booked it on my credit card without hesitation. And as we made our way across the city centre I made sure I didn't think about Vicky, William or even my friend Tony.

In fact, I made sure I didn't think at all.

Melissa

A bus pulled up at the stop where we were all standing. Before its hydraulic doors had even fully opened a trio of teenage boys streamed onto the pavement shouting and yelling abuse at the driver. The driver, a young guy with a shaven head and pierced eyebrow, refused to let the fact that he was in uniform get in the way of taking some form of retribution and coolly brandished the middle finger of his right hand in their direction. The boys, unsettled by his action, jeered him in an attempt to save face. But it was too late. The bus was already pulling away and the driver was no longer looking in their direction. Stubbornly refusing to give in to defeat they chased after the bus but gave up after twenty yards before changing tack and hurling abuse at the back of the bus until it had disappeared from view.

'I'd better go.' Hannah hazarded a brief glance in my direction but I said nothing. I wondered if Paul wanted to say something reassuring to her. That he'd call her. That they would talk later. That somehow this mess would get sorted out. But I knew he wouldn't say a thing for fear of appearing disloyal. Hannah must have understood his predicament because she waited for a mini-cab to pass by, then crossed the road towards her car.

Suddenly every movement she made seemed to be imbued with some extraordinary significance. I could barely take my eyes off her as she opened up the car and put on her seat belt. It was almost as though I was expecting something out of the ordinary to happen now that the laws that governed the everyday activities of life had been irrevocably broken. But nothing out of the ordinary happened. A pretty young girl simply turned on the ignition of her car and cast a last glance across the road at us before driving away.

Vicky

It was getting late and a fair number of people had already made the decision to go home. Chris, Laura, Cooper and I searched around for Melissa and Paul without success, then came to the conclusion that they must have left and right now, as Cooper tastefully put it, 'were probably at Melissa's going at it like there was no tomorrow'. Chris hadn't seemed his usual self since I'd met up with him after my conversation with Tony, and when I asked whether he thought I should send Melissa a text to see if she was okay, his response was to shrug and tell me to do whatever I wanted. I made a mental note to text her when we got home just to be on the safe side.

We got our coats and went to find Charlotte and Cameron to say our goodbyes. I told Charlotte that I would ring her later in the week to arrange a venue for me, Melissa and Laura to meet her for lunch the following weekend. Cameron suggested to Chris and Cooper that if we girls were meeting up for 'one of those lunches that go on until just after midnight' all the boys should meet up for a big night out as compensation. Cooper agreed straight away, jokingly telling Cameron that they should all pay a visit to a new lap-dancing club that had recently opened up in town. Cameron roared that he was definitely up for something like that but Chris barely reacted, and when pushed by Cooper to sign up for their boys' night out would only say that he would have to see how things were nearer the time.

Chris stayed quiet in the car all the way home. He was so lost in his thoughts that as we approached a pedestrian crossing he drove right through, much to the ire of a group of students who had been about to cross. They all managed to get out of the way but one hurled the bag of chips in his hand at the car as it passed by.

'What are you doing?' I yelled. 'You could've killed someone.'

Chris said nothing.

'Look, are you okay, Chris? Do you want me to drive? You haven't seemed right all night.'

'I'm fine. Just leave me alone, okay?'

'No, it's not okay,' I replied. 'If you want to be left alone, you're out of luck because I'm not going anywhere.'

Chris slowed down and pulled over to the side of the road.

'What are you doing? We're only a few minutes from home.'

I put my hand on his shoulder. 'Talk to me, sweetheart. What's the matter? You haven't been right since we left the party.'

'I'm fine,' he said but I could see that his hands were shaking.

'Look, you're not fine at all. Just tell me what's going on.'

'Nothing's going on, okay?' He closed his eyes

and began rocking backwards and forwards, then without warning let out a groan from somewhere deep inside his chest. His hands clenched, he rained blow after blow down on the steering wheel in front of him until, exhausted, he finally broke down in tears.

Melissa

Paul and I stood in silence, staring at the pavement, the road, the trees and the cars around us — anything but each other. A group of lads were chatting at the bus stop about the night out in front of them.

Paul lifted his head and looked at me. 'You must be freezing.'

'I'm fine.'

'Are you sure?'

'I said I'm fine.'

Paul took off his coat and put it around my shoulders. I hadn't even realised that I was cold until I felt the weight of his coat warm with the heat of his body. For a few moments I felt comforted, as though he had put his arms around me and was holding me close. But when he tried to do just that a few moments later I flinched away from him the second his hand touched my shoulder.

Paul looked hurt but I didn't care.

'Did you cheat on me again?'

'No, of course I didn't. You don't really believe that, do you? You must know I'd never do that to you again.'

'So how many weeks gone is she?'

'I don't know exactly,' said Paul. 'It wasn't that kind of conversation.'

'And . . . and you're sure?'

'That I didn't cheat on you? That it's mine? Or that she's telling the truth?'

'All of the above.'

Paul shook his head. 'I didn't cheat on you, Mel, I promise. And as for the other questions I wish I had some reason to doubt her in either scenario but I haven't.'

So there it was. The last possible escape route closed off. I looked at my watch. 'Everybody will be wondering where we are.'

'Do you want to go back to the party?'

I shook my head and finally let out all the tears I'd been holding back.

'Why did this have to happen now? We were going to be so happy. We were going to make everything right.'

'We still can be happy,' said Paul, putting his arms around me. 'We can still make everything right.'

I shook my head. 'How long has she known?'

'She took the test just after New Year.'

'So why didn't she tell you earlier?'

'She said she needed time to sort her head out.'

'So what does she want from you now?'

'I really don't know. Like I said, it wasn't that kind of conversation.'

'So you'll be seeing her again to clear up the details?'

'I'll have to . . . you understand that, don't you?'

'Is she going to keep it?'

Paul said nothing.

I repeated the question. 'I said, is she going to keep it?'

'She doesn't know,' he replied.

I felt as though I was going to be sick. Everything was becoming too real. Too intense. I wanted the emotions boiling up inside my chest to go away. I wanted to be back in control of my life and all the things I was feeling. I closed my eyes, momentarily blocking out the world.

'So what does she want from you? You're not hers any more. You're mine. Why is she involving you in all this? Does she want you back?'

'This is a mess,' he said quietly. 'I know it is. I screwed up. But we'll sort it out, I promise. We'll be fine.'

'But that's just it,' I replied. 'We won't be fine. We won't be fine at all. You've been telling me for the longest time how you're ready to settle down. Ready to grow up and be more responsible. This could be just what you need. A fresh start. A new beginning . . . ' I could barely get the word out, ' . . . a baby.'

'You're my fresh start, Mel. You're my new beginning. I don't want her. I want you. You are all that matters. Just you and no one else.'

I wanted to believe Paul. I wanted to believe him so much that the desire to be proved wrong was like a burning ache in my chest.

'I love you,' said Paul.

'But that's not enough any more.' I broke away from his embrace. 'What do you think she'll do if you don't go back to her?'

Paul shrugged, the hopelessness of the situation apparent in the dullness of his eyes.

'It's out of my hands,' he said.

I exploded in anger. 'How dare you say that! How dare you! It's not out of your fucking hands. It's not out of your hands at all!'

The students at the bus stop were looking at the two of us with embarrassed amusement. I struggled to catch my breath through my tears. 'She won't have the baby if you don't go back to her. She won't go through with the pregnancy. She'll get rid of it if she thinks you're never coming back. She'll get rid of it because she'll think she has no choice.'

Paul cut me short, his eyes flashing with indignation. 'You don't know that for sure. How could you? No one knows what's going through Hannah's head right now apart from Hannah herself.'

I looked down at the ground: it seemed the safest place for my eyes to rest. 'But that's just it. I know exactly what she's going through because I've been there too.'

'What are you talking about?' asked Paul. I could see a car crash of questions piling up in his head, one after the other hitting the inside of his skull at maximum velocity. 'What is it you're trying to say? I don't understand.'

'No, you don't,' I replied. 'And I don't expect you ever will.'

Then I turned round and walked away.

Three Months Later

Cath and Simon's Fancy-Dress Party

April 2006

Cooper

It was just after six on the Saturday of Cath and Simon's party when I finally arrived home shattered after having spent the afternoon trudging round jewellery shops on Kingly Street trying to find the perfect engagement ring in order to propose to Laura on her birthday at the end of the month.

I was about to head straight upstairs and hide the box when Laura called from the living room.

'Coop? Is that you, babe?'

'Yeah.'

'The internet has gone off again. Can you fix it for me?'

Stuffing the engagement ring deeper inside the pocket of my leather jacket I made my way to the living room to find Laura sitting at the dining-room table with her laptop in front of her. She stretched her arms out towards me for a kiss. 'Hey, you. Did you get anything good?'

'Nothing much,' I replied as I squeezed her tightly and kissed her on the lips. 'So you've killed the internet connection again?'

'It wasn't me. I didn't touch it.'

Leaning over her shoulders I studied the screen for a moment before solving the whole problem with three clicks of the mouse.

Laura laughed. 'I was just about to do that.'

'Bet you were,' I replied noticing what was on the screen: one of those last-minute-holiday-type booking websites. 'What were you looking at anyway? Holiday porn?' I sighed and rubbed her shoulders affectionately. 'I don't know why you do this to yourself when you know we can't afford it.'

'But that's just it,' replied Laura. 'There are lots of deals on here and we've got loads saved up already. There's stuff on here that's dirt cheap. We could be somewhere better than this dump by next week if you let me make a booking.'

'We've been here before, babe,' I replied, willing the conversation to end as soon as possible. 'The money we've saved isn't there for a weekend at a posh hotel, or a new car, or even some cut-price holiday in the sun. It's for a house. A house for me and you. And I don't understand why you don't get it. House prices round here are going through the roof. And if we don't buy soon then we'll never get a place of our own.'

Laura stood up from the table abruptly and walked over to the bay window. She stood glowering out into the dark street. 'And would that really be so bad?'

'So you're saying you want to rent forever?'

'It has its plus points.'

'Like?'

'Well, for starters not having to save up for deposits that only half of us are interested in.'

'Right, so it's just me that wants to stop

messing around and put down some proper roots?' I sat down on the sofa and tried my best to stay calm. This wasn't what I'd been expecting from the evening at all. I'd just spent a month's wages on a engagement ring. I was planning to ask Laura to marry me. All I wanted to do was sort out some kind of a future for the two of us and she was making me out to be the bad guy.

I looked up at her. 'So you're telling me you'd rather trade sorting out our future for a week's holiday that'll be nothing but memories the minute we land back at the airport?'

There was a long pause and I sensed that she was about to drop some kind of bombshell. 'Well . . . if we're putting all our cards on the table then the truth is I was actually thinking a little longer than a week.'

'What? Like a fortnight?'

She shook her head. 'I was actually thinking more like a year. Come travelling, Coop! You've never been. You'll love it. We could have the best time. We could go anywhere you wanted: Australia, Vietnam, Thailand, Japan . . . you name it.'

'I think we're a bit long in the tooth to be taking a gap year.'

'People our age do it all the time.'

'Do they now?' I hated sounding like I was Laura's dad but I also hated listening to her banging on like a spoilt teenager. In the last year she had given up a well-paid job as a biology teacher at a rough comprehensive school in Preston citing 'unrealistic levels of stress' in order to teach yoga. But then she needed to

107

undertake a week's crash course in how to teach yoga — a course that cost me, not her — the best part of five hundred quid. And since then she had managed to pick up the sum total of three yoga classes a week each paying the princely sum of forty pounds a session.

I needed to calm things down a little. 'So what brought all this on?'

'I've been thinking about it for a while. But I only really made up my mind on New Year's Eve.' She smiled softly. 'Look, I'm not saying we have to go straight away.'

'But a year?' I replied. 'You want to go for a year?'

'Anything less wouldn't be worth it.'

'But why a year? I'd have to give up my job and everything. I mean, are you serious about this? This isn't just some sort of whim?'

'You mean like all my other flighty plans?'

I didn't rise to the bait. 'All I'm asking is are you sure?'

Laura nodded. 'I've checked the prices for the tickets we'll need and we've got more than enough money saved to buy them and cover spending money for a whole year. Look, it will be one last blast of freedom and then we'll come back to England and put down roots as deep as you like wherever you like.'

'But my job . . . I can't . . . ' my voice trailed off. 'I'm not like you. I can't make snap decisions just like that.'

'And you don't have to. All I'm asking is that you think about it. Seriously think about it. We've got the rest of our lives to settle down. But right now I feel like this is our last chance. Our last chance to do something fun.'

Melissa

Lying in bed watching mindless early evening TV on the portable that lived on top of my dresser I was thinking to myself how I was probably due yet another call from Vicky when my mobile rang. I looked at the screen and raised a small smile when I saw that it was indeed Vicky calling.

'Are you dressed yet?'

'No.'

'Why not?'

'Because nothing's changed since our last conversation half an hour ago, or the one we had half an hour before that or the one half an hour before that.'

Vicky laughed. 'But aren't you sick of me calling you like this? I know I would be. I know for a fact that I can be really, really annoying when I want to be. Chris tells me I am all the time.'

'Look, Vicks, I know you're trying to be nice and everything but I can't begin to tell you how much I don't want to go out tonight and even if I did feel like going out, a fancy-dress party would so not be my thing right now.'

'But it's Cath and Simon's birthday party. Cath loves you. She specifically called me this afternoon to make sure that I brought you along.'

'But I've given you a card and a present to give to her — what more does she want?'

'You, to come out tonight, instead of festering in that bedroom of yours like you have been all these weeks. I bet you're even tucked up in bed right now watching one of those ridiculous celebrity talent shows that are always on.'

I picked up the remote and switched off the TV.

'Look, none of this matters as I don't actually want to come out. Why can't you just let me be?'

'Because I don't understand why you're still letting him rule your life like this. You aren't coming tonight because you don't fancy it, you're not coming because you think that Paul's going to be there. And it's not like I blame you because it must be awkward. But things are always going to be like this when the two of you have so many friends in common. So what are you going to do to escape them? Move back to Swindon? Cath and Simon are your friends as well as Paul's. He doesn't own them so I don't see why you're handing them over to him on a plate.' Vicky sighed as though coming to the end of her argument. 'Come out, Mel. You know it'll be a laugh. I'll personally make sure that they play *Abba: Gold* from beginning to end so that we can dance all night if you'll say you'll come. Think about it. When was the last time we all went dancing?'

'I'd love to, babe, I really would, but I just don't feel up to it.'

'But you've done nothing wrong, Mel,' pleaded Vicky. 'It should be Paul avoiding you, not the other way round. It was his mistake, not yours.'

'But that's not really fair, is it?'

'I'm not trying to be fair. I'm trying to be a friend. And if Paul really was trying to be a friend to you he wouldn't come tonight anyway.'

'But that's not what I want either. You, Laura, Cooper and Chris are his friends as well as mine and he's not been in contact with any of you since it all happened. And I don't want him to feel like he's alone in all this. That's not what I want at all.'

'So what do you want?'

'I don't know,' I sighed. 'And that's why I think it's probably best if I don't come tonight. If I see him I don't know what I'll do or say so I think it would be best for all of us if I stayed away.'

Chris

It was just before seven and Vicky and I were in our bathroom getting ready to go to the party. William was in bed, Vicky's mum was downstairs watching TV and we were both standing at the sink brushing our teeth when out of the blue, her mouth full of toothpaste, Vicky said to me, 'I love this, you know.'

I spat my toothpaste into the sink. 'You love what exactly?'

Vicky spat her toothpaste into the sink, rinsed her mouth and then dried her face on the hand towel behind her.

111

'You'll think I'm stupid.'

'Try me.'

Vicky grinned shyly. 'We were just brushing our teeth in time with each other.'

'Were we?'

'It was just a nice moment, that's all.'

'You're easily pleased tonight.' I glanced in the mirror at the freshly shaven skin on my chin. I looked old. I barely recognised this haggard-looking version of myself. 'What's brought this on?'

'Nothing really . . . It's just . . . you know . . . having someone brushing their teeth in unison with you . . . it's nice. And I'm just glad I'm me and that I've got you and William, that's all.' She paused again and looked up to see if I was following her argument. 'Does that make any sense?'

'Yeah,' I replied. 'It does.'

Vicky had been saying stuff like this about 'being happy' and 'how lucky she was to have me and William' in her life on a regular basis since the night when I'd lost the plot coming back from Charlotte and Cameron's. I explained it away at the time by telling her I was really stressed at work, which wasn't hard to be convincing about as I *was* really stressed at work. Looking back, I can sort of see that the real reason for my episode came down to a simple truth of life: you can only manage a certain amount of holding in of things before the pressure builds up, finds a weak spot to exploit and finally makes an exit.

Melissa

Sitting in the darkness staring out of my bedroom window at the passing traffic, I thought about what Vicky had said about hiding myself away from my friends all this time. She was right. It was true. I was hiding. I wasn't sure that I could face seeing him and Hannah. Not enough time had passed to ease the pain I felt. The memories of the night we split up were still my constant companions.

Returning alone to my flat that night I'd felt as though my whole world had ended. I just hadn't known what to do with myself. I called Vicky and told her the vague details and in a matter of minutes she arrived in her car at mine insisting that I came back to hers so that she could look after me (even though, as I later learned, she'd had a few problems of her own to deal with that night.)

I came home the next day and set about writing the essay that I was supposed to hand in on the Monday but I didn't get further than the title before I gave up, decided that a change was as good as a rest, packed a bag and caught the train to Swindon to see my mum and dad. I only stayed there a week. Just long enough to get myself together and try to put Paul out of my mind for good. It was wishful thinking of course. The second I arrived back at Piccadilly he was everywhere I looked, from places we'd been together that I passed in the taxi on the way home right through to the unread newspaper that lay on my bedside table, which he'd left the

113

last time he had stayed over.

The thing that surprised me most was that he hadn't tried to get in contact. From the moment that I'd left him standing alone in the middle of the street that night I'd expected a phone call or a text at least to try to bring me round but there was nothing. News about what he was up to was impossible to come by as even Chris, the closest thing he had to a best friend, hadn't heard from him despite leaving dozens of messages on his voice-mail. None of us knew whether he and Hannah had got back together or whether they had split up for good. We were all completely in the dark. Then at the beginning of February, a few days before my thirty-fifth birthday, as I sat on a bench in Chorlton Park with Vicky and William attempting to enjoy the first signs of spring, I got a text message from Paul out of the blue. All it said was: 'You deserve better.'

I didn't text him back.

Thinking about that message now as I sat looking out on to the street, it occurred to me that he was absolutely right. I did deserve better. Much better. And that was the moment I decided that my first step towards my goal of getting 'much better' would be to stop hiding from both Paul and the world at large. Vicky had been right. It was Paul's mistake, not mine. He should be avoiding me, not the other way round. I picked up my mobile and dialled Vicky's number. She didn't pick up so I left a message.

'It's me,' I said. 'Listen, I'm sorry about

earlier. You were right. I do need to get out more. So if there's still room in the car, there's nothing I'd rather do than join you, Laura and anyone who is up for it in some of the cheesiest dancing the world has ever seen.'

As I put down the phone, I suddenly remembered that thanks to my focus on avoiding Paul, one particularly important fact about Cath and Simon's party had slipped my mind: it was fancy dress. And now that I'd agreed to go I had exactly an hour and ten minutes to come up with something roughly approximating a costume that fitted the theme of the party: 'Hollywood or Bust'.

Hannah

Paul's mobile was ringing.

'Aren't you going to answer it?' I asked when after four rings he hadn't moved off the bed.

'No need,' he replied. 'It'll only be Chris to see if we're coming tonight.'

'So why not put him out of his misery and tell him that we are?'

Paul shrugged, picked up his phone from the bedside table and switched it off. 'Job done.'

'He's probably just worried about you, that's all.'

'Well, I'm fine, so there's nothing to say to him, is there?'

I could tell that Paul wasn't in the right frame of mind for this conversation, so I walked over to the long mirror on the wardrobe to examine my costume: a black dress and cape, red striped tights and a pair of flat red shoes. Paul had guessed 'The Wicked Witch of the West' the second I'd shown him what I was wearing but made no mention of the rather obvious joke that this was how his friends thought of me now that I had succeeded in taking him away from both them and Melissa.

Paul and I had been back together for a while now. He'd called me the evening after I'd told him I was pregnant and we'd talked on the phone for nearly three hours. He told me that he and Melissa had split up although he didn't offer me any details and I hadn't pressed him for any either. I said that it made no difference to me one way or another: I hadn't contacted him with the idea of us getting back together, that I had contacted him because I thought he had a right to know.

Not once that night did he ask me if I was going to go through with the pregnancy. And not once did I seek to reassure him either way. The truth was I hadn't known myself. I just wanted to do the right thing, whatever that might be, and to do it with as much dignity as possible given the circumstances.

I told Paul that I needed time alone and that I was going to stay with my parents in Malvern. I suggested that we meet up when I got back, by which time I hoped to have made my decision. Paul didn't say much in reply. He told me that whatever my decision, he'd guarantee his support.

My parents were taken aback at having their

116

eldest daughter back home again so soon after my recent Christmas visit and I could tell they sensed that something was wrong but they didn't pry much beyond a small amount of cursory questioning.

It was good to be home. When I wasn't helping Dad in the garden or being shown off to nearby relatives and friends by Mum, I wandered around the house in which I'd grown up, deliberately trying to evoke memories of my own childhood: the chipped figurine of a horse in the hallway damaged when my younger sister Jessica and I knocked it over during an impromptu wrestling match; the football stickers I'd stolen from my brother Tim and secretly placed on the rear of what used to be my bedside table; the sad-looking pink glazed piggy bank that I'd got for Christmas the year I turned eleven that I'd found abandoned in the garden shed.

By the time I was ready to leave I was in no doubt that I would continue with the pregnancy. I told my parents the real reason for the visit and although I could see that Mum was disappointed that I hadn't done things 'the right way round', I felt that by the time I was due to get the train back home to Manchester they had come to terms with the idea that whether they liked it or not their little girl had finally grown up.

Paul came round the evening I arrived back in Manchester and we talked until the early hours. He admitted that he had made a lot of mistakes in his life and hurt a lot of people along the way.

He said he wanted all that to end and that the baby would be an opportunity for a new beginning for the both of us. I told him that although I'd decided to keep the baby, we shouldn't try to make any promises now but deal with each day as it arrived. Not once in all the time we spoke, did he mention Melissa. I guessed that he had his reasons and although I wanted us to talk it through I feared that somehow this would be a step too far. I could see that Paul genuinely wanted to make things right between us. Maybe we could be like we were before, I told myself. Maybe we could fall in love all over again. Either way I owed it to myself at least to give him the opportunity to try.

★ ★ ★

I turned to face Paul who was still lying on top of his bed: 'Do you think I make a good witch?'

He got up from the bed and put his arms around me from behind so that we could see each other in the mirror.

'I think you make the best witch.'

I studied our reflection. We looked happy. We fitted together like two parts of a jigsaw puzzle. Maybe things would be different this time.

'Let's not go tonight,' I suggested. 'Let's just stay in. Just the two of us. What do you think?'

Paul tried hard not to show the obvious relief he felt.

'That's a great idea,' he replied. 'Let's order in something to eat, watch a bit of telly and get an early night.'

Cooper

It was just after eight as Laura and I pulled up outside Cath and Simon's house in Altrincham having not said a single word to each other since Laura had raised the subject of us going travelling together. For most of the evening until we went out I sulked in the living room under the guise of listening to music. And the more I sulked, the more Laura stomped around the house as if she was in a bid to shake it down to its very foundations.

Laura turned to look at me.

'Are we okay now or what?'

'What do you think?' I snapped.

'I think you're being a complete and utter idiot about this.'

'Cheers, thanks for letting me know.'

Laura tutted under her breath. 'I hate it when you're like this.'

'When I'm like what? You mean not giving in to your every whim?'

'What's that supposed to mean?'

'Nothing.'

'No, go on, Cooper. If you're going to have a go at me at least be man enough to say it to my face.'

I really didn't want to go there. It was time to defuse things like I always did.

'Look,' I began, 'I'm sorry, okay? I was just a bit annoyed, that's all. I thought I was doing what's best for us but you've obviously got other ideas.'

'And that's your idea of an apology?'

119

'Well, it's all you're going to get.'

'Fine.' Laura climbed out of the car and slammed the door behind her. 'Just so long as we both know where we stand.'

Melissa

The second I saw Cooper and Laura through the window of Chris and Vicky's car I could tell that they had had some kind of row. We all kissed our hellos and I watched as Vicky and then a few moments later Chris picked up on the tension between Cooper and Laura. In a bid to lighten the mood I suggested that we all try to identify each other's costumes, so we started with Laura who was wearing a cropped checked shirt, tied up high over a red bikini top, home-made denim hotpants and a pair of seventies-looking wedge heels.

'Daisy Duke from *The Dukes of Hazzard*,' said Chris straight away as Laura gave us a twirl.

'I should've known you'd get it straight away.'

We then all looked at Cooper who was wearing motorcycle leathers that clearly didn't fit him and holding a toy rifle.

'Is it the cop from the Village People?' asked Chris grinning.

Cooper, offended, protested it wasn't.

'I haven't got a clue,' said Vicky.

'He's Australian,' said Coop offering up a clue.

'The guy from *Mad Max!*' said Chris.

'You should've known that,' said Cooper. 'It was our favourite film when we were kids.'

Next up was Vicky. Her outfit was strange to say the least. Under her cream coat (which wasn't part of her costume) she was wearing a pink T-shirt, pink jeans and pink shoes.

I guessed Alicia Silverstone in *Clueless* and Cooper guessed Little Bo Beep in *Toy Story*, but we were both wrong.

'You've got to think whole film rather than a single character,' prompted Chris.

With that I got it straight away. '*Pretty in Pink!*'

Next for our scrutiny was Chris who looked completely normal until he opened his jacket. He was naked from the waist up and across his torso were various words and sentences scribbled in black marker pen.

'That's a no-brainer, you're the bloke out of *Memento*.'

'Got it in one,' replied Chris. 'Which means you win tonight's star prize.' He threw his arms round me and squashed my face into his naked chest until I screamed.

'So what about you?' asked Cooper once Chris had finished torturing me. 'Who have you come as?'

As I straightened myself out my friends looked my ensemble up and down: a shirt, tie, waistcoat, cream wide-legged trousers and flat black shoes.

'You look like a clown,' said Cooper. 'Are you Charlie Chaplin?'

'First off,' I replied sternly, 'no, I do not look like a clown and secondly, Charlie Chaplin's got a moustache.'

'Julie Andrews in *Victor/Victoria*,' suggested Laura.

'Never seen it.'

'Barbra Streisand in *Yentl*,' guessed Vicky, 'or possibly Barbra Streisand in *What's Up Doc?*'

'Wrong on both counts.'

'I've no idea,' said Chris. 'Give us a clue? Are you supposed to be male or female?'

'I'm saying nothing until somebody guesses.'

'If Paul was here,' laughed Chris, 'I bet he'd get it straight away.'

Everyone looked from Chris to me and back again and Chris looked as though he wanted the earth to open up and swallow him.

'Look, it's fine,' I said as everyone waited for my reaction. I looped my arm through Chris's. 'We all know he's right: Paul probably would guess it in a second but . . . you know what? I don't care. For the first time in a long while I feel really good and whether Paul's here with Hannah or whether he doesn't turn up at all it doesn't matter. All that does matter is that I'm here, I'm with my friends and no matter what it takes I'm going to have a brilliant time.'

Chris

I'm not sure that any of us really believed Melissa's little speech, least of all Melissa herself, but we all nodded and agreed with her anyway. Collecting the booze we'd brought with us from our various cars we made our way to Cath and Simon's three-bed semi and rang the

122

doorbell. Within seconds the front door was flung open to reveal Cath in a big white flouncy-looking dress which, according to Vicky, made her Maria from *The Sound of Music*. Simon greeted us wearing a black hooded top with a grey T-shirt underneath, ridiculously tight jeans and white Adidas trainers. I hadn't clue who he was supposed to be but then I noticed the black stick-on moustache he was sporting and the toy pistol sticking out of his back pocket. 'You're Axel Foley from *Beverley Hills Cop*,' I pronounced triumphantly.

Cath and Simon then took their turns guessing our costumes. But when it came to Melissa's they too were stumped.

'One last go,' demanded Simon, whose guesses so far had ranged from Melanie Griffiths in *Working Girl* through to Anne Hathaway in *The Devil Wears Prada*. 'Is it Stan Laurel?' Melissa scowled and informed Simon in no uncertain terms that she was not 'Stan-sodding-Laurel', and that if people weren't going to guess properly she was going to go home.

Relieved to have got all of the guess-who stuff out of the way for the time being, Cath invited us to head to the kitchen for a drink. I'd been about to go along with everyone else when Vicky pulled me aside.

'What's up?'

'What do you mean 'what's up?'.' she replied. 'Didn't you see how Cooper and Laura were?'

'I'm guessing they've had some sort of row. And?'

'Well, aren't you worried?'

123

'About what?'

'About what they've been fighting about?'

'No, not really.'

'Why not?'

'Because I'm sure at some point tonight Laura will give you a blow-by-blow breakdown of everything that happened.'

'Well, don't you think you should find out Cooper's side too? Make sure he's okay? Don't you remember how he was after he split up with Angie?'

Angie was Cooper's last proper girlfriend and the reason he left Derby to join me in Manchester. They were sort of childhood sweethearts who were together from the age of sixteen until they both turned twenty-eight when she left him for some guy that she had met at work. It had taken him years to get over her and even now there were times when I wasn't one hundred per cent sure that he had fully recovered.

'I'll have a word with him later, okay? Come on, this is a party, isn't it? So why don't we just try to enjoy ourselves?'

Melissa

For the first couple of hours at the party I really did try my best to have a good time. Initially I stuck with Vicky and Laura while they circulated catching up with all the usual suspects but I barely contributed anything to the conversations. For the most part my mind was focused on whether or not Paul would arrive with Hannah and how I would be when I finally saw them face to face.

Leaving Vicky and Laura exchanging work anecdotes with a group of Cath's friends I was about to go in search of Chris when out of the corner of my eye I saw a face that I recognised. It was Billy, the young guy who had tried to chat me up at Ed and Sharon's New Year's Eve party. He waved and came over to talk to me.

'*Annie Hall*,' he said with a grin.

For a second I was confused but then I realised he was talking about my costume, and gave him a round of applause.

'Finally,' I replied in relief. 'I've been here since eight and you're the only person that's got it right. You wouldn't believe some of the guesses I've had. When I was getting myself a drink some guy actually asked me if I'd come as Dustin Hoffman in *Tootsie*. Can you believe it? *Tootsie*? I can tell you they got a kick in the shins for that one.'

'They must be mad,' laughed Billy. 'First off, Dustin Hoffman in *Tootsie* was a bloke dressed as a woman and second, you look nothing like Dustin Hoffman dressed as a man either. *Annie Hall* should have been easy. I mean, isn't it in everyone's all-time top ten films?'

'Well, the answer to that is obviously a big fat no. If it isn't, I must have come up with the worst fancy-dress costume in living history.'

'So come on then. Return the compliment. Who am I?'

'Okay,' I mused looking Billy up and down.

He was wearing black shoes and trousers, a white short-sleeved shirt with a striped tie in two different shades of red and looked like he was some kind of shop assistant. The icing on the cake was the patches of red marker pen all over the shirt that I guessed was supposed to be blood.

'When we met last time didn't you tell me your name was Billy?' I asked, pointing to the green Curry's electrical store name badge on the front pocket of his shirt which said: 'STEVE BAMFORD.'

'It is . . . and before you ask, no, I don't work at Curry's. I bought it off eBay from this Bamford guy.'

I wracked my brains for the answer. His costume was ringing a bell but I couldn't place him. 'I take it it's from some kind of action film?'

'Action-ish,' shrugged Billy. 'Though it's probably more cross-genre.'

'Action crossed with what?'

'That would be telling.'

'I have no idea,' I replied, still drawing a blank. 'You'll have to give me a clue.'

'Okay, here's a clue. Are you ready?'

He let out a long groan that was so loud, it took both me and the group of people around us more than a bit by surprise. Billy was not only unfazed by the looks he was receiving but appeared to be relishing the attention.

'What was that about? It sounded like you were about to throw up.'

'It was a clue.'

'You groaning was a clue?' A picture slowly

126

began to form in my head. I knew the film. It was about zombies and starred the bloke who used to be in a sitcom that Paul and I used to watch sometimes on a Friday night. I could even see the cover of the DVD from when Chris, Vicky and I had rented it from Blockbuster when it first came out. Finally it came to me.

'*Shaun of the Dead.*'

Billy gave me a small bow.

'I wasn't the first to get it right though, was I?'

'It doesn't matter that you weren't the first to guess,' grinned Billy, 'the bottom line is you've managed to win tonight's star prize.'

I was well aware that this was probably the lead up to the world's cheesiest line but I didn't entirely mind because Billy had already begun to grow on me.

'Okay then,' I replied. 'What, pray tell, is tonight's star prize?'

With a theatrical flourish as much for his own amusement as mine, he reached into his pocket and pulled out a keychain with a red plastic lobster at the end of it.

'The perfect present for Annie Hall,' he said and handed it to me. 'From Alvy Singer with love.'

Billy

Melissa's face when she saw the lobster was priceless.

'How did you do that?'

'Do what?'

She narrowed her eyes at me. 'The lobster, it's

127

a reference to the bit in *Annie Hall* where Alvy tries to cook live lobster for Annie and they end up escaping. Now either you constantly walk around with red plastic lobsters in your pocket or somehow you guessed that I was going to come as *Annie Hall* . . . which is impossible because I only came up with the idea half an hour before I left my flat.'

'The truth is I have the gift,' I replied. 'Either that or I'm a dab hand with smoke and mirrors.'

Of course Melissa didn't fall for any of this but that didn't really matter because I was making her smile and, given that this had been my main objective since I hatched this plan several weeks ago, I considered the mission to have been accomplished very well indeed.

The whole lobster thing came about as a result of a chance mid-week night out with my house-mates Seb and Brian. Seb worked in the accounts department for a firm of solicitors in town and he'd recently been up for promotion, so when he came home one night and told us he'd got it and wanted to celebrate we all agreed to go out with him. For a change Seb suggested that we go to Blue-Bar on Wilbraham Road rather than the Duck and Drake. I tried to talk him out of it because Blue-Bar was one of Freya's favourite places and as I was still trying to avoid her I didn't really fancy it but Seb wouldn't budge. Half an hour later we arrived at the bar, and as I walked in I was completely blown away because the first person that I saw (standing behind the bar pulling pints, no less) was Melissa.

Melissa had been on my mind off and on ever

since we'd met on New Year's Eve. Even though nothing had happened between us she had made a real impact on me and so seeing her working in this bar that we didn't normally go to suddenly didn't seem like any random coincidence. It seemed like something bigger. Like it was all part of a plan. And the fact that she looked just as amazing as she had done on New Year's Eve was the icing on the cake.

I could barely take my eyes off her, and before long Seb and Brian noticed my distraction and tried to cajole me into going over to talk to her. But then I told them about my opening salvo the first time we'd met, about our matching Converse. Once the boys had finished laughing, I added that Melissa might also have a boyfriend so talking to her would hardly be worth the bother. But then Brian volunteered to do some digging with Martha, a Polish girl he'd been after for the longest time, who occasionally worked in Blue-Bar at the weekends.

Brian called Martha and reported back everything he had learned. Melissa was a student at Manchester university. She worked six shifts a week at Blue-Bar. She was popular with customers. She liked music and cinema. She lived in Chorlton. Her flatmate was a bit strange. She had a bit of a complicated relationship with her ex-boyfriend but was currently single. The biggest revelation was the fact that Melissa (who on the night we'd first met I'd guessed to be somewhere between the ages of twenty-five to twenty-eight, tops) was actually 'somewhere in her mid-thirties'.

I think this was more of an issue for Brian and Seb than it was for me as for the rest of the evening their running joke became, 'So if you two get hitched, when you're thirty-five she'll be forty-five,' followed by 'when you're forty-five she'll be fifty-five,' and then finally 'when you're one hundred and ten she'll no doubt be dead.' The bottom line was that I didn't care how old Melissa was, all I knew was that I liked her, and that given that she wasn't seeing anyone I was more than prepared to have a go at trying to make her like me in return.

Later that night I called my sister Nadine and asked her to invite me along the next time her mates had one of their get-togethers. She guessed straight away that my interest was more than likely due to my being 'in pursuit of skirt' and when I told her how old 'the skirt' was she duly informed me that I had no chance.

In a bid to prove her wrong I attended three birthday parties (two in Withington and the other in Didsbury), and an engagement party in Stretford. And while it was interesting to discover that my sister's group of friends had a more happening social life than I'd first imagined, it failed to result in a single sighting of Melissa. For a while I began to think that perhaps Nadine's friends had less crossover with Melissa's friends than I had imagined but then Nadine told me about a Hollywood-themed fancy-dress party in Altrincham and I just knew in my gut that Melissa would be there.

The second I saw Melissa arrive with her friends it occurred to me that I hadn't really thought about what I would do once we were in the same room. But as she took off her coat in the hallway, I spotted her costume and guessed that she had come as Annie Hall. I knew then that I had the perfect way to make a better second impression if only I could find the right prop.

I made my way up to Simon and Cath's bathroom, locked the door behind me and started looking for anything that could be used to help me in my endeavours with Melissa. As I frantically scanned the room, opening cupboards left, right and centre, I came across air fresheners, loo rolls, a copy of the *Guinness Book of Hit Singles*, a box of tampons, a spider plant and two issues of *Heat* magazine, but not a single thing that might have had a Woody Allen connection no matter how tenuous. But as I sat down on the loo to take stock I glanced up at a shelf on the wall and spotted a red plastic lobster keyring dangling from the wall bracket. Cheap and tacky looking, it couldn't have been more perfect for what I needed and I knew this would be the best-ever way in with Melissa. Delving into the pocket of my jeans I pulled out a tenner and left it on the shelf by way of recompense, then made my way back downstairs.

Vicky

I was in Cath and Simon's kitchen talking to them about the plans they had for renovating the room when Chris appeared from nowhere

131

looking incredibly pleased with himself, as though he had some kind of news. I could tell right away that it wasn't meant necessarily for Cath and Simon's ears, so making an excuse I took him to one side.

'Okay, what is it you've seen or heard?'

'Brace yourself for it because it's big news. I'm not sure but I think our small but perfectly formed friend Melissa has just pulled some bloke.'

I couldn't think who it might be.

'It's not Simon's friend Alex, is it? I remember he was sniffing round her last summer but I'm pretty sure he's got a girlfriend now.'

'No, it's not him,' replied Chris. 'It's some young-looking guy I've never seen before.'

'And they were kissing?'

'No, but you could tell something was going on. He was doing that thing blokes do when they're trying to give girls the impression that they're really listening to every word they're saying.'

'Is he good looking?'

Chris shrugged. 'Maybe, if you like that sort of thing. He's tall-ish, all-right looking and he's dressed like a bit of an idiot — but I'm guessing that's just his costume for tonight. He's definitely toy-boy material though. Mid-twenties tops.'

I was shocked. 'I have no idea who this guy could be.'

'Do you think he knows how old she is? I suppose to be fair to him Melissa is quite well preserved for her age but even so . . . he'd have to be blind to think that she was under thirty.'

I punched Chris in the arm as hard as I could but he didn't even flinch.

'Don't be so mean. If he's as young as you say she's probably just basking in the glow of a bit of male attention. I know I wouldn't mind having some young guy trying to chat me up instead of just holding doors open for me or telling me that I remind them of their mum. I can't even remember the last time I got wolf-whistled by a builder.'

'Maybe Melissa's new bloke has got a friend for you?'

'Don't think you can palm me off that easily,' I replied narrowing my eyes. 'You, I'm afraid, are stuck with me for life.'

For a second I thought I detected a small flash of unease on Chris's face, but when I looked for it again it was gone and I told myself I was being silly.

'Are you okay?' I asked, thinking not for the first time in recent weeks about the episode in the car coming back from Charlotte and Cameron's party. 'Things are all right with you, aren't they?'

'I'm fine,' he said. 'Really I'm fine,' and then he kissed me and headed outside for a cigarette.

Melissa

Billy and I had been talking for quite a while.

Somehow or other we went from talking about who we knew at the party to talking about the weather, which in turn had led us to the topic of 'Places that we'd go if someone handed us the keys to a Doctor Who-style Tardis'. I'd told Billy how I'd want to go somewhere nice and warm where the sun would bake me — like Ibiza maybe — where Vicky and I had taken our first holiday together. Or even Woolacoombe Bay on a good day like the August bank holiday a few years back when Vicky, Laura and I had spent an entire 'boy-free' weekend on the beach soaking up the sun. At a push, I told him, I would accept being in bed at my gran's house in Aberdovey because even if it was freezing outside, my gran's house always felt warm and cosy. Billy asked if he could come and see it with me one day and I replied probably not unless we could get our hands on an actual Tardis as my gran had died a few years back. There was an awkward silence and then he asked if I wanted another drink.

It was really odd. I think we both knew that his question had a deeper meaning behind it. Something along the lines of: 'I'd like to carry on talking to you but I'd also like to give you the opportunity to walk away if this isn't really happening for you', and the truth was I didn't know whether this was happening for me or not. He was good looking, funny and polite. And he'd made good conversation without trying to pummel me to death with his opinions or jokes. But the big problem was that he was young. Young enough to have prompted me to do some subtle investigation during our conversation. Young enough for me to guesstimate that he was somewhere between twenty-four and twenty-six.

And therefore young enough for me to think twice about whether or not it would be a good idea to let him get me another drink.

He must have sensed my hesitation because rather than wait for me to answer he said, 'Look, this might be a little too much information given the short amount of time we've been talking but my bladder is full to bursting.'

'That's good to know.'

'The thing is,' he continued, 'my full bladder is actually your fault.'

'How come?'

'Well, I would've gone earlier but I was enjoying talking to you too much to even think for a second about how I needed to answer the call of nature. Anyway, here's my point: given that I'm going to have to join what will undoubtedly be the world's longest queue for the toilet, I may be some time. So how about this: I'll go to the loo and then get us a drink — and here's the good bit — you can feel free to use this pause in the conversation to make a break for it and run for the hills or not. If you're here then great, if you're not then I completely understand.' He paused and held out his hand for me to shake, 'If I don't get to speak to you again, Melissa Vickery of Chorlton-cum-Hardy, it was nice talking to you.'

I waited until he had completely left the room before I covered my face with my hands, lowered my head and laughed with a mixture of shame, embarrassment but above all delight. It had been a long time since I'd met someone like Billy. A long time. And although there were a million and one reasons why he was completely unsuitable for me I was finding it hard to escape the feeling that after his ridiculously charming exit I didn't really care. I thought again about Vicky telling me I needed to move on and how in the space of a single short conversation Billy had made me feel more attractive and more wanted than I'd felt in ages.

Still undecided about whether I had the guts to be here waiting for him when he returned, I decided to seek out Vicky and Laura for their advice. But in fact Vicky was standing right in front of me.

'I was just about to go looking for you.'

'Oh, really?' She eyed me suspiciously. 'Why would that be? You look guilty, Mel, what have you been up to?'

For a moment or two I wondered if I really did look guilty but then a smile cracked across Vicky's face and she was unable to stifle her laughter any longer.

'Who told you?'

'Chris, about ten minutes ago and I've been hanging around by the door keeping you under surveillance ever since. So come on then, what's going on?'

'Nothing really. It's ridiculous.'

'That goes without saying.'

'Okay, do you remember me telling you about the guy from Ed and Sharon's New Year's Eve party who just appeared from nowhere and started going on about my Converse?'

'Are you saying that's him?'

I nodded.

Vicky laughed. 'But didn't you say he was a bit weird?'

'Only because I didn't know him. He's actually really nice and I'd be really happy if there wasn't one small problem ... he's twenty-five.'

'And does he know that you're ... you know ... not so twenty-five.'

'I told him I was a mature student, but I couldn't seem to find a way of dropping the words, 'Oh, by the way I'm whole decade older than you,' into the conversation. This is so shameful. I can't be carrying on with guys young enough to still be doing paper rounds. It's unseemly.'

'You must get chatted up at university all the time.'

'Not at all.' I shook my head. 'If being back in full-time education has shown me anything it's this: that in the university pecking order mature students are the lowest of the low. Not that I fancy them at all but I'm completely invisible to the guys in my classes. They only ever notice me if they want to borrow my lecture notes.'

'They're intimidated by your wealth of life experience.'

'No, I think they're just afraid of catching old-people disease. I used to be the same when I was their age. I remember the mature students on my first course freaked me out a bit too.'

'But age thing aside, is he nice?'

'He's really funny and sweet,' I replied, 'and he did this weird thing with this,' I dug into my pocket and showed Vicky the red lobster key chain, 'which I'll explain another time. If I'm being honest, Vick, if he was just five years older I wouldn't have a problem with him at all.'

'So what are you going to do?'

'I don't know.'

Vicky raised her eyebrows mischievously.

'Are you sure you don't know or are you just saying that? It would be one to tick off the list after all.'

'You're loving this, aren't you?'

'I can't help it,' said Vicky. 'Things like this never happen to me. Where is he now anyway?'

'Gone to the loo then off to get me a drink.'

'So he could be back any minute? Do you want me to stay?'

'No.'

'Are you sure?'

'Absolutely sure.'

Vicky's mobile phone rang from inside her bag. She took it out and checked the screen. 'It's our home number, so I'd better take it even though it'll probably just be Mum calling to ask where I keep the 'good' biscuits.'

Vicky

'Hi, Mum. Everything all right?'

'Everything's fine. It's just William. He woke up about half an hour ago saying that he was thirsty, then when I gave him water he said he needed a wee, then after he had a wee he said that he was too wide awake and could he stay up with me, and when I said that not being tired

138

wasn't a good enough excuse he started crying and wouldn't stop until I said that I'd let him talk to you. He's upstairs at the minute. Shall I put him on?'

None of this was a particularly big surprise. William hadn't been sleeping well for a few weeks now. He'd regularly been waking a few times in the night with a head full of suggestions, comments and questions as though his young brain was working at such a high capacity that it was unable to contain itself.

Listening to the sound of static as Mum made her way upstairs to William's room I thought about how it had taken me nearly half an hour to settle him down for bed, and how as I'd crept out of his room, all I'd wanted was to crawl into the bath and then fall into bed myself. Yet here I was, late at night, at a fancy-dress party trying my best to prove that I still had what it took to have a good time.

Mum put William on the phone.

'Hello, sweetie. What's up, my baby?'

'Why aren't you and Daddy here with me tonight, Mummy? I don't like it when you go out.'

'I've already told you a million times, sweetheart,' I replied. 'Mummy and Daddy are at Cath and Simon's house for a party.'

'But why are you at a party?'

'Because we're celebrating,' I replied.

'Celebrating what?'

'Their birthdays. Cath and Simon have just turned thirty-five.'

'But why?'

William could play the 'why?' game for hours without getting the slightest bit jaded. Normally I would have cut him short and insisted that he go to bed but my mind flicked forward to a row we'd had earlier in the day when I'd caught him banging one of his toy cars on the brand-new units in the kitchen and making a big black mark on the door. I well and truly lost it and ended up yelling at him so loudly that he burst into tears. Despite apologising profusely and taking him to the newsagents to buy a Mini Milk I could still feel the guilt lurking deep within me and I hoped that by indulging him in a few minutes of 'Question Time' I might be able to somehow end the day guilt neutral.

'Everybody has birthdays, William,' I explained. 'And Cath and Simon have had one just like you had yours.'

'Did they get presents?'

'Probably.'

'Did they get a Dalek piggy bank like me?'

'I doubt it, sweetheart. Daleks can be very scary you know. They say: 'Exterminate! Exterminate!', don't they?'

William giggled. 'What does 'Exterminate' mean?'

'It doesn't mean anything,' I replied even though I'd told him the answer to this question pretty much every day since his birthday back in November.

'Yes, it does,' he said. 'It means: 'Kill'. I know because Daddy told me.'

'Well, it's only a pretend sort of killing. And they don't do it to nice people. Only naughty aliens.'

140

'I love my piggy bank.'

'I'm sure you do, sweetheart.'

'Will you put some money in it for me one day?'

'Maybe when Daddy and I get home.'

For a moment it seemed as though he might have run out of questions but then he suddenly sparked to life again.

'Mummy?'

'Yes?'

There was a long silence. He was clearly still thinking of a question.

'Who's at the party?'

'That you know? Well, there's Mummy and Daddy, Uncle Cooper and Auntie Laura and of course, your favourite Auntie of all, Auntie Melissa.'

There was a long silence and then William said: 'But where's Uncle Paul'

'He's not here.'

'He should be, shouldn't he? Where is he? Why hasn't he come?'

'I don't know, darling,' I replied sadly. 'I really don't know.'

Melissa

I think Billy was more surprised than I was to see that I was still standing in exactly the same spot that he had left me.

'I know this isn't going to sound very cool,' he said handing me a bottle of Budweiser, 'but I didn't think you'd be here. In fact I'd have bet a

141

fair wedge of cash that you wouldn't even still be at the party. Out of curiosity, what made you stay?'

'Just that,' I replied. 'Curiosity.'

We talked a lot more and in between we made several trips to the kitchen to get more Budweiser and eventually, having exhausted nearly every remaining avenue for polite conversation and drunk enough to more than loosen our tongues, we reached the inevitable point in the evening where people, such as ourselves, who had spent most of the night wrapped in conversation with a single party began to share more than just basic biographies and so I told him about my relationship with Paul in some of but not all its gory detail.

'And so that was the guy that you were talking to on New Year's Eve?' asked Billy when I'd finished.

I nodded.

'That was the night he and I got back together.'

'You must have really loved him,' said Billy.

'What makes you say that?' I asked.

'After everything he did you still went back to him.'

I thought for a moment how odd it was to see my life through Billy's eyes.

'I did love him. I loved him a lot.' I suddenly flushed with self-consciousness. 'I'm guessing I must seem more than a little bit pathetic to you.'

'No, not at all,' replied Billy. 'I get it. We've all been there, haven't we?'

I laughed. 'I'm guessing right now you must

142

be really regretting coming over to me. I know I look normal on the outside but inside I'm probably about this far,' I held up my thumb and index finger with barely any space between them, 'from being sectioned.'

Billy laughed. 'First off, if you're really that close to being sectioned then I'd happily be carted off with you and secondly, this might sound cheesy but I could never in a million years regret coming over to talk to you because I think you're great.'

I was momentarily stumped for a response and when I did come up with one: 'Why are you being so nice to me?' I couldn't actually get the words out so instead I offered to take my turn in liberating another pair of Budweisers from the kitchen.

Cooper

It was just coming up to midnight and Laura and I still weren't speaking to each other. In fact for most of the party we'd been in separate rooms and on the rare occasions that we had been in the same room she had gone out of her way to ignore me.

Having reached my limit on what I was prepared to take, I decided to go home, so went in search of Laura to let her know. She was in the kitchen deep in the middle of a conversation with Cath and Simon.

'It's up to you whether you stay or go,' I spat in Laura's direction much to the alarm of Cath and Simon, 'after all, I wouldn't want to stifle your 'independent spirit', would I? But I thought it only polite to let you know that I'm off this very second and if you want a lift back home you'd better get ready.'

This was plainly a red rag to a bull. As Laura stormed after me I was already regretting my ultimatum and would've apologised to her on the spot were it not for the fact that she practically blew up before I could get a word out.

'I can't believe you just spoke to me like that in front of Cath and Simon,' screamed Laura as she finally caught up with me by my car. 'How dare you do that! Who do you think you are? My dad?'

'Well, if I did think I was your dad then there would only be one person that I could blame for that and that would be you!' I yelled. 'Do you know what, Laura? I'm sick of this. I'm sick and tired of always feeling like I'm the responsible adult in this relationship! How come I never get to just quit my job on a whim? How come I don't get to suggest that we blow all our savings on a stupid bloody holiday? How come I'm the one who always has to worry about the future?'

Laura's eyes widened in hurt. 'No one's asking you to do any of those things.'

'No, of course not because they'll just take care of themselves won't they?'

'How would you know if you never let them?'

'And how would you know if you always rely on someone else to be your safety net?'

'What's that supposed to mean?'

'Look.' I was tired of us having a go at each other. I wanted this all to stop. 'I'm sorry, it was

144

nothing. Let's just go home, eh? Sort things out there.'

'It wasn't nothing though, was it? Deep down it's what you really think, isn't it? That you're my safety net and that without you I'd be lost?'

'No, it's not what I think.'

'Say it.' She pushed me hard in the chest forcing me to take a step backwards. 'Say it if you mean it. Go on! For once in your life say what you mean.'

Straight away I was back to being angry. Angry at the situation, Laura's response, and most of all angry at myself.

'Yeah, you're right,' I snapped. 'I do think that you get to act the way you do because you can rely on other people to pick up after you. Me, your . . . mum and dad . . . your brother . . . even your kid sister. It doesn't really matter who does the picking up as long as it's not you.' I waited for her retaliation but there was none. She looked at me in disbelief. 'So that's it? You've got nothing to say? I tell you a few home truths and you just clam up like you can't be bothered to talk to me any more?'

Laura looked away. She'd started crying like she always did when we argued. I hated seeing her cry. I was wishing that the whole thing would just go away when she mumbled something incomprehensible.

'I can't hear you,' I replied, 'speak more slowly.' I took a step towards her and reached out to wipe away her tears.

'The engagement ring,' she said looking up at me. 'I said I found the engagement ring.'

'When?'

'Tonight.'

'How?'

'I went looking through your things while you were upstairs trying to find proof that you'd been wasting money too.'

I closed my eyes. This wasn't the way I'd imagined proposing to her.

'Look, I'm sorry, okay?'

'What for?'

'For everything.'

Laura shook her head. 'But I don't want you to be sorry.' She took hold of my hands. 'I love you, Cooper. More than you'll ever know. You're the sweetest, kindest, most patient man. Even if I lived to be a hundred I'll never be able to repay you for everything you've done for me. And yes, one day I really would like to marry you. But what you said just now is true. I *do* depend on other people. You *are* my safety net. Without you I've got no one to catch me if I fall. But tonight you've made me realise that I can't be with you unless I can catch you too. And I'm not that person right now. And I'll never be if you're always by my side.'

'So what are you saying?' I took a breath. 'That it's all over?'

'No,' she said quietly, 'I'm saying that I need to stand on my own two feet. I'm saying that I am going to go travelling, but I'm going to go without you. And while I'd love you to be here and still be in love with me when I get back, I'll understand if you're not. Either way this is something I just have to do.'

146

Melissa

It was quarter past midnight, I'd returned to the living room with two Budweisers and Billy and I were now talking about his past relationships.

'Since I turned seventeen I've had a total of four 'proper' relationships,' began Billy. 'The shortest lasted about four months and the longest a year a half.'

'Who was the year-and-a-half girl? A sixth-form sweetheart?'

Billy looked puzzled. 'How did you guess?'

'It's always the way,' I replied. 'Life's so much easier when you're seventeen.' I smiled and encouraged him to carry on.

'Well, on top of the longest and the shortest relationships there are probably between six and eight what you might call 'improper' relationships most of which to a greater or lesser extent I now regret.'

'I've had a few of those,' I replied. 'Anything else?'

Billy shrugged and sighed. 'I wasn't going to tell you this because I didn't want to get into it but in the spirit of full disclosure I think I ought to confess that prior to meeting you on New Year's Eve I was deeply 'in like' with a girl called Freya.'

'Sounds like a game girl. So what happened?'

'Do we have to do this?'

I shook my head. 'No, but I can tell you want to.'

'You can read me like a book, can't you? Okay, well it went like this: we'd been mates for a while, things sort of came to a head around Christmas when a late night kiss goodnight got quickly rebuffed.'

'I'm assuming by her?'

'You assume correctly. I haven't seen her since then and to be truthful I've sort of lost interest in her.'

'Because she knocked you back?'

Billy shook his head. 'No, because on New Year's Eve I went to a party with my sister and met a girl wearing red Converse baseball boots who had great eyes and a nice smile. I've sort of sworn myself off all other girls until I've made Converse Girl my own.'

I didn't know where to look. I was fancying him more and more with each passing second but I couldn't escape the feeling that this was all going to end badly.

'Look, Billy,' I began, 'you do realise that Converse Girl is a good ten years your senior, don't you?'

'I don't care if she's forty years my senior,' replied Billy. 'I think she's ace.'

Ace! I couldn't remember the last time someone my age had used that word let alone in reference to me. While my inner reaction was embarrassment my outward reaction was to roll my eyes in a comedy fashion.

Billy's reaction was far more bold: he simply leaned over to me and kissed me very softly on the lips.

'Wow, I wasn't expecting that.'

'Me neither. I was sort of making it up as I went along. Was it okay?'

'It was very satisfactory.'

'Good.' He kissed me again. This time a long, slower kiss than before.

'For future reference,' asked Billy as I reflected on just how good this second kiss had made me feel. 'You know that night when we first met . . . the dangling my foot in the air thing . . . that didn't really work for you, did it?'

'It wasn't the best chat-up attempt I've ever experienced but it was definitely one of the most unusual.' I looked at Billy, shook my head in disbelief and took his hands in my own. 'Look, you'll have to forgive me but this is all just a bit weird for me,' I began, 'the thing is . . . well, the thing is . . . '

'What?'

'The thing is you were born in the Eighties.'

'And?'

'Well, I wasn't. And it's just sort of strange thinking that people born the year I turned ten look like you now. In my head I'd just assumed people born in the Eighties would still be at school studying for GCSEs rather than hanging around fancy-dress parties in the suburbs of Manchester getting off with girls old enough to be their older sisters.'

'Is this contagious?' asked Billy. 'When I'm in my thirties will I automatically start getting freaked out when people born the decade after mine start joining the police force?'

'It is sort of inevitable,' I replied. 'In fact it's obligatory. Don't you get it? Your view of the world is completely different from mine.'

'So what if it is?'

'I don't know. It's just that I'm guessing it will matter at some point.'

'Like when you make jokes that include references to TV programmes I don't remember? It won't happen. Everything's repeated these days. I remember the seventies without ever being there and if there is anything you say that isn't covered by watching UK Gold, I'll look it up on the internet.'

'I'm not making any sense, am I?'

Billy shook his head. 'Not really, but I'd put that down to the Alzheimer's.'

'Listen here, you young whipper-snapper,' I protested. 'My memory is perfect, okay? Look, you know what I'm saying. I just don't understand why you're sitting here with me when there must be tonnes of girls your own age who would snap you up in a second.'

'First off, which tonne of girls, where? I haven't see them so I don't know how you have. Second, even if they did exist, I know for a fact that they would all be inferior to you, because . . . they just would, wouldn't they?' He paused, clearly pondering a big question. 'Look, this might be a bit forward or whatever but I'm starving. I don't suppose you fancy sharing a cab back to Chorlton and getting something to eat? Neelams on the Borough Road is great. What do you think?'

I assessed the situation: here I was about to leave a party with a guy ten years my junior who I'd only properly met a few hours before. This wasn't me. This wasn't the kind of thing I did at all.

'Do you know what?' I replied, thinking how good it felt to have my mind occupied by someone other than Paul. 'Right now I can't think of anything in the world that I'd rather do.'

Two Months Later

Laura's Leaving Do

June 2006

Melissa

It was a lovely warm Saturday evening, I was feeling lighter than air having handed in the last of my course work for the academic year and Billy and I were walking hand-in-hand on our way down to Laura's leaving do at Blue-Bar. It was hard to believe that in a matter of days Laura would be off for a whole year. A year seemed too long to be bearable.

'So where is it she's going on her trip?' asked Billy.

'She's flying into Mumbai on Tuesday, seeing a bit of India, then she's moving on to south east Asia, then Australia, New Zealand, the US, Cuba and South America for the final leg.'

'And she's going without her boyfriend . . . what's his name . . . Cooper? How does he feel about that? He can't be best pleased, can he?'

'No.' I took the time to put myself in Cooper's shoes. 'I don't think he is. But they'll get through it. I know they will.'

I could tell that Billy had something else on his mind and I knew what it was: Paul. Since I'd passed on the news that Paul was definitely coming to the party, Billy had seemed a little on edge.

155

'Everything's going to be fine, you know,' I said squeezing his hand. 'I'm over him. He's over me. We've both moved on.'

'When is his kid due again?'

'Some time in September.'

'And it doesn't bother you?'

'It did, but it doesn't now.'

Billy sighed. 'Look, you know I'm not trying to put a downer on things, it's just . . . you two had this big thing and now you're seeing him for the first time in ages. I just don't want to feel like a spare part, that's all.'

We both came to a halt as we reached the entrance to the bar. I stood up on the tips of my toes and kissed him. 'We're fine, okay? I promise you. There's absolutely nothing to worry about.'

'You're right. Let's just forget about all this and have a good time.'

Entering the bar I suggested to Billy that we head straight to the downstairs bar where the party was being held but before we could even make a step in that direction, we were pounced upon by Seb and Brian. I'd met Seb and Brian a couple of times at Billy's and though he had warned me that they could be a bit juvenile, I'd found them a harmless, good-natured pair even though they both insisted on holding a conversation with my chest whenever I spoke to them. What was most intriguing was that even though they were the same age as Billy there was no way in the world that I could have imagined going out with either of them. This reassured me that rather than having a burgeoning fetish for younger guys, what I had was a burgeoning fetish for younger guys who happened to be like Billy.

Suggesting that Billy stay and chat to his mates I made my way down the stairs to the basement bar. Cooper and I had spent most of the afternoon here decorating the walls with home-made banners, pinning up maps of the world showing the route Laura would be taking and even connecting Cooper's laptop to a projector so that everybody on the dance floor could be entertained by a rolling gallery of Laura's best photographic moments.

Even though it was relatively early the bar was already pretty packed and I immediately bumped into a few of Laura's old work friends who I'd known quite well at one point, but who were now virtual strangers. As we caught up with each other's recent history I couldn't help but notice how perfectly presented they were compared to me, especially given that I was back in the very same red Converse that I'd been wearing when I first met Billy. Filling them in with the details of my life (yes I was seeing someone at the minute, no I wasn't still working at the art gallery gift shop, yes I did think it was sad that Cooper wasn't going with Laura) I made an excuse and headed back to the stairs. I looked up and was frozen to the spot by the sight of Claudia Harris, the one person in the world that I least wanted to see, coming the other way.

Nine months after Paul and I split up the first time round, and having properly shored up our new friendship, we both decided that it was time that we saw other people. I started seeing Ben, an old housemate of mine who I'd fancied years ago (needless to say it didn't work out) and Paul started seeing Claudia Harris. I didn't know Claudia at the time and was only vaguely aware of her through friends of friends as being both incredibly beautiful and the type of person who was always name-dropping about DJs she knew, bands she was friends with and clubs that she could get in for free. Her thing with Paul only lasted a matter of a few weeks. As pretty as she was Paul got bored of the way she only ever talked about herself and he called the whole thing off. Claudia refused to believe that Paul could possibly have come to this decision on his own and accused me of engineering the destruction of their relationship. Ever since she'd made it her mission to bad mouth me amongst our mutual friends. Claudia was one of the few people that I could honestly put my hand on my heart and say I hated. And while normally I would have felt guilty feeling this way about another human being I was well aware that it was completely mutual.

'Melissa,' said Claudia greeting me with a kiss. 'How are you?'

'I'm fine,' I replied. 'And you?'

'Couldn't be better.'

'You look amazing,' I replied.

'You too,' she smiled. 'I really love what you've done with your hair.'

I hadn't done anything with my hair apart from putting it in a ponytail.

'Thanks,' I replied. 'How's work?'

'Brilliant,' she replied and then proceeded without further prompting to enter into a long

158

and involved story about how fabulous her life was (she did something in TV down at Granada studios) and how she and a few of her DJ friends were heading out to Ibiza at the end of June. She pointedly didn't ask me about my life and I didn't offer any information because all I wanted to do was escape from her clutches. Then she moved on to talking about Laura's trip and how sad it was that she and Cooper had split up and how awful break-ups are when you're our age especially when the couples in question have been together a long time. And it was then, as she paused for breath, that I suddenly realised that everything that had gone before had just been a warm-up so that she could move in for the killer blow.

'So how are you coping?'

The subtext was clear: 'The only reason I'm talking to you is because I heard that you and Paul split up and I'm here to gloat.'

'I'm good, thanks.'

'Really?'

'Yes. Really.'

'It's just that I heard about everything that happened — you know how people talk around here — and obviously I know that you and Paul used to be really close.'

'We still are,' I replied.

'So you've worked things out?'

'No. I'm seeing someone else.'

Claudia seemed surprised. 'Congratulations.'

Life was just too short to spend a second longer with someone I loathed as much as Claudia and I was about to walk off when with a perfect sense of timing Billy appeared at the top of the stairs. 'Babe,' I said beaming a smile so intense in Claudia's direction that I hoped it would make her melt, explode, combust or whatever else happens when pure evil is vanquished. 'I'd like you to meet Claudia, a really, really old friend of mine.'

Cooper

Standing upstairs watching Laura and a bunch of her friends sobbing in each other's arms about how much they were all going to miss each other I wondered how much of this I could take. Just as I thought I could stand no more Chris and Vicky finally arrived. Relieved at the prospect of some male company I offered to get them a drink before they had even properly registered that it was me.

'So what's going on over there?' asked Chris peering over my shoulder. 'Someone died?'

'It's just girls being girls. One of Laura's mates said something nice to her. Laura said something nice in return and they've been trapped in a cycle of sobbing and hugging ever since.' I gave Vicky a deliberately condescending wink. 'You should join them, mate, you know you want to.'

'If I didn't suspect that deep down you're as upset as we all are you'd be in big trouble right now.'

'Yeah,' I replied dejectedly. 'I cry all my tears on the inside.'

Vicky rolled her eyes and crossed the room to

be sucked into Laura's never-ending group hug.

I turned to Chris and shook my head in despair. 'They'll be like that all evening.'

'More than likely.' He looked at the pint in my hand. 'So what about that drink then?'

I nodded and we made our way to the bar.

'So how's it going then?' asked Chris as we waited to be served.

'As well as it can when I know that my girlfriend is buggering off around the world in less than a week.'

Chris seemed to pick up on my reluctance to elaborate and moved straight into a discussion about a bunch of films he'd recently rented and this carried us through the wait to get served, finding somewhere to sit upstairs and half way through our pints.

'Laura said Paul was coming tonight,' said Chris setting down his pint on the table.

'That's what his text said,' I replied. 'Have you seen much of him lately?'

'I spoke to him on the phone a few times but that's it,' said Chris. 'Why he thinks that he has to drop off the face of the earth just because of what happened is anybody's guess.'

'I suppose it's a guilt thing.'

'Maybe.' Chris lit up a cigarette. 'Reading between the lines it sounds to me like he and Hannah are getting on okay which has got to be a good thing. He's been going with her to her scans and apparently a few weeks ago he even met her parents.'

'I bet they were thrilled, 'Ah, so you're the young man who's knocked up our daughter.

161

How lovely to meet you.''

Chris took a drag on his cigarette. 'I definitely wouldn't have wanted to be in Paul's shoes during that particular dinner.' He paused and looked at me directly. 'If it makes you feel any better I wouldn't be over the moon either if it was Vicky that was going away for a year. I know Laura keeps going on about how she's got to get this travel thing out of her system but all the time I'm thinking, why? Why can't you just go on a normal holiday like everyone else? What's the big deal about tramping around south east Asia with all your belongings on your back? It's not like you're going to some undiscovered country somewhere. It's just an over-extended, heavily disguised package holiday for the terminally work-shy.'

'Look, she's not 'work-shy' she's just 'creative', okay?'

'Whatever, I'm just glad she's not my girlfriend.' Chris took a sip of his pint. 'So anyway, tell me, just how *is* this year apart going to work? You know, you being here and Laura being halfway around the world?'

I shrugged. 'She'll have her phone with her so she can send me texts, there are internet cafés all over the place so she can always email me, there are loads of those cheap call places dotted about too and . . . fingers crossed, if work'll let me jam all of the holiday I've got left into one month I'll be with her for the whole of August in Thailand.'

'And that'll be enough?'

'To do what?'

'I don't know . . . to keep you connected?'

162

'Your guess is as good as mine. I'm hoping so. The deal is when she gets back we'll buy a place, she'll get a proper job and then we'll get married.'

Chris didn't offer any reaction which made me suspect that he thought it was all going to end in tears but didn't want to be the one to say it. 'I'm going to the loo,' he said standing up. 'When I get back we'll finish up here and then head downstairs, okay?'

I pondered my brother's lack of response. 'Yeah,' I replied, 'you do that and I'll see you in a second.'

Chris

On my way to the toilet I thought to myself about how weird it was that the bar that was hosting Laura's leaving party was the very one in which Cooper and Laura had met for the very first time.

Unlike me, Cooper had left school at sixteen with only a handful of qualifications and had spent the best part of a decade flitting between occupations. In his time he had been everything from a care assistant in a nursing home right through to a security guard looking after an empty office block in the centre of town. But at the time he met Laura he had just moved to Manchester and got his first job in sales for a paper recycling company based outside Oldham. It had been a job that he had hated from his very first day and one that he only endured because

163

the money was half decent.

That night in Blue-Bar Cooper had been chatting with me and Paul when I saw him catch the eye of a pretty blonde talking with her mates on the other side of the bar. I was right there next to Cooper when the girl told Cooper that she liked his glasses and asked if she could try them on. I knew for a fact that he hated letting people try on his glasses and yet not only did he let her, but he even laughed when her mates started saying she looked like Vic Reeves in them and started shouting out catchphrases from *Shooting Stars*. That was it. Their first meeting. Temporary loan of a pair of spectacles. Yet from that moment onwards Cooper had been under her thumb.

Cooper

When Chris returned from the toilet we drank up straight away. We'd barely stood up from the table however when Paul appeared in front of us carrying three pints. He looked well. But different from how I remembered him. His hair seemed shorter, he looked as if he hadn't shaved in a week and also appeared to have lost some weight.

Chris adopted a comedy Yorkshire accent straight out of Monty Python. 'I'd given thee up for dead.'

'No such luck,' replied Paul. 'I wasn't sure I was going to come. You know how it is: the last thing I want to do tonight is cause trouble but I wanted to be here for Laura, you know?'

'She'll be really pleased that you made it, mate.'

'So how is she?' He sat down in the seat next to me. 'All ready to go?'

'As ready as she'll ever be.'

Paul glanced around the bar. Chris picked up on it straight away. 'If you're looking for Mel I think she's downstairs.'

'Does she know I'm coming?'

'Laura told her.'

'And what did she say?'

'I'm guessing she probably said a lot of stuff but I don't think any of it was bad. She'll be pleased that you're, you know . . . alone.'

'A room full of my ex-girlfriend's best mates. I think even Hannah knew it would be a nightmare.' He paused. 'So is Mel alone?'

Chris shook his head. 'She's been seeing some new guy for a while. I've met him a few times. He seems okay . . . if a little on the young side.'

'How old?'

'I think Vicky said he was twenty-five.'

'And they're happy?'

'How should I know? She looks fine to me.'

'That's good to hear,' said Paul. 'She deserves to be happy.'

'How about yourself,' asked Chris. 'You still doing okay?'

'Hanging in there. Hannah's good and everything's still cool with the baby. We had a scan last week.' A smile broke out across his face. 'It was brilliant. Best thing I've seen in my life.'

Chris smiled. 'I remember that moment with

William. I'm really pleased for you, mate. It's great to hear some good news for a change.'

'How is William? Is he still mad about Daleks?'

'He's obsessed. He gets more and more fun with each passing day.'

'It must feel good to be so sure about something,' said Paul. 'To have no doubt in your mind that William's everything to you. I'd kill to have something I could be that sure about. I'd kill to know one hundred per cent that the way I felt was the way I would always feel.' He paused, obviously hoping that Chris or I would chime in with something that would make him feel that we were on his wavelength.

'I know what you mean,' I replied, even though I wasn't sure that I did. 'It is hard to be sure about stuff sometimes.'

'I think I'm already feeling what you're supposed to feel,' said Paul. 'I know it's only early days, but when this kid . . . this baby . . . when it's actually there in my hands and not just on some monitor or kicking out in Hannah's belly . . . I feel like I'll know for sure. That's all I want. That's all I've ever wanted.' He laughed self-consciously and then drained his pint. 'Here endeth the sermon,' he said setting the glass firmly down on the table. 'Who wants another one?' Before we could respond he was making his way over to the bar.

'This doesn't bode well.' I watched him waiting to be served. 'I've seen him like this before.'

'Like every day after he and Melissa split up

the first time round,' agreed Chris. 'And the way he's knocking back the drink . . . I'm guessing he's definitely on a mission to forget.'

'Absolutely, let's just hope that this time round he doesn't do too much damage to himself or anyone else along the way.'

Billy

It was just after midnight, I was more than a little drunk and I was standing out of the way of the crowded upstairs bar while Melissa got us some drinks. The evening so far had been good given that I was meeting so many of Melissa's friends for the first time. Laura, whose party it was, had seemed the most fun. But then again that could be because she was really fit and looked like a cut-price Jennifer Aniston. Her boyfriend Cooper seemed a bit grumpy but warmed up when I told him I was a City supporter, while his brother Chris had seemed okay, if somewhat distracted. Chris's wife Vicky seemed lovely and had even joked to Melissa about taking me on a date to the Cornerhouse if they ever showed a revival of *The Graduate*. But the person I was most curious to meet (albeit for the second time) was the one proving to be the most elusive. And although I'd heard that Paul was actually here at the party I'd yet to see him and I got the impression from the others that he was doing his best to avoid both me and Melissa.

Just as I was working out what to say to Paul if I ever did get to meet him again, I felt someone reach around the back of me and put their hands over my eyes. In a pitifully disguised voice my mystery assailant whispered: 'Guess who?' I knew straight away that it was Freya and before I could say a word she threw her arms around my neck in her usual overly familiar flirtatious way. Part of me wanted to peel her off me but most of me would've been happy to let her stay.

'It's packed in here tonight,' she said looking around the bar. 'It's never usually this crowded.'

'There's a party on downstairs.' I noticed that she had moved one arm down to circle my waist.

'Who are you here with?' she asked. 'Seb and Brian?'

I felt odd talking about Melissa to Freya.

'I'm actually with another mate tonight,' I replied.

Freya raised her eyebrows suggestively. 'Girlfriend?'

I nodded guiltily. 'Look, it's early days . . . but, yeah, I think I could describe her as my girlfriend.'

'Well done you,' said Freya as though I'd won a competition that had more to do with luck than actual skill. 'I'm really thrilled. Who is she? Do I know her?'

I shook my head and Freya gazed around the bar clearly trying to spot Melissa. 'At first I thought it might be that girl over there,' she pointed to a blonde in a cream beanie hat, 'but then I realised she wasn't quite right so I thought it might be that girl there.' She pointed to a pretty girl with black hair and a severe fringe. 'But I was wrong again. That's when I realised that it's that girl over there with the brown hair and the denim jacket?'

I was confused by her accuracy. 'How did you . . . ?'

'Easy. She looks exactly the kind of girl you'd go for. She works in here sometimes, doesn't she?'

'Just part-time. She's actually at the university studying Art History.'

'And she's how old?'

I was surprised by Freya's directness.

'Why do you ask?'

'Now you've made me really want to know. Come on, how old is she?'

'Why does it matter?'

'Well, it obviously matters to you if you won't tell me. She's easily over thirty.'

'She's thirty-five,' I said finally.

Freya nodded sagely. 'Good for you.' Something in her face changed as though she was hatching some kind of plan. 'Well, I'm here with Gina and Lou. We're heading off up to the Jockey in bit. You should come . . . bring your girlfriend too.'

'Thanks, but no thanks,' I replied, unsure whether I should be relishing the thrill of turning down Freya. 'This is sort of an important night for Mel and me, so I'll have to give it a miss this time.'

Melissa

I'd been contemplating the sorry-looking gerbera floating on the surface of the water in the pint

169

glass that we used as a tip jar and wondering why no one had thought to put a fresh flower in there — when I looked over at Billy and saw him talking to a pretty girl in her early twenties. I guessed straight away that the girl was Freya, as she looked exactly as Billy had described her: 'cool', 'pretty' and 'more than a bit self aware'.

Much to my amusement the second Billy saw that I was looking over at them his whole being seemed to cringe, as though he imagined I might think that there was something going on. The truth couldn't have been further from my mind. Seeing Billy with this girl made me realise how much he was unlike any guy I'd ever been out with. I didn't feel any pangs of jealousy. I didn't feel the slightest bit insecure. And it wasn't as though he wasn't a catch — more than once when we'd been out I'd spied girls eyeing him up — it was more to do with the fact that I knew that I could trust him completely.

'Hi,' I said with a smile, 'you must be Billy's friend Freya.'

Freya looked as though she hadn't expected Billy to have been open enough to tell me about her. 'I am,' she replied. 'And you must be Melissa. I was just saying to Billy that he must be really mad about you because I haven't seen him in ages. He always used to be hanging around somewhere handy but not any more.' She laughed, as if to make it clear that she was joking. 'Anyway, it's really nice to meet you.'

'What are you up to tonight?'

'Freya's just off to the Jockey,' said Billy,

clearly trying to minimise the amount of time that she and I shared the same air space.

'You should stay,' I said to Freya. 'My friend's having a leaving do downstairs and friends of ours are DJ-ing. It's been a great night so far. You and your friends should come down for a while. I'm sure no one would mind.'

'I'd love to,' replied Freya, 'But like Billy mentioned, my friends and I already have plans.' She nodded over to where a group of ridiculously pretty girls were pretending that they weren't watching us. 'Maybe next time. It was nice to meet you.' She looked at Billy. 'And good to see you too.'

'I had no idea she was going to be here,' Billy said quickly. 'That wasn't too awkward, was it?'

I laughed. 'It was fine.'

'And when you say 'fine' do you mean 'fine' or do you mean something else?'

'I mean 'fine' as in it was fine. She is pretty though. I can definitely see what you saw in her.'

'Yeah, well I'm glad I've moved on,' said Billy uncomfortably. 'Shall we head back downstairs?'

Billy took my hand. It was then that I saw Paul. He was over by the cigarette machines, standing with Claudia and a bunch of her other friends as though he had been hijacked on his way to somewhere else and he was looking directly at me.

I didn't want to talk to him right now. The whole thing would be too awkward.

'What's up?' asked Billy.

I shook my head. 'Nothing, I'm fine. Let's just go.'

Chris

I'd lost Paul almost as soon as we'd come downstairs to the party; Vicky and Laura were constantly flitting about in a triangle consisting of the dance floor, the toilets and the collection of sofas at the far end of the bar; Melissa seemed to be surgically attached to her new boyfriend and so by default I'd spent most of the evening together with Cooper floating in and out of conversations with Laura's mates' boyfriends.

Now I was at the bar waiting to be served in a queue three people deep. The longer I waited the more people gave up and headed upstairs in the hope of getting served more quickly but I was glad of the opportunity to have some time on my own to think through the decision that I'd made to finally finish with Polly.

Over the past few months this thing between us had become out of control. Each time I saw her I took greater and greater risks, the most recent of which had seen me inventing a conference I had to attend in Brighton when in fact Polly and I were planning to drive down to London and spend the night together in a hotel.

Everything had been fine on the journey down but when we reached London I realised that I had left my work mobile — a phone on which I fielded an average of thirty to forty calls a day — at home. Even though I'd booked the day off work, all it would take for me to get caught out would be for a single person to call me. Part of me had wanted to drive back up to Manchester straight away but Polly begged me to stay, assuring me that everything would be all right. We did stay but the night away was ruined. Back at home I searched high and low for my phone only to find it switched off, on the table in the hallway. When I asked Vicky if it had rung at all, she said that just after I had left someone had called but she had missed them as she had been upstairs getting William dressed. Reasoning that I could probably do without the disturbances she had simply turned off my phone and gone back upstairs.

Then a week ago Vicky complained that we still hadn't booked a summer holiday, so the very next evening we devoted ourselves to looking through brochures and the internet trying to find somewhere to go. Nothing. It felt as though there were far too many choices to even begin to narrow it down. But the whole evening had got me questioning what I was doing with Polly. It made me think about the fortnight William, Vicky and I had spent in Sardinia the previous summer. How much I had enjoyed having every day with William unimpeded by the distractions of work and how well Vicky and I had got on together. And it occurred to me that if I carried on down the route I was travelling with Polly that kind of holiday would never be repeated. I didn't want that to happen. I wanted William to have good memories of his childhood holidays just like I did. Mum, Dad, me and Cooper stuck in a static caravan in Tenby. The funny-smelling toilet. The tall grass growing out of the sand at the beach. The wind that made the sea feel ten times colder than ice even on a sunny day.

Holiday memories I could never forget.

But the one thing above all others that convinced me it was time to end things with Polly was a conversation I overheard in the toilet at the party. Two guys had joined me at the urinals. Standing either side of me, they swayed gently from side to side, very much the worse for wear as they began talking across me about a girl that one of them had just met. The guy on my right asked his friend if he thought the girl fancied him and his friend replied he thought she did. The guy on the left said that he thought she had a great arse and followed up by asking if his friend was going to do anything about it. Right guy smirked and said: 'It would be rude not to.' Left guy asked if he was bothered about his girlfriend finding out and the guy on my right sniggered and said, 'Well, she never found out all the other times,' and then they both cracked up.

I didn't want to think that I had anything in common with either of them: I was me and they were something different entirely. But like it or not, my affair with Polly meant that I was treating Vicky with the same brand of contempt that the guys in the toilet had used on their girlfriends. I'd turned my life into a big fat cliché: bloke halfway through his thirties has crisis of confidence, goes in search of the meaning of life between the thighs of another woman and risks family, home, reputation — in fact pretty much everything that he'd worked so hard to create — in order to indulge himself, if only for a moment, in the fantasy that the last ten years hadn't happened. My fling with Polly had been nothing more than an attempt to prove to myself that time wasn't moving forwards. That things weren't changing. And the months we'd been together were essentially nothing more than an aid to memory — like a photograph, a memento or a diary — to help me recall the highs of my twenties, underscoring in my mind the flawed belief that my best days were behind me.

But the best wasn't behind me, I knew that now. The best was right in front of me all the time. It was Vicky and William who gave my life meaning. They gave me a reason to carry on. And right there on the spot I decided that what I needed to do was end things with Polly as soon as possible and prepare myself for the mammoth task of trying to make up for everything I'd done wrong.

Cooper

Standing at the edge of the dance floor watching Laura and her mates enjoying themselves I reflected on the question Chris had posed earlier in the night: just how were Laura and I going to make this thing work when we were on opposite sides of the world? Though we'd been adamant that we weren't splitting up, neither of us seemed to have the least idea what that meant in reality, other than relying on what Vicky had described as 'the ancient art of finger crossing'. There had been a number of times I'd wanted to sit Laura down and make her sign some sort of agreement that she wasn't just using this whole trip as a way of getting away from me; that she would be faithful to me; and above all that she did indeed love me like she said she did. But there was no agreement. And even if there had been, it wouldn't have been worth the paper it was written on. When you're in love you're supposed to be able to trust one another. But though I hoped for the best I couldn't help but have doubts not just about Laura but about myself too. Did I really have what it took to live like a monk when Laura was on the other side of the world? I hoped so but I wasn't sure. I looked at her again on the dance floor — head thrown back, completely and utterly carefree and more beautiful than I'd ever seen her — and I realised that I just couldn't let her go without a fight.

I waved but she didn't see, so I walked over and grabbed her by the hand as she danced.

'What is it?' she asked. 'Is everything okay?'

'No,' I replied. 'Things aren't right. They're not right at all.'

Chris

As I stood outside Blue-Bar calling Polly I watched people passing by — a young couple dressed as though they had been for a big night out in town, a gang of indie kids looking like they were on their way to a party, and a group of lads in search of the nearest curry house — and I wondered whether any of them had noticed me or given any thought to why I was standing

176

outside the bar. Maybe a few thought I was waiting for a taxi or calling my girlfriend to let her know I was on my way home. I doubted any of them would've guessed that I was about to make a call that would put an end to the five months of deceit that had been part of my life since Christmas.

She finally answered.

'Polly, it's me.'

'Where are you? At Laura's leaving do?'

'Yeah.'

'I can't tell you how much Tony wanted to come tonight. We had a big row and now he's in the living room pretending he's watching a DVD but really he's just sulking.'

I swallowed. This wasn't going to be easy.

'I think we should stop seeing each other,' I said quietly. Polly said nothing. 'Look, I'm sorry, but you must know as well as I do that this has got to stop. It's getting too dangerous and I've . . . ' I corrected myself, 'we've both got too much to lose to even think about carrying on.'

Polly found her voice. 'So this is it? You just want to walk away? I understand it's difficult for you, Chris, I do. But whatever it is . . . whatever the problem . . . we can work something out. There's always a solution.'

'I don't think so. Not to this one.'

'And that's it? Your mind is made up? I don't understand why you're giving up so easily. What about everything we talked about? What about the times you told me you loved me?'

'I know,' I replied. 'I'm sorry. I don't know what else to say.'

177

'Maybe that's because there is nothing left to say,' snapped Polly, and then she put the phone down.

Cooper

I took Laura over to one of the quieter corners of the bar that was insulated against the music by virtue of being so tucked away. There were a couple of sofas covered in our friends' coats and bags. I made a space for us and sat down.

'What is it?' asked Laura. 'What's wrong?'

'Look, I've been thinking and well . . . I don't want you to go.'

Laura looked confused. 'I don't understand. What do you mean?'

'Exactly that. I don't want you to go travelling. I want you to stay here with me. Don't worry about the money we've spent on the ticket. Don't worry about any of that. And if you want we can blow every last thing we've saved on the holiday of a lifetime — wherever you want — New York, Japan, the Caribbean — anywhere. Just don't go travelling. Stay with me.'

'What's brought all this on?'

'Everything.'

'But you're not making any sense.'

'What's not to understand? I love you and I thought that you loved me so why are you going off halfway around the world without me?'

'We've talked about this. I thought you were fine with everything.'

'Why would you think that? Because I told

you? I tell you that it's fine if we don't get married and you believe me. I tell you that it's okay to go off around the world and you think I'm fine with it. Is there anything you wouldn't believe?' I grabbed hold of Laura's hand. 'I'm telling you now, Laura, I don't think I've got what it takes to make this work with you not here with me. I'd miss you too much. I want you to stay.'

'Or what?'

'You think this is a threat?'

'Well if it isn't, what is it?'

'It's a declaration of love. It's me asking you to stay because you love me.'

'And if I don't stay?'

'Why wouldn't you?'

Laura sat there staring at me with tears in her eyes. I was about to say again how much I needed her. How I'd got it all wrong. How she was my safety net just as much as I was hers but then Alistair and Baxter went from playing 'She Left Me on Friday' to 'Waterfall' — a song to which the opening bars seemed to demand the attention of everyone who had ever danced to it at the Student Union on a Friday night — and within seconds the dance floor was flooded. Jumping up and down to the music like drunken teenagers Laura's friends Davina and Alexa tripped on the carpet and came crashing to the floor at our feet. Picking themselves up with the minimum of fuss they were back dancing within seconds and their delight in seeing Laura was matched only by their delight in dancing to this long-forgotten student anthem. Ignoring Laura's resistance they grabbed her by the hands and re-entered the fray leaving me to stand on the fringes of the frenzy looking on until Laura was swallowed up in the crowd. I stood watching the space where she had been, occasionally buffeted by the people around me but I couldn't see her, and so, grabbing my things, I drained the last dregs of my pint and left.

Melissa

It was just after one in the morning and I was dancing with Billy to the Happy Mondays — my fifth song in a row — and though I was getting tired Billy showed no signs of flagging.

'Do you fancy a drink?' he asked as the Happy Mondays faded into The Inspiral Carpets.

'Vodka and Coke would be wonderful.'

'Vodka and Coke coming up.' Billy looked over at the crowded bar. 'I think I'm going to head upstairs. I'll be ages down here.' He smiled at me and we kissed.

I made the decision to retire from the dance floor and scanned my surroundings for someone to talk to. Who was I kidding? Not just someone: I was looking for Paul. Laura and Vicky had told me that they had spoken to him at various points during the evening and that he had seemed okay if a little the worse for wear, and the knowledge that he was here and alone made me want to see him even more. I had been thinking about him all evening: about everything that we had once meant to each other and why it had fallen apart.

The pain when we'd first split up and the worse pain the second time. And I thought about how even now I still felt that there was a bond between us that couldn't be destroyed. It would always be there. Primed. Ready. Waiting. I told myself firmly it was time to make our peace, time to stop hanging on to the past and move on. With this in mind I went in search of Paul.

When a cursory look at the dance floor revealed nothing, I began asking around. Sightings with various degrees of reliability had Paul pinpointed everywhere from a queue in the men's loos right through to the side of the DJ booth. Chad and Liam (who were admittedly very drunk) claimed to have seen him upstairs on his own looking like he was very much the worse for wear. I checked all the downstairs locations without success and was heading for the staircase when I was frozen to the spot by the sight of Paul and Claudia Harris kissing like a pair of drunken teenagers.

Billy

It had been nearly three quarters of an hour since I had left to get Melissa a drink. I would have gladly latched myself onto her for the entire night and it required every fibre of my self control not to do so. After all, Melissa was everything I wanted in a girlfriend — cool, funny and I felt like I could talk to her about anything at all and she would just get it. Time away from her seemed wasted.

181

When I locked eyes with Melissa's friend Vicky, she mouthed, 'Have you seen Mel?' across the room. I shook my head and shrugged, then walked straight into Brian and Seb standing near the exit.

'I thought you two were heading to the Jockey with Nathan and that lot?'

'It was crap so we came back,' replied Brian.

Seb raised his eyebrows. 'Where's the bird?'

'Probably with her mates.'

'Look, you don't have to act all casual for our benefit. We both know you're under the thumb.'

'Yeah, that's me, under the thumb.'

'So if you're not, what do you reckon then?' Seb nodded in the direction of a group of girls near the bar.

Though mindless banter was all part of what Brian and Seb were about, it had been a while since I'd been out with them and I felt a bit alienated.

'Seb reckons the bird on the left is the fittest,' said Brian. The girl in question was in her mid twenties and wearing a John Lennon-style Working Class Hero T-shirt.

'Tell him he's wrong, it has to be the one near the jukebox surely? She looks like an Indian Cameron Diaz.'

I looked over at the 'Indian Cameron Diaz', a tall-ish girl in a fitted black T-shirt. She was indeed Indian and very attractive, but she looked nothing like Cameron Diaz. I was filled with despair at the thought that if things didn't go well with Melissa all my future Saturday nights would end up like this: standing in cool bars with my two daft mates, making comments about girls we would never talk to in a million years while gradually drinking ourselves into a stupor. Melissa had saved me from this life. She had saved me from a lifetime of empty Saturday nights with my nose pressed up against the sweet shop window.

I pulled out my phone and dialled Mel's number. 'Hey, Mel, it's me,' I said when her voicemail kicked in, 'Where are you? I've done so many circuits of this place that I keep getting mistaken for a glass collector. No one seems to know where you are. Give me a ring when you get this, okay? I just want to know you're all right.'

Melissa

I fished out my keys from my bag, opened the front door and stepped into the darkness of the hallway. Turning on the lights, I glanced in the hallway mirror and was surprised to see tears were running down my face. The faster I wiped them away the faster they fell until I couldn't suppress them no matter how hard I tried.

I still found it hard to believe what I had seen. How could Paul have done that in the middle of a bar filled with people who had come to say their goodbyes to one of our friends? And with that bitch Claudia of all people? It had obviously all been her doing, her vicious way of evening the score. It made me sick to think about her lips touching Paul's. It made me want to vomit at the thought of her hands on his skin. But Paul was no innocent victim here. Drunk as he undoubtedly was, it was still no excuse. He had not only betrayed Hannah, he had failed to show any respect for the sacrifice I had made either. And it was this more than anything that had made me boil up inside. I'd stepped aside and relinquished all claims on him. I'd made things easy even though he hadn't asked me to. I'd put him first when all he had ever done was think about himself. And once again he'd let me down.

It hurt to think that the person I'd cared for so deeply was prepared to act in such a staggeringly shallow manner, risking his chance of happiness, and for what? For Claudia? I really hated him at that moment. Hated him more than I thought possible. And I wanted to hurt him. I wanted to hurt him the way that he had hurt me time and time again.

★ ★ ★

The second Paul saw me he'd pushed Claudia away as though she was nothing to do with him.

'Stop, Mel,' he said grabbing my wrists. 'Look, I can explain.'

'Explain what?' I broke free of his grip. 'Explain why you think so little of me that you'd do this? Go on, Paul, explain away.' Before he could reply I threw back my arm and slapped him across the face as hard as I could. I didn't care that everyone was watching me. I didn't care that the security staff were on their way towards me. And I didn't even care that Claudia was looking on with a smug expression fixed to her fake-tanned face. I just wished I'd hit him harder.

I was already on my way out by the time Steve and Georgie, Blue-Bar's regular door staff, caught up with me. They could see I was upset and they obviously weren't sure what to do.

'What's going on, Mel?'

'Nothing,' I replied. 'It's all over and I'm leaving. But if you want to be sure that there isn't any more trouble then the best thing that you can do is make sure that the guy I just hit doesn't try and come after me because if he does I will not be held responsible for my actions.'

Cooper

Things between Laura and me really were over. No question. This trip had never really been about her wanting to see the world, it was about getting away from me. Even though I knew in my heart that she loved me, I was also well aware that she wasn't *in love* with me. Or at least not as *in love* as you're supposed to be when you're planning the rest of your life with someone.

Heading home I thought about the ring. How long had I peered through the the jeweller's window trying to pluck up the courage to go in? There had been a dozen rings I'd had my eye on, varying in style and cost. Having come to a completely arbitrary decision that one of them would be the one that I would buy for Laura, I had ventured into the shop and asked the girl behind the counter to show me a few. As big decisions went I was pretty sure this wasn't the best way to go about purchasing something that was supposed to be a representation of my love for Laura, but better to get the job done badly than not done at all.

I was after something that looked expensive without being gaudy, and cheap enough that I could afford it without taking out a crippling bank loan. I'd had a figure in mind. Earlier in the week it had been much smaller but when I had written it down on a Post-it note at work it had seemed woefully inadequate for something that was supposed to last a lifetime. I doubled the figure I'd first thought of (taking me well out of my comfort zone) and this new amount had seemed far more appropriate.

As the shop assistant showed me the rings, I'd begun to worry that I might actually be overstating my case. While I'm all for extravagant gestures I'm not particularly keen on spending money for money's sake and all the obvious questions sprang up in my head. Would Laura really appreciate the five-hundred-pound difference between one ring and another? Would she be quantifiably happier? If I could have been sure that she would be happier then I would gladly spend the money. But if not, then wasn't I simply throwing away good money for no reason? The only way to be sure was for Laura to choose her own ring and this would have been my ideal scenario, except that the whole point was for it to be a surprise. I'd wanted to do the whole get-down-on-one-knee thing and open the box, slip the ring on her finger and see the smile on her face. That would have made it all worth it.

By the time I'd reached home I knew what to do. I stuffed the ring, still in its box, into my pocket and made my way through the quiet streets towards Maitland Avenue and the boundaries of Chorlton water park.

Melissa

I let my phone ring out until the caller gave up. I saw I had a voicemail message from Billy, the third he had left in the last hour asking me where I was. Just hearing the concern in his voice made me sad, but what was even sadder was that he hadn't even crossed my mind until I'd got home.

Things had been great between Billy and me since the night we got together at Cath and Simon's. Though we'd talked about going to Neelams to get something to eat, the plan changed. As I called a mini-cab to take us to Chorlton I began thinking about where all this was going with Billy. What I wanted — or at least what I thought I wanted — was a bit of fun and no more. I certainly didn't want to get into another long-term relationship. So when the cab finally turned up I gave the driver my address and suggested we order a takeaway to eat at mine instead.

I'd been pleased to see that Creepy Susie and her boyfriend were nowhere to be seen and I'd led Billy to the kitchen and pulled out the drawer

187

where we kept all the takeaway food menus.

'Pick what you like and I'll order it.'

As Billy flicked through the menus I became aware of the gulf between what I thought I wanted to happen and what I actually wanted now that thought was about to turn into action. Billy seemed far too nice a guy for a one-night stand and although he hadn't said anything specifically I could tell that he wanted something more than a meaningless fling.

'Do you fancy a beer? I'm pretty sure I've got a couple of Becks left in the fridge.'

'Yeah, that would be great.' He looked concerned. 'What's wrong, Mel? Is everything was okay?'

I wanted to tell him I was fine. I wanted to tell him everything was okay. But instead I found myself saying: 'I'm really sorry, Billy, but I don't think this is going to work.'

'I've been expecting you to say something like this,' he sighed. 'Is it anything to do with your ex?'

I nodded. 'It's sort of complicated.'

'It always is.' He put the menus down on the kitchen counter. 'Look, it's been great, Mel, but I think I ought to be going.'

I gave him a hug and kissed him on the cheek. Part of me was already regretting letting him go but I knew I was doing the right thing. 'I'm really sorry, Billy. You have no idea how gutted I'm going to be in the morning knowing that I've let you go like this.'

Billy didn't reply. My words seemed to have made things more awkward rather than less.

At the front door he paused to do up his jacket. 'Look, Mel, is it okay if I give you a ring later in the week so we can go out as friends — 'no-strings attached'?'

The thought of seeing Billy again really appealed to me. And while I'll admit that part of it came down to vanity — the novelty of basking in his adoration had yet to wear off — the rest of me genuinely liked him. He was funny, he was good company and he seemed more honest and open than most guys I'd met in years.

'That would be great. I'd really like that.'

After he left I set about clearing up in the kitchen, which was a mess. I got bored of that almost immediately so opened the fridge instead, took out a half drunk bottle of Chardonnay and poured myself a glass. As I took my first sip I reached into my pocket and pulled out the novelty keychain that Billy had given me and couldn't help smiling, still baffled by how he had managed to come up with such an appropriate gift. Pulling out my phone I typed out: 'The lobster. How did you do it?' in a text message and pressed 'send'. Sixty seconds later I received the reply: 'A good magician never reveals his tricks.'

Billy called next day and we arranged to go out for a drink the following week 'just as friends'. We met up at Sam's Chop House on Chapel Walks and talked all night, barely drinking because we had too much to say and too many jokes and bad puns to share. By the end of the night it was completely obvious to me that we would end up being more than just good

189

friends. Something about him clicked with me. The chemistry between us felt natural and easy in a way that I'd never imagined was possible with anyone other than Paul. And although nothing happened on that first night — we didn't even kiss again — I knew that something would happen soon and it would feel right.

A few weeks later, Billy invited me to the cinema on Sunday night. By this time we were already spending so much time together that when I wasn't at university, working at Blue-Bar or asleep, chances were that I would be with Billy. But in all this time I'd never been to his house. When I pointed this out to him after the film, he confessed that it had been a deliberate strategy because he was embarrassed. I playfully pushed as to why but he seemed to go into a bit of a mood so I dropped the subject, but then out of nowhere he said, 'Do you fancy coming back to mine now?' He seemed agitated so I felt bad for teasing him and said we didn't have to, but he insisted so we caught a cab back to Withington.

We stopped off on the way at the twenty-four-hour grocery shop around the corner from his house and bought two bottles of red wine, a four-pack of Red Stripe and a family-sized bag of crisps and then made our way back to his place.

The house was part of a huge Edwardian terrace in a dilapidated state of repair. Paint was peeling from the windows and a pane of glass in one of the upstairs windows had been smashed and replaced with a piece of cardboard gaffer-taped in place. It reminded me of the kind of place that I had lived in when I was in my twenties. The kind of place that in my thirties I'd never dream of moving into on pain of death.

Billy's flat was much nicer than the hallway with its two seemingly abandoned mountain bikes and three full black bin bags had led me to believe. In the living room there was a big brown sofa, a seventies-looking armchair and a large tiled-top coffee table. The only adornment on the magnolia walls were a number of film posters, the titles of which I could've guessed without even seeing them: *The Godfather II*, *Pulp Fiction*, *Reservoir Dogs* and *Goodfellas*. Classic boys' films, each and every one. I could've been standing in the very same flat that Paul and Chris had been sharing back when we all first met. Nothing changes.

'Do you fancy a drink?' He didn't bother to hide his relief that his flatmates were out.

'Why don't we make a start on one of those bottles of red?'

Billy disappeared into the kitchen in search of some glasses and I followed. He began rooting around in the various kitchen drawers for a corkscrew before somewhat explosively giving up and kicking one of the cupboard doors in anger.

'What's wrong?'

He shook his head and sighed. 'This is why I didn't want you to come here.'

'Why?' I tried to lighten the mood by making a joke. 'Because you don't have a corkscrew?'

Billy shook his head like I was missing the point. 'Forget it, Mel, maybe you should just go.'

Now I really was confused.

191

'Look, I was just joking, Billy. This isn't a big deal.' And because I could tell he didn't mean it about me going, I put my arms around him and then after a short while we started kissing.

When we stopped, eyes closed, foreheads touching, he murmured, 'I didn't want you to come here because I didn't want to give you another reason not to like me,' he said quietly. 'I didn't want to give you another reason to walk away.'

For Billy, the flat was hard evidence of the age gap between us, it was proof that we were at different stages in life. I was living in a nice purpose-built flat in Chorlton while he was in a student hovel that didn't even have a corkscrew.

If ever there was a single moment when the way you perceive a person changes so dramatically that it's like seeing inside their soul, this was it. In that second, I really liked him. And it didn't matter about what anyone thought, whether he would still love me when I was forty-five, about my biological clock, if he wanted kids or even that I was still in love with Paul. All that mattered was that I liked him and he liked me.

Cooper

Standing next to the water's edge watching the reflection of the moon scattered in front of me I thought about all of the times that Laura and I had stood in this very spot. The last time had been only a few weeks earlier when, inspired by a small flash of early summer that had gripped the nation, we'd sat in the sun watching the light reflecting off the water and planning the itinerary for her trip, while making sure also to talk about our plans for life after her return. But that was then and this was now. Now it was all over.

I took the box out of my pocket and held Laura's engagement ring between my thumb and forefinger before clenching it in the palm of my hand. I threw back my arm to throw the ring and everything it represented into the water but at the last minute, just as the ring was supposed to have been tracing the arc that would have led it some twenty feet into the middle of the water, I closed my fist tightly and refused to let go. It wasn't the cost of the ring that stopped me, the pointlessness of such a gesture or even the sense that I might regret the decision. It was that I still loved Laura and whether she was right here in Manchester or halfway across the world, I wasn't sure that would ever change.

Melissa

The sound of a police siren roused me from my thoughts of Billy. I suddenly missed him, so I tapped out a quick text telling him that I had felt a bit ill and had gone home but would call him in the morning. I pressed 'send' and was about to put the phone away and go to bed when the intercom near the front door buzzed. Assuming it was just some random drunk having a laugh I ignored it and carried on towards the bathroom but a few moments later it buzzed again, this time more insistently. I stomped my way to the hall and pressed the button that opened the front door, hoping that would be the end of it. People visiting other flats were forever pressing the wrong buzzer in the hope of gaining entry and as I had yet to discover that I'd accidentally let in a mass murderer rather than a bunch of my neighbours' drunken mates, I reckoned it wasn't worth losing sleep over.

Brushing my teeth at the sink going over the entire evening again in my head I was startled by an abrupt knock on the front door. My heart began pounding at the thought that perhaps I had after all let in some random nutter from the street. Fuelled by anger and tiredness I called out in no uncertain terms that whoever was knocking should leave the building straight away as I was already on the phone to the police. The second I heard the voice on the other side, however, I put down the phone and opened my front door, sure that my mind was playing tricks on me. But it wasn't. It really had been Paul's voice and now he was standing right in front of me. One look at the sadness in his eyes told me why he had come.

'I want to talk about our baby,' he said. 'I want to talk about our baby that never was.'

Two Months Later

Chris and Vicky's Anniversary Party

August 2006

Melissa

It was just after nine on the morning of Chris and Vicky's anniversary dinner and I was flitting around the flat doing several things at once badly to get ready to go into town. As well as finishing off my make-up in the mirror near the bedroom door, I was also trying to locate the matching shoe to the one I had in my hand, plug in the charger for my mobile phone and chat to Billy, who was sitting patiently on the edge of the bed watching me with a bemused grin. Without any warning he stood up and kissed me.

'What was that for?'

'That wasn't exactly the reaction I was looking for. I was hopng for something a little more . . . I don't know . . . effusive.'

'I'm just suspicious of your motivation, that's all.' I eyed him with mock suspicion.

Billy whispered in my ear in a pseudo-Barry White voice: 'I think you'll find, Ms Vickery, that you're all the motivation I need.'

The cheesiness of the line had me doubled over with laughter.

'Too cheesy?'

'Like gone-off Stilton!'

I carried on with my make-up but Billy still had that same bemused look on his face.

'So you like your men to be a bit less effusive with their compliments, is that it?'

'And which men would these be?'

'All men. Everywhere. You have no idea how great you are, have you?'

I pretended to continue with my eyelashes while wondering what he was going to say next.

'I've embarrassed you haven't I? Admit it, Mel, you have no idea how to take a compliment.'

'Look, mate.' I waved my mascara brush menacingly. 'Some of us just aren't used to them, that's all.'

'Well, you really should be.'

I looked at him through the mirror on the wardrobe door. 'I love you,' I said quietly. 'I've never said it before but I just want you to know.'

'I know,' he replied. 'And what's really funny is that I probably knew before you did yourself.'

Hannah

Paul and I were in bed together when I turned to him and said 'So tell me again, what's the name of the restaurant where Chris and Vicky's thing is going to be tonight?'

'La Galleria.'

'I thought that was the one. I was telling some friends at work and they were saying how amazing the food is. Apparently it's quite pricey though.'

'Chris said the starters alone are enough to break the bank.'

I laughed. 'Do you think we'll be flashing the cash like that when we're celebrating our tenth wedding anniversary?'

'Maybe,' said Paul grinning. 'If you're lucky.'

★   ★   ★

It was hard to believe that Paul and I were now married. Especially given the casual manner in which he asked me.

'What do you think about getting married?' he asked a few days after Laura's party.

'I think it's a bad idea,' I replied, thinking that he was joking. Paul rolled over on his side away from me and only then did I realise that he was serious.

'Why would you even think of such a thing?' I asked, still unable to believe what he was suggesting.

'Because we're having a kid,' replied Paul, 'and call me old fashioned but I like the idea.'

I was sceptical about Paul's reasoning. Paul hadn't said much about Laura's party other than that it had been 'good to catch up with a few people'. Not wanting to make a big deal out of things I hadn't asked about Melissa specifically even though I knew that she would be there. But when this proposal came out of the blue I began to wonder whether perhaps his impulse to get married had more to do with seeing Melissa with her new younger boyfriend than it had with him wanting to spend the rest of his life with me.

'There are a lot of things wrong with us making a commitment to each other just because there's a baby on the way. A piece of paper isn't going to make any difference if things start to fall apart.'

A week passed and Paul continued to pester me, stressing the practical and financial implications for our baby should anything happen to us in the future. Gradually, possibly more for pragmatic reasons than romantic ones, I came round to the idea but with certain conditions. It was to be a register office wedding. No ring. No friends. No family. Just us, the words we wanted to say, and the requisite number of witnesses to make the whole thing legal. When it was done, we would keep it to ourselves so that it would always be our wedding and nobody else's.

So one rainy Tuesday afternoon at the register office on Lloyd Street, following on from a second marriage between a publican and a nursery nurse twenty years his junior, wearing our normal everyday clothes Paul and I made our vows. Paul promised to look after me always and try his best to be the man who would make me proud, while I vowed to be both his friend and lover for as long as we both continued to live. The two security guards had clapped when Paul and I kissed and after they had witnessed the signing of the register had hung around, even though they hadn't needed to, curious as to how our wedding had come about. They'd laughed when I'd told them that we were going to keep our wedding news to ourselves, but then a few moments later (having had time to mull the idea over) the chubbier of the two told me that he thought it was a good idea. 'After all,' he said, 'at the end of the day what goes on in a marriage is nobody else's business but your own.' After the register office we went for something to eat at an upmarket pizza place on Clarence Street and whiled away the afternoon eating and talking. I can't say that this had exactly been my dream scenario when I was a little girl but I was a grown woman now and although things were far more complicated than I ever could have imagined as a child, the truth was it all felt right.

Melissa

Billy and I spent the best part of the morning looking in what felt like every shop in Manchester city centre for a present for Chris and Vicky before settling on vouchers for his and hers facials at a beauty salon in town. After a slight detour to the university library to pick up some books to help me with my dissertation, we had lunch at Pizza Express on South Street and because it was a beautiful day — one of those days when you feel sorry for anyone who has to be inside working — we decided not to go home and spent the rest of the afternoon sitting outside Manto on Canal Street. Armed with drinks and nothing pressing to do we sat outside enjoying the sun, people-watching and talking about things that made us smile. At around four as the sun began to hide away behind the clouds we decided it was time to make plans for the evening ahead. Billy would go back to his place to get ready, then come round to mine just before seven so that we could get a cab into town together and be at the restaurant for half past. Arriving home I'd not even kicked off my shoes when Creepy Susie called from the living room. The last thing I wanted to do was get embroiled in a fully fledged conversation with her, but I reluctantly poked my head round the door.

'Hi, Susie, everything okay?'

Susie's face was the very picture of worry. 'Sort of,' she replied, looking up from the sofa. 'I was just wondering . . . have you got a minute? It's just that I've got some news that I'd like to share with you.'

Having no choice I warily entered the living room and sat down in the armchair next to the TV. In the short space of time before she put me out of my misery I ran through a couple of possible scenarios for what Susie's so-called 'news' might be. My first choice was the arrival of an extraordinarily large gas bill. Susie and I had run the central heating in the flat almost solidly throughout the winter and had been sending in badly estimated readings until a couple of weeks ago when a meter reader finally came round and took an official reading. This could only mean trouble and I wondered whether we'd been landed with the kind of crippling bill that would require extra shifts at Blue-Bar for the rest of the year in order to pay it off.

My second choice for the bad news was to do with a rise in my monthly rent. Even before I'd moved in I'd been well aware that Susie was asking less than the going rate for a room in

Chorlton and had been wondering ever since when she might cotton on to this fact. At the beginning of the new academic year I'd even earmarked a small portion of my student loan to cover this possibility but that emergency fund had long since been eaten away by a whole string of more pressing emergencies (buying text books that were always on loan in the library, replacing lost bus passes and paying back Paul some money I had borrowed from him over the summer).

Given a choice, I preferred the rent-rise scenario, if only because I couldn't work out how I'd manage to finish off all of my course work and work practically fulltime at Blue-Bar to cover the gas bill while still having time for frivolities like eating and sleeping.

Susie was still looking at me expectantly and so I said: 'Fire away. I'm all ears.'

'It's about Steve.'

Immediately my stomach went into freefall because I knew exactly what was coming next.

Susie's big news had nothing to do with gas bills or rent rises . . . it was about love. The clues were all there. Susie and Steve had been together for two years. Susie had been saying for ages now how much she wanted to stop living like a student (which was both ironic and insulting given that Susie worked in a bank and had never actually been to university). But the biggest clue was the fact that for the past few months Steve had practically become a third flatmate. The only reason I hadn't complained about his omnipresence was because I thought it would prevent the very thing that was about to happen.

'What about Steve?' I asked carefully.

'Well, the thing is Steve and I have been talking — '

' — and you want me to move out so that he can move in?' I made things easier for her.

Susie nodded sheepishly. 'We've been together ages and he's practically here all the time anyway. You do understand, don't you?'

I nodded calmly even though what I really wanted to do was go on a rampage in Susie's bedroom and amputate the limbs from every single one of her teddy bears and cuddly toys.

'How long have I got?'

'Oh, there's no rush.'

I could see she was lying. From the moment of making the decision to let Steve move in, Susie had spent day and night dreaming about a life of domestic bliss.

'How long do you think you'll need?' asked Susie.

I sighed. 'It's been a while since I had to room hunt. How about the month after next? That'll be the end of October.'

'Oh, right.' Susie did not even bother to hide her disappointment. 'That long? I was sort of hoping . . . '

'Fine,' I said flatly, 'I'll be out by the end of the month. Is that okay?'

'Oh that's perfect,' beamed Susie. 'I can't tell you how nervous I've been about telling you. You really have been so understanding.' She fixed me with an odd stare. 'It's quite funny actually, the only reason I even thought about Steve moving in was because of you.'

'Me? What did I do?'

Susie seemed unsure how I might react to what she had to say. 'I hope you don't mind . . . it's just that a couple of weeks ago I came across that old shoe box of yours with all your photos in it. You'd left it on the coffee table. You'd obviously been looking at them the night before and left the lid off.'

I cast my mind back to the night in question. It had been the Tuesday that Billy had been away visiting his grandparents in Chester and Susie had stayed over at Steve's. With nothing to do and the rare opportunity to have the flat to myself I'd stayed in and drunk half a bottle of red whilst watching a documentary about kids with cancer. I'd sobbed from the moment it had started right through to the credits at the end. The kids had been so brave. The parents had been so brave. What problems did I have compared to them? That's when I'd dug out the shoebox with old photos of me and Paul. Ones taken before things had fallen apart. I know I shouldn't have done it, especially with things so good between me and Billy. I knew no good could come of it but I just couldn't help myself. I'd flicked through all the pictures of the two of us searching for the one in which we looked most happy. It had been a close call between one in the garden at Laura and Cooper's barbecue (Paul was lifting me in the air while I was screaming with laughter) and another of us kissing underneath a large spring of thyme in lieu of mistletoe at Chris and Vicky's one

Christmas. I'd stared at the photos for hours before falling asleep on the sofa. When I woke up in the middle of the night I'd dragged myself to bed leaving the photos and the open bottle of red behind.

'I hope you don't mind me saying,' said Susie, 'but you looked ever so happy in those pictures. Really bright and bubbly. And because of that I thought to myself maybe it's time Steve and I moved things on a bit.' Susie pulled her 'sad face', then stood up and walked over to me with her arms open for a hug. I allowed her to embrace me.

'I'll really miss you,' said Susie. 'You aren't just a flatmate: you are my best friend too.'

This was just too much to take. It wasn't enough that Susie had a leering boyfriend, a steady job, a mortgage and a flat in a nice part of south Manchester. No, now, she wanted to add the indignity of indignities of pretending that we were friends? I was too annoyed for restraint.

'Do you know what, Susie?' I said extricating myself from her embrace. 'I know this is going to make me sound like an embittered old hag, and on behalf of my conscience — which I know will be troubled by what I'm about to do — I apologise, but if I thought for even a fraction of a second that I really was your best friend I'd have to end it all now.' I headed out of the room slamming the door behind me with all the fury of a petulant teenager, then surprised myself by picking up my phone and calling not Vicky, Cooper or even Paul but Billy. And that was a real shock. I was turning to someone other than my closest friends for comfort. I was relying on someone I hadn't known an entire lifetime. It felt perfect, normal even, and the way things should be. Within half an hour of talking to him, listening to him tell me how it wasn't anything to worry about, assuring me that I would find something better and promising to take time off work to help me find somewhere, I was calm. Calmer than I had been in a long, long time.

Vicky

It was just after five and I was sitting on the loo with the lid down staring blankly at the pregnancy-testing kit in my hand when I heard Chris at the door.

'Are you all right in there, babe?'

I looked from the kit to the door and back again.

'Yeah, I'm fine. I think I probably ate something funny at lunch today.'

'Do you feel really ill?'

'No, just a bit queasy.'

'Do you want me to get you something? There might be a couple of paracetamol in the drawer in the kitchen if that's any use?'

'No, it's not that bad.'

'Good. It won't stop you from enjoying tonight, will it? I think we could both do with a proper drink.'

I had to take a few moments to compose myself and get the pitch of my voice right before I replied.

'Sounds great. I won't be long, honestly. Just give me a few minutes to sort myself and I'll be out, okay?'

'No problem,' said Chris. 'Your mum, sister and Daniel have just arrived. I'll settle them with a cup of tea until you're ready.'

Twenty-four hours had elapsed since I had first begun to suspect that I might be pregnant. I knew it was far too early to get excited but I couldn't help myself: my period had been due on Wednesday and was still nowhere to be seen.

It had been Chris's idea that we should start trying for a brother or sister for William. Until he'd raised the subject I'd been sure that I only ever wanted one child and Chris had always assured me that he felt the same. But a few weeks after Laura's leaving do Chris surprised me with a weekend in Paris and had even arranged for his parents to look after William while we were away. We had the most amazing time and he kept saying he had neglected us and wanted to make things right. We got talking about the future and what we wanted from it and while we were sitting in a café in Montmartre he just came out with it. 'I know we've always said that we only want the one, but maybe we ought to try for another baby. What do you think?'

I didn't have a moment's hesitation. 'I think that's the best idea I've ever heard, and weird because I've been thinking the same. I love William so much . . . how incredible would it be for us to give him a brother or sister?'

I stopped taking my pill the very next day and

even though it had been such a short time trying, and even though I knew it was more than likely a false alarm, I wanted to be pregnant so badly that the idea that the test might be negative was unbearable. I didn't want to let Chris down.

I'd bought the kit from the big Superdrug near Piccadilly rather than Boots in Chorlton so there would be less chance of me bumping into anyone I knew. I'd told Chris that I was nipping into town to get William's feet measured for a new pair of shoes and he'd barely looked up from his newspaper. With my cover story in place I'd taken William into town on the bus and made our way through the busy Saturday morning crowds to Superdrug. For good luck I'd selected the same brand of test kit that had predicted William's arrival. Throwing a few other items into my basket as camouflage (handcream, cotton buds, fragranced panty liners and a small bar of Green and Blacks dark chocolate) I'd made my way to the till and paid, scrutinising the face of the teenage Saturday girl serving me for any signs of recognition. But there was none. She failed to raise even so much as an eyebrow over the pregnancy test — it must be part of their training. Then we had a wander around the Arndale Centre and a drink in the BHS café before going home. I sent William in search of his father while I hurried upstairs and hid the test kit at the bottom of my wardrobe, where it had sat in its plastic carrier bag for several hours, slowly burning a hole in my brain.

Now I located the little tear strip on the

Cellophane and screwed the whole lot into a tight ball. I opened the box and removed the contents. I was going to cast aside the instruction leaflet but had a change of heart as I took one of the plastic sticks out of its foil sheath. Just because I wasn't a pregnancy-test novice didn't make me an expert. Things might have changed in the world of pregnancy tests since the last time and I doubted I could stand the shock of any false test result brought about through my own lack of care.

Reading through the instructions as carefully as I could given that my heart was racing so much, I tried to hold back the deluge of questions that threatened to overwhelm me. When would I get the chance to tell Chris? Would William react badly to the idea of having a brother or sister? How would I cope with motherhood the second time around? Would the pregnancy go as smoothly as before? Would labour be as difficult as William's had been? Would I ever get the hang of breast-feeding?

There were too many questions and too little time to deal with them all with my family sitting downstairs. I dropped the plastic stick back into the box, returned the box into its carrier bag, and tucked the lot right at the back of the cupboard underneath the sink, behind the bleach, the bathroom cleanser and a half-empty bottle of Milton's sterilising liquid. I pressed the flush firmly, washed and dried my hands and tidied away the Cellophane at my feet. I would take the test later. Later, when I had more time.

Cooper

It was five minutes past seven and I was following the waiter to the private dining room at La Galleria. It looked as though I was the first to arrive and as I waited for the others I thought how much things had changed these past few months since splitting up with Laura.

Drunk and dispirited after my failed attempt to throw away Laura's engagement ring, I'd woken up late next morning to discover that Laura hadn't been home. Her mobile was switched off and after phoning around her friends I eventually discovered that she was staying at Davina's house, so I called there.

'Hello?'

'Hi, Davina, it's me, Cooper, is Laura about at all?'

Davina was really shifty. 'Look . . . she's . . . er . . . I don't think she can come to the phone right now. Can I take a message?'

This was ridiculous. I could hear the sound of Laura frantically whispering in her friend's ear.

'I'm not stupid, Davina. She's right next to you, why don't you just put her on?'

'She won't come to the phone.' Davina seemed relieved she no longer had to lie to me. 'She's really upset with you right now, so maybe it's best if you leave things for a while.'

'Fine,' I was barely able to conceal my fury that Laura had dragged one of her friends into the middle of our relationship, 'get her to call me when she's ready.'

An hour later I was lying on the sofa watching

TV and wondering what was going through Laura's mind when my mobile rang. Laura.

I got in first. 'I'm sorry. I'm sorry for everything.'

'There's no need to be,' she replied. 'It was as much my fault as yours.'

'Are you going to come home then?'

'No. At least not right away. I've been trying to see if I could get the date of my flight moved forward.'

'You don't have to do that.'

'I know, but I want to and anyway, it's all done.'

'So when do you go?'

'Tomorrow.'

'Tomorrow! You can't go tomorrow. You weren't supposed to be going for another week.'

'I'm going tomorrow, Coop. And I'm coming round to get my stuff some time this afternoon so it would be really great if you could just give me the space to get what I need and go.'

'You mean you don't want me to be here?'

'I mean that I think it would be best for both of us if we didn't have a big scene. What's done is done. We've both got to move on.'

She meant every word, so once I'd recovered from the call, I got myself invited round for Sunday lunch at Chris and Vicky's, and by the time I got back home Laura's rucksack had gone and there was a note waiting for me on the stairs. The note was short and to the point. It simply asked me to look after the rest of her stuff until she returned, but if that was going to be too much of a problem she would arrange for her dad to take it back to Bristol with him. There was nothing about me or how she felt or about how things had ended. I'm guessing she was feeling too angry to bother trying to condense her feelings so that they would fit on the back of the envelope for the electricity bill — an electricity bill which incidentally she hadn't paid.

I didn't sleep much the first few nights after Laura's departure from a combination of guilt and uneasiness about the way things had ended between us. I felt even worse that she'd had to leave without saying a proper goodbye to her friends and sent dozens of text messages to say so. I didn't hear anything for a month — none of us did. Then out of the blue I received an email. The good news was that she was fine. She was in Mumbai and planning to work her way down the country towards Sri Lanka. She had spoken to lots of people, hadn't made any friends, though sounded pretty optimistic. She apologised for the way things ended and for not replying to my texts.

I replied immediately, updating her with everyone's news and finishing off that I missed her (which was true) but even as I pressed send I was regretting it. I expected the reply to be an intricate dissection of our relationship but there was no mention of my parting line, just a few reminders about what to do with her post and a long account of the things that she had done the day before.

After that we exchanged the odd email but it seemed that Laura saw us more as friends now than anything else. Our relationship, along with

213

her life at home, had been left behind. There was a subtext to her email that now she was somewhere else I should be too. Bizarrely, this made me miss her all the more. Her life was filled with new experiences while mine was pitted with huge holes where she had been. She wasn't there when I woke up in the morning. She wasn't there when I got in from work. She wasn't there for me to cook for during the early evening and she wasn't there when I watched TV late at night. And yet everywhere I looked she was always there.

★ ★ ★

The waiter opened the door and in walked Vicky in a stunning long black dress.

'Hello, sweetheart,' she said warmly, kissing me on the cheek. 'How are you?'

'I'm all right.' I gave her a wink and handed her the present I'd bought. 'This is for you and him indoors. Be careful though, it's fragile.'

'Can I open it now?'

'I shouldn't bother,' I replied. 'Once you've seen one set of wine glasses you've pretty much seen them all.'

Vicky laughed and Chris came over to say hello. Once we'd done the blokey pat-on-the-back-hug thing he went to say hello to Vicky's family while I made my way to greet my mum and stepdad.

'All right, Mum?' I said kissing her on the cheek.

'Looking well, David.' I shook my stepfather's

214

hand. I sat down next to David and prepared to ask about his journey because he always liked telling travel horror stories when Mum interrupted us.

'You can't sit there.'

'Why not?'

'We've all got place settings.' She pointed to the name cards on the table.

'Where am I sitting then?'

'Over there.'

I walked over to my place and looked at the cards on either side. Vicky had sandwiched me between Melissa's boyfriend Billy and some woman I'd never heard of called Naomi. My gut feeling told me that she was one of Vicky's pre-school mums' crowd and I envisioned a whole evening of being forced to listen to the ins and outs of her child's development from foetus to terror toddler without a single opportunity to get a word in edgewise.

I was reaching out to swap with Billy so that at least I could spend the evening talking to Melissa when Vicky slapped my hand and I turned to see her standing with a woman I had never seen before. She had black hair, light-brown skin and was so well groomed that I couldn't imagine for a moment that she was single.

'Cooper, this is Naomi, one of my old work mates from St James's. Naomi, this is my brother-in-law, Cooper.'

'Hi,' I said, instinctively glancing around the room for her partner. 'Nice to meet you.'

'You too. Vicky's told me so much about you.'

There was something about the way that she

said this that made everything fall into place.

This girl didn't have a partner.

She was here alone.

I glanced from Vicky to Naomi and back again and caught a flash of guilt in her eyes. It was the guilt of carrying a secret that affected someone else. And that someone was me. Naomi was here because Vicky had decided that I needed to move on. And the most obvious reason for her to have come to that conclusion was because she knew that Laura had already done some moving on of her own.

Vicky

Cooper's face looked like thunder. As much as I knew it might not work, I still felt that easing my own brother-in-law back into the real world by setting him up with the prettiest single female I knew was the right thing to do — especially as the plan had only come about after Laura had sent an email detailing her exploits with a young Australian called Sean.

'How have you been, Vick?' asked Naomi, setting into her chair.

'Fine, how are things with you? Are you busy?'

'I'm decorating at the minute. Once Ray finally moved all of his stuff out I could see just how badly my place was in need of a good spruce up.'

Cooper threw a loaded glance in my direction. I ignored it. 'What can I get you to drink, Naomi? Red? White? Both are open.'

'Red, please.'

I looked enquiringly at Cooper. 'White,' he replied pointedly.

I reached across to one of the open bottles of Merlot just as the waiter re-entered the room, this time leading in Melissa and her new boyfriend.

I handed Cooper the Merlot with instructions to look after Naomi while I went over to say hello. Melissa greeted me with a huge hug and I noted that Billy was taller, more self assured and more good looking than I remembered; he also had on a great suit.

He noticed me staring. 'Melissa chose it for me. I normally wouldn't go anywhere near one unless it was for an interview but she's got such great taste I could hardly say no.'

'Well, you do look fantastic in it,' I replied as I kissed him on the cheek. He smelt faintly of expensive aftershave.

'This is for you and Chris as a token of mine and Billy's esteem.' Melissa handed me a large envelope which piqued my interest.

'Can I open it now?'

'No,' protested Melissa. 'Do it when I'm not here in case you hate it.'

'Never in a million years. Let me go and put it with the other presents and I'll be back with you in a second.'

By the time I returned Chris had engaged Billy in conversation leaving Melissa free to talk to me. Part of me wanted to share the news that I might be pregnant right away but this was neither the time nor the place.

'I've missed you, you know.' I looped my arm around Melissa's waist. 'It feels like I haven't seen you properly in ages.'

'I know. We should go out next week for a bit of a social. Just the two of us. We could have a really nice dinner and get well and truly drunk. I could definitely do with a night like that after the day I've had.'

'Why? What's happened?'

'It's Creepy Susie, she's kicking me out.'

Melissa proceeded to fill me in on her flatmate's plans for domestic bliss.

'And you said that right to her face?' I asked incredulously as Melissa concluded her tale of woe.

'I couldn't believe the words were actually leaving my lips,' she admitted. 'It was like a scene from a film.'

'Definitely what you'd call memorable dialogue.'

'But in a film that would've been the end of the scene. The camera wouldn't cut away with Susie looking horrified and me looking pleased with myself before moving on to the scene where I find a fabulous new pad. But since I wasn't in a film I was left looking at Susie's crestfallen face. It was horrible, Vick. Really horrible. Once I'd talked to Billy I calmed down a bit and I went back to apologise to her, but she wouldn't let me in, so I had to talk to her through the door, which made me feel like an idiot. We then had a ridiculous shouty conversation where I apologised while she spilled her soul open for my benefit and told me about how she had issues about her self-esteem because her older sister was so much prettier and her younger sister was so much cleverer. Honestly, I looked at my watch at one point and she'd been rambling on for nearly an hour. It was like a bad version of Oprah. All that was missing was the whooping audience.'

'So how did you leave it?'

'I told her that I really valued her friendship and promised we'd keep in touch.'

'And will you?'

'I'd sooner have lunch with a serial killer than share a sandwich with Susie. This could only happen to me.'

'You're right. This kind of episode is definitely your niche. You should be pleased. It takes most people a lot longer than thirty-odd years to find their unique selling point,' I teased. 'Well, you know that whatever happens you're always welcome to stay with me and Chris. I really mean that, you know.'

'I know you do.' Simultaneously we both looked over at Billy.

'So things still going well with The Boy?'

'Couldn't be any better.'

'And you're all right about seeing Paul and Hannah tonight? They're both definitely coming.'

'Yes, I'm fine about it, honestly.'

I glanced over at Billy again. 'Looks like you've managed to bag yourself a good one this time.'

Chris and Billy's conversation seemed to have come to a conclusion so I led Melissa over to Billy and showed them where they were sitting. There was a lot of hand-shaking, kissing of cheeks and the beginnings of polite conversation and I relaxed, sure that we were in for the most amazing evening together celebrating mine and Chris's anniversary. Then the waiter arrived at the door with Paul and a heavily pregnant Hannah in tow and all such feelings of warmth vanished in an instant.

Melissa

From the moment of Hannah and Paul's entrance I felt as though everyone in the room was watching me like a hawk in order to gauge my reaction. As they came in and took off their coats I kept my head down to disguise my feelings, especially since I knew Billy would be studying my every expression, ready to pinpoint any look or gesture that might puncture his ego. I couldn't win — I couldn't look happy without being accused of pretending and I couldn't look sad without seeming to be still in love with Paul. There wasn't a thing I could do or say that wouldn't be open to misinterpretation.

Eventually I knew I had no choice but to face up to the inevitable. I looked over at Paul, held his gaze without flinching, and offered a brief smile. It was a small victory. I didn't doubt for a minute that it would be a short-lived one but I still allowed myself a moment's satisfaction. I had handled myself pretty well. And though the worst was over, as the waiters began to serve the first course my heart was thumping as if I'd just run a marathon. Under the guise of needing

the loo I excused myself from the table and left
the room.

Hannah

It was a little after eleven o'clock. The meal was
over and the empty dessert dishes had long since
been cleared away. I tried to take part in the
conversation going on around me but my body
was one huge ache. The baby had been unusually
active all evening, regularly thumping my insides
with various tiny body parts. I was worn out and
I wanted to fall fast asleep as quickly as humanly
possible. I looked over at Paul and mouthed: 'I
think it's time to go,' in his direction.

Turning to Naomi, who had been my main
partner in conversation for the evening, I smiled
apologetically and told her it was time that Paul
and I went home.

'Of course,' she replied. 'You must be worn out.'

I shuffled to the edge of my chair and tried to
stand up. Within seconds I was inundated with
offers to help me to my feet, which made me feel
vulnerable and ungainly but also strangely comforted. When I had just been Paul's girlfriend I
had felt like an actress auditioning for a bit part
in his life. But things were different now. I no
longer had anything to prove to his friends. My
status amongst them was assured.

'It really was lovely to meet you,' said Naomi.
'I'll get your number off Vicky and give you a call
about meeting up some time before the baby's
due.'

'I haven't really had much of a chat with you tonight,' said Cooper. 'Paul's been monopolizing me.'

'Well, you're welcome at ours anytime,' I replied.

Out of the corner of my eye I saw Melissa and her boyfriend approaching and I don't know if it was hormones but I suddenly wanted to make peace with her.

'I just wanted to come over and wish you all the best for the birth,' she said warmly.

'That's really nice of you. I hope you'll come and visit us when the baby's here.'

'Wouldn't miss it for the world,' replied Melissa. She looked at Paul. 'It was good to see you too.'

He moved to kiss her on the cheek and I automatically felt my goodwill evaporate.

Melissa

By the time Billy and I decided to leave the restaurant, nearly everyone else had already gone. While Billy went to the loo I stood outside looking up at the stars.

'Anything good up there?' asked Billy emerging on to the pavement.

'Not really.'

Billy juggled his mobile phone from hand to hand as though waiting for me to make a decision.

'So what next? Yours or mine?'

'I don't know. I can't see a cab anywhere.'

Billy shrugged. 'Do you fancy walking for a bit?'

I looked down at my feet. 'In these shoes?'

'I'll carry you.'

'You're on.'

'You think I'm joking, don't you? Well I'm not.' Billy picked me up and ignoring my screams of laughter started walking towards Deansgate.

Vicky

Chris and I were in a black cab on our way back home.

'Tonight was good, wasn't it?' said Chris. 'Everyone seemed to enjoy themselves.'

'Nearly everyone.'

Chris nodded. 'You mean Melissa?'

'She put on a brave face but I could tell she was miserable. I hate the way things are. I hate that I don't see Paul any more. I hate that Melissa's got so much pain in her life. I hate that Laura's gone and that Cooper's on his own. Why can't things just stay the same? Why does everything have to turn upside down?'

'It doesn't,' said Chris. 'We're proof of that, aren't we? Ten years under our belt. We're good. We haven't got any worries.'

Now was my chance. 'I think I might be pregnant.'

There was a long silence while I waited for his reaction.

'Are you sure? I mean, is it definite?'

223

'I'm only a little bit late. It's probably nothing.'

'Is that what you really think?'

'No. I don't know why I feel like I am, I just do. I tried to take the test earlier tonight but I couldn't do it. The stuff's in the bathroom at home. You haven't changed your mind about another baby, have you?'

'No, no, of course not.'

'So what's the problem?'

'Nothing,' he replied. 'It's just a bit of a shock that's all.'

I snuggled closer to him.

'It's okay to admit to not being fine, Chris. It's okay to feel helpless sometimes.'

'I know. I never thought I wanted more than one kid. I thought I'd try fatherhood, tick it off the list and then be happy with my lot. And when William came along I couldn't imagine loving another child as much as I love him. But I don't want William to grow up alone. I want him to have someone in his life who will always be connected to him. Someone he can always turn to when you and I aren't around.' He kissed the top of my head. 'Baby or no baby, I couldn't possibly love you more than I do right now.'

Arriving home, hand in hand we headed upstairs and as I took the test in the bathroom Chris waited outside. Emerging moments later with the test in my hand we stood wrapped in each other's arms waiting for the result to appear. I could barely breath as I waited, wishing, hoping, praying for the thin blue line to appear that would change our futures forever.

And as it slowly became clear that my eyes weren't playing tricks on me, that the blue line on the test really was real, I felt so completely and utterly relieved that I just sat down right where I'd been standing, closed my eyes and sobbed my heart out.

Hannah

'I really enjoyed tonight,' I said as, standing in the kitchen, Paul opened the fridge door and pulled out a bottle of Red Stripe. 'Everyone was really nice to me and the food was fantastic.'

'You're not wrong about the food,' he replied. 'That dessert you had was amazing.' He rummaged in the cutlery drawer for a bottle opener. 'And it was good to see everyone on such really good form.'

'Apart from Melissa.'

'How do you mean?'

'Oh come on, Paul. Don't tell me you didn't notice the look on her face when we walked in tonight? She looked distraught.'

Paul opened his beer and took a sip. 'I doubt it.'

I stared at Paul. I couldn't believe he was being so wilfully ignorant when it came to Melissa. I couldn't believe that he was going to make me spell it out: if we were going to work as a couple then he had to find a way to close the door on his past so that I wouldn't have to spend every waking moment fearing he was going to walk back through it.

'You know she's still in love with you, don't you? She's never completely got over you.'

'What do you want me to say?'

'Do you still have feelings for her?'

'No.'

'None at all?'

'Not in the way you mean. Melissa and I are friends. Nothing more. To be truthful I'm actually not even sure we are friends any more. We barely said a word to each other tonight. I've moved on. She's moved on. End of story.'

'I'm not attacking you.' I made a bid to bring the conversation back from the edge of an argument. 'It would be understandable if you did have feelings for her.'

'Well, I don't.' Paul set the bottle down on the kitchen counter and put his arms around me. 'Melissa's part of my past. I can't change my history any more than you can change yours. But right now I love you. And I know that us having a baby is the best thing that has ever happened to me.'

I wanted to believe his words. If I could I would finally be able to relax and enjoy what we had instead of fearing from moment to moment that something terrible was about to happen.

'I'm not going anywhere. I'm here with you for good.' Paul lifted up my chin.

'I know you are.'

'So you trust me?'

I couldn't bear to voice my affirmation when so many doubts remained in my mind so I simply nodded.

'I'm sorry, Paul, I really don't know what's got

226

into me. I know we're supposed to be seeing my friends tomorrow night but let's cancel, shall we? Let's stay home and not see anyone before Monday. I'm tired of sharing you with other people. I want to be selfish. I want to feel like you're mine and nobody else's.'

'You're worrying about nothing.' He kissed me gently on the forehead. 'I *am* yours and nobody else's.'

'Then prove it by promising that you'll never see or speak to Melissa ever again. I know I'm asking a lot. I know you two have a history. I know you're friends. But every time I see the look on her face when she's in your presence, it tears me up inside. And I don't want to feel like that for the rest of my life, Paul.' I watched his face for any sign that my words had hit home but his features were blank, unmoved. I almost dared not to breathe until he spoke.

'Okay, if you want it you've got it. If it's what you want I promise I won't see or talk to Melissa again.'

'It *is* what I want,' I replied.

'Then it's yours.'

'This is a new beginning for us. A new start. No baggage. No history. Just me, you and our baby.'

Melissa

Much to my relief Billy put me down after less than twenty feet and we made our way hand-in-hand through the streets towards the

227

taxi rank. It was nice being in town this late at night watching groups of glammed-up boys and girls on their way to the nearest bar or club.

'So is it still the end of the month that you've got to be out by?' asked Billy as we walked past a group of indie girls laughing and joking as they waited in the queue outside 42nd Street.

'With the way things are with Susie? I was thinking more like the end of next week. Vicky has insisted that I stay with her and Chris but I can't do to that to them, they've got William to look after. I know that this is a bit mean but I'm guessing with Laura gone Cooper might be up for having a house guest for a while.'

Billy was quiet for a few moments. 'What about me?'

'What about you?'

'Why don't you stay at mine?'

'I can't.'

'Yes, you can.'

'I'll do whatever you want me to do.'

He meant it too. 'Look, Billy, it's lovely of you to offer but you know . . .'

'What?'

'Please don't make me spell it out?'

'But I need you to,' he replied. 'I need to know why.'

I looked into his eyes and could see that he genuinely believed there was no good reason for me not to say yes. And right there on the spot I wished that I had Billy's confidence in us. I wished that I shared his confidence in me.

'I can't move in with you because I'll mess things up like I usually do.'

'You think I'm trying to rush things, don't you?'

'Well, aren't you?'

'Look, I'm not trying to overwhelm or confuse you or anything like that. I just want you to know how serious I am about you — about us. That's not a crime, is it?'

'Of course not,' I stumbled, unable to find the right words, 'These past few months have been amazing, Billy, but that's all they've been . . . a few amazing months.' I willed myself to continue, fearing that I might be about to hurt him. 'Paul really broke my heart you know, Billy. He broke it and there were times when I thought it would never recover.' I closed my eyes and exhaled. 'I'm sorry.'

'Don't be, it was something I needed to hear. But you seem to be forgetting that I'm not Paul. With my hand on my heart, Mel, I promise you I'd never hurt you in a million years. And what I'm really trying to say to you is this: I don't really want you to move into mine — I want us to look for a place for the two of us to live together. Not flatmates or housemates. Just you, me and . . . a cat.'

'A cat?'

'Of course we'd get a cat. We'd get a cat and we'd call him something like . . . I don't know . . . Charlie. And the place we'd get would be in Chorlton and okay . . . maybe it wouldn't be the biggest place in the world but it would be ours and we wouldn't have to share it with teddy-bear-collecting freaks or even Seb and Brian and their film-poster collection.'

Listening to him paint this picture of the future made me realise that I didn't want to view a million and one unsuitable flats just to find a half-decent room in one. And I didn't want to have to share a flat with complete strangers. What I wanted was a life. A proper life. With someone I loved and who loved me right back. So without wasting another moment I found myself saying yes.

Three Weeks Later

Melissa and Billy's House-Warming Party

September 2006

Melissa

It had been a long road that Billy and I had had to travel in order to make it to the moment when we could finally throw a party of our own. On the night of Chris and Vicky's anniversary we'd gone back to mine. Still feeling bad about my earlier argument with Creepy Susie I asked Billy to go and make us both a cup of tea while I knocked on her door and apologised to her again for the way that I'd spoken to her earlier.

Susie's eyes lit up when I told her the news. She got so carried away with the romance of it all that she even told me to forget everything she'd said earlier and take as long as I needed to find a place of my own. I promised Billy and I would start looking first thing in the morning and that hopefully it wouldn't take too long.

The very next day Billy and I started flat hunting and within a week we'd found a one-bedroom flat five minutes from my old place that we could just about afford. It was in a Victorian house conversion and as flats went it wasn't exactly huge but it was clean, bright and well maintained and more importantly, it was going to be ours. On the morning that we were supposed to drop off our deposit with the letting agent, however, they called with some story about a mix-up that had resulted in another couple also being shown 'our' flat. According to the agent this other couple were prepared to pay a hundred and fifty pounds a month more than we were! At first Billy wanted to match the offer because he knew that we'd never find a flat as nice as this one again but I hated being held to ransom and persuaded him that the best thing to do was to tell the agents what they could do with their 'accidental mix-up' and carry on looking.

A week later, still with no success, we decided to drown our sorrows and take ourselves off for a night of good food and drinking. Starting at Neelams with a quick curry we gradually gravitated towards Blue-Bar where we bumped into Billy's sister Nadine. Nadine was out with Karen, an old university friend, and while we were talking it came out that Karen was a lawyer, who had just got a promotion that would involve her being relocated to Singapore for six months. She was worried about her cat because she couldn't take it with her and asked us if we had any trustworthy friends who wouldn't mind baby-sitting a cat in return for cheap rent in a nice house. Before she had even finished her sentence we'd practically jumped down her throat and begged her to let us have it.

The house was much more impressive than the flat we'd lost out on. It was a beautiful three-bedroom Edwardian terrace on a great road just opposite Chorlton Park. The ceilings in all the downstairs room were really high and the windows so large that they flooded the front sitting room in light. Once we'd had the guided tour, Karen took us out to the utility room at the back of the house and introduced us to Thomas, her three-year-old Chartreux, who was lying in a fur-lined basket on top of the washing machine. He was, as cats went, pretty ordinary looking, with light grey fur, green eyes and a low-slung stomach. Karen obviously adored him so Billy and I tried our best to adore him too but he didn't appear all that interested in us. I think this gave Karen the reassurance she needed that whilst most cats might be fickle, she was undoubtedly number one in Thomas's heart. Satisfied with our cat-keeping capabilities she handed us a set of keys and asked us if we had any questions. I was about to say no, when Billy piped up, 'I know it's a bit cheeky but would it be okay if we throw a party here?'

For a moment I thought that Karen was going to change her mind and throw us out on the spot but she just laughed and told Billy she had thrown more parties here than she cared to remember and that as long as nothing got stolen, the place didn't get wrecked and Thomas was okay we could do whatever we liked.

We moved in the next day. And for that short time I was happier than I ever thought might be possible. Everything was going right for me. At long last I'd managed to put the past behind me and the party, mine and Billy's party, was supposed to be the icing on the cake, a celebration of everything we were and everything we hoped to be. But then while I was out getting things for the party, I took the phone call from Chris telling me that Paul had died and after that nothing was ever quite the same again.

Paul's Funeral

September 2006

Chris

It was just after nine in the morning and I was sitting at the dining table struggling to finish the eulogy that I was supposed to be delivering in a few hours at Paul's funeral service. Everything I wanted to say sounded insincere and clichéd the second I'd written it down. It was as if the very act of picking up a pen rendered me incapable of writing a sentence without resorting to something that I'd seen in a film or watched on a soap opera. What I really wanted was to say something from the heart — something that would do justice to the memory of my friend. But nothing I could ever hope to write could achieve this most impossible of tasks.

I'd been at work when I got the call from Hannah's mother.

'Hello,' she said. 'I was wondering whether I might be able to speak to a Mr Christopher Cooper?'

My first thought was that I was being cold-called by one of those dodgy companies that are always flogging replacement mobile handsets. I seemed to get a dozen or so of these kinds of calls a week and each one only served to make me wish that I had an air horn at the ready so I could blast it down the phone. I was a split second away from cutting her off altogether when she told me she was calling with regard to 'a Mr Paul Rogers' and that was when I finally realised that the woman's voice (grave, middle-aged and well spoken) was unlike that of any cold-caller I'd ever encountered.

She told me she was Hannah's mother and was calling on her daughter's behalf, then went on to say — and these were the exact words she used — that she had 'some rather awful news'. My first thought was that something had happened with Paul and Hannah's baby. The last time I'd seen Paul he'd told me that Hannah's due date was only a few weeks away. Maybe there had been some kind of complication and Hannah was in hospital. With Vicky being pregnant too the thought that something bad might have happened to Paul and Hannah's unborn child made me feel doubly sick to my stomach. I braced myself for the 'awful news'.

'It's about your friend Paul. I'm sorry to have to say that he was involved in a car crash on the south-bound carriageway of the M6. It happened just after eight this morning. A lorry crossed the central reservation. Paul was one of six fatalities.'

Everything after this point was a blur. After I'd put down the phone I remember colleagues gathering round me asking what had happened. All I could say was: 'It's my friend. He's gone.' Helping hands ushered me into the corridor. A cup of ice-cold water from the dispenser was pushed in my hand. 'Drink it and you'll feel better.' Even at the time I thought that that was

240

asking a lot of a simple paper cup of water but I did as instructed. And while it didn't make me feel better this simple act brought me to my senses enough to realise that it was up to me to call the others and let them know what had happened. And Melissa would be the first person that I would call.

★ ★ ★

That was less than a week ago and now here I was trying to write my best friend's eulogy. Sensing that I was no longer alone I looked up to see Vicky standing in the doorway of the living room wearing a long black dress. She looked beautiful — her face, her smile, everything about her — just too perfect for words.

She came over and draped her arms around my neck. 'Everyone is on your side, Chris,' she said quietly. 'Whatever you say will be right for Paul.'

'I still can't believe it. I'm going to bury my best friend.'

'I know, sweetheart. I know.'

'None of it seems real.'

'I know.'

'He's never coming back.'

'You're right,' she said softly. 'He isn't coming back. And there's nothing we can do about it. We just have to hang on to each other as tightly as we can and hope that through some miracle tomorrow will be better than today.'

As Vicky kissed the top of my head the front doorbell rang.

'That'll be Melissa,' said Vicky, looking over at the clock on the wall. 'You go upstairs and get ready and I'll let her in.'

Melissa

My finger was still hovering over the bell as Vicky opened the front door. We hugged on the doorstep and I followed her into the kitchen. She asked if I fancied a tea and although I declined, that didn't stop her from taking three mugs out of the cupboard above the kettle.

'Is the third one for William?'

'It's for you.'

'You won't take no for an answer, will you?'

She shook her head. 'So Billy decided not to come after all?'

'He wanted to . . . you know, for me . . . but this morning I asked him not to. Do you think that was the wrong thing to do?'

'It's complicated, isn't it? The important thing was that he wanted to do what was best for you. You can't ask for more than that.'

I watched her take the milk out of the fridge and set it down on the surface next to the mugs. 'Where's Chris?'

'He's upstairs getting ready.'

'And William?'

'Upstairs probably talking to Chris about how much he likes it at Grandma's.' Vicky smiled. 'We're dropping him at my mum's on the way to the church.' She paused. 'And how are you? Did you sleep at all last night?'

'Not really.'

'Chris didn't either.'

I nodded.

'Has he finished writing his thing yet?'

'No, but I'm sure he'll be fine.' She hugged me tightly. 'I'm here for you, you know? If you want to talk . . . or you feel like it's all getting a bit much just say and I'll straighten everything out.'

'You've been really great this past week, Vicks.' My voice started to crack. 'The absolute best. I don't know what I would've done without you.'

Since Paul died I'd spent a lot of time at Chris and Vicky's. After Chris's phone call I caught a cab straight over to theirs because it seemed like the only place to be. And by the time I'd arrived Cooper was already there and the four of us did our best to comfort one another. As news of what had happened spread across south Manchester and everyone started calling for further information, Chris did his best but when it reached the stage that the phone was ringing literally every five minutes Vicky made the decision on Chris's behalf to turn on the answer phone and let him get some rest. The most surreal moment was at six o'clock when we turned on the news and there was a three-minute report on the crash. Paul's name wasn't mentioned directly, instead he became, 'a thirty-six-year-old social worker based in south Manchester'. Vicky and I left the room before the report had even finished and sank down on the stairs sobbing in each other's arms.

As the kettle came to a rattling boil Vicky

dropped tea bags in each of the mugs and poured the water over them and as we waited for the tea to brew we talked about normal things like Vicky's pregnancy and for a few moments I forgot what this terrible day was supposed to be.

★ ★ ★

'I'd better go and finish getting ready. Will you be all right entertaining yourself for a little while?'

'I'll be fine,' I said as the kitchen door burst open and William walked in. He was wearing jeans and a green tracksuit top with red piping that was zipped up right underneath his chin. A toy dinosaur dangled from his right hand.

'Auntie Mel!' he screamed throwing his arms around my legs.

'I wish everyone greeted me like that.' I bent down and kissed the top of his head. 'Hello, William.'

Vicky kneeled down to talk to him. 'Sweetheart, can you do something for Mummy? I need you to look after Auntie Mel while Mummy and Daddy finish getting ready. Can you do that?' He nodded. 'Okay.' Vicky looked up at me. 'Just give me a shout if he's too much trouble.'

'We'll be fine,' I replied. 'You go and do what you've got to do.' Vicky took the two mugs of tea and left the room leaving me alone with William. I held out my hand. 'Can I have a look at your dinosaur please?' William offered it up to me without protest and I made a great show of examining it carefully. 'It really is a lovely dinosaur. Is it new?'

'It's not lovely,' he corrected. 'It's very angry.' To illustrate the point he screwed up his face, curled his fingers and roared. I pretended to be terrified and cowered, pleading with the dinosaur not to eat me, which amused William greatly.

'I'm not really a dinosaur, Auntie Mel. It's just me: William. I was pretending.'

'Oh, I can see that now. So what are you?'

William thought for a moment. 'A boy.'

'That's good to know.'

William examined the horns on his dinosaur. 'Do you know what these are?'

'They're pointy bits so the dinosaur can pick up his dinner.'

'Like a fork?'

'Like a fork.'

I reached down and gently stroked William's hair.

'Auntie Mel?'

'Yes?'

'Are you sad?'

'Why do you ask?'

'Mummy said you might be sad today.'

'Yes, I am a bit sad today.'

'Because of Uncle Paul.'

'Yes, because of Uncle Paul.'

There was another silence.

'Auntie Mel?'

'Yes?'

'Mummy says it's okay to be sad sometimes.'

'Does she?' I spoke as brightly as I could.

William nodded. I thought I would break down in tears if he didn't stop soon. 'Mummy said that when sad things happen you're allowed to be sad because it's not good to keep it all in.'

'No, it isn't.'

William waved his dinosaur in my direction and roared. Grateful for the opportunity to scream rather than listen to a small child discuss techniques for coping with grief I threw myself into the role of a potential meal for the roaming dinosaur. I ran from the kitchen into the living room where William chased me round the coffee table. After several revolutions I finally allowed myself to be caught. William and his dinosaur began tickling me. Then out of the corner of my eye I caught sight of a photo on the wall that I'd seen a million times before. It was a picture taken on New Year's Day three years ago of the six of us: me, Vicky, Chris, Cooper, Laura and Paul all bunched together on the beach at Barafundle Bay in Pembrokeshire. We had been larking about and had asked a woman walking her dog whether she would take the picture. Cooper and Laura were on one side, Chris and Vicky were on the other. And in the middle were me and Paul. Everyone looked happy. Everyone was smiling. Everyone looked young and trouble free. And at the sight of all this lost happiness I became horribly aware of a rush of saliva into my mouth.

'Auntie Mel's got to go to the loo,' I said. I made my way to the downstairs bathroom, locked the door behind me and promptly threw up into the sink.

Cooper

I felt a bit weird as I rang Naomi's front doorbell. Because of one thing and another we had only been out together a handful of times since Chris and Vicky's anniversary dinner and yet here I was taking her to the funeral of one of my closest friends. It might be okay to go on your own to the pictures or for a walk in the park but it seemed weird to turn up at the funeral of one of your best friends alone, and as none of us had seen or heard from Laura since it had happened, almost by default Naomi became my number-one choice.

Despite the occasion, when Naomi answered the door dressed in a black sleeveless knee-length dress I couldn't help but think how gorgeous she looked. She greeted me with a kiss and invited me in. I watched as she checked her hair and make-up in a heart-shaped mirror before grabbing a denim jacket from the hat stand just next to her.

'Sorry about making you wait.'

'No problem.'

Naomi bit her lip as if trying to make a decision. 'So, how are you feeling?'

'Okay,' I replied. 'Not brilliant. But okay. Does that make any sense?'

'I know what you mean. The last funeral I went to was my granddad's three years ago. I remember feeling really weird on the day because I didn't feel as upset as I thought I ought to be. The funeral should have been this big focal point but for me it just wasn't. Then seven months later on my birthday my gran called me and I completely broke down. You see, after I left home it was always my granddad's job to call and wish me happy birthday on behalf of my grandparents. Whether I was up at Cardiff doing my degree, down in London in my first job, or even on holiday in Australia — Granddad always called to wish me happy birthday. I think Gran thought she was doing the right thing but it just wasn't the same.'

I pulled Naomi closer and we held each other tightly for a few moments before loosening our embrace to kiss each other properly.

'You know you really don't have to come with me today.'

'But I'd like to, if that's still okay by you.'

'Of course.'

'You don't think it's too weird then?'

I managed a small laugh. 'It's not weird at all. I invited you. We're friends. What else is there? Anyway, I'm sure if Paul were here he'd say it was a case of 'the more the merrier'.' Naomi seemed to relax a little. 'We'd better go,' I said looking at my watch. Despite everything that was going on, being with her made me feel happy because I wasn't quite so alone any more.

* * *

Despite being annoyed with Vicky for trying to set me up with Naomi on the night of their anniversary party, out of politeness I had offered to share a cab back to Chorlton with her. For most of the journey we talked about Vicky but as we warmed to each other we began to share a bit more background about ourselves and despite the awkward start to the evening we were actually beginning to get on.

'This might be a weird thing to say,' I began as we pulled into her road, 'but I'm really glad we got a taxi back together.'

'Me too,' she replied. 'Although if I'm honest I thought you were more than a little bit frosty towards me earlier tonight.'

'Yeah, sorry about that. That was nothing to do with you and everything to do with me being an idiot. Maybe you'll let me take you out for a drink sometime to apologise.'

'Yeah, I'd like that, unless . . . look, say no if you want to but you're more than welcome to come in for a drink now if you like.'

I was seriously tempted but the more I thought about it the more sure I was that we'd both regret using the loneliness we both felt to justify falling into bed together.

'I'd love to, but I can't. I'm supposed to be up early in the morning to spend the day with my mum and stepdad. Maybe we should just exchange numbers and I'll call you some time in the week?'

Even as the taxi pulled away I knew that I wouldn't be calling her. Monday would come along and I'd look at her number sitting in my SIM card on my mobile phone and I could see myself deleting it rather than finding the courage to take a risk. Returning home from work on the Monday evening, however, I opened the front door to find a hand-delivered postcard from

Vicky on the mat. On the front of the postcard was an old black and white photograph of a elderly couple sitting at opposite ends of a park bench and on the back Vicky had written a quotation that I later learned was from Tennessee Williams: 'When so many are lonely it would be inexcusably selfish to be lonely alone.' Leaving the rest of my post on the floor at my feet I called Naomi that instant and arranged a date for the very same evening.

It had been on the eve of our fourth date that I had received the call from Chris about Paul's accident. I'd been at work, about to leave the office in order to go and meet a client, when my mobile rang. I half expected Chris to be calling on Vicky's behalf to find out how things were going with Naomi. The news had stunned me. The abruptness of Paul's death seemed to render words meaningless. I cancelled my meeting and made my way to Chris and Vicky's. That seemed the natural place to be. With my friends. With my family. It was only once I was there that it occurred to me that someone needed to let Laura know what had happened. Chris and Vicky had offered but I felt the news would only seem right coming from me. I called her mobile and left a message for her to call. I emailed her saying the same. After a few days with no response Chris and Vicky tried to contact her but with no success. I began to worry but then Chris put forward so many plausible reasons why Laura might be out of reach that even though we agonised over how hurtful it would be to receive the news via the internet, I decided to detail everything that had happened in an email to her and wait for her to get back to me. But she never did.

★ ★ ★

Parking the car in one of the streets behind St Jude's, Naomi and I walked hand-in-hand towards the church.

'We should go away after all this,' I said noticing the weather for the first time. The day was cold but dry and bright. I squeezed Naomi's hand. In a short space of time she had proved herself indispensable. I could barely believe that I had got a second chance at happiness. 'You know, just you and me, somewhere warm. Recharge our batteries.'

'That would be lovely. We could both do with getting away for a while.'

As we got closer to the church I spotted Chris, Vicky and Melissa amongst the crowd and picked up my pace but before I reached them everyone turned as one to face the road. Following their line of sight it was easy to see why: a slow-moving procession of funeral cars was making its way towards the church.

Hannah

I knew that if I looked up I would see a thousand pairs of eyes staring back at me. I knew that to everyone gathered here to say goodbye to Paul I was a lesson learned. A timely reminder of the cruel blows that life sometimes dealt — a reason never to take anything for granted. People had said as much to my face. Told me how what had happened had helped them to see the light. From now on they would change. They would love harder and stronger, vowing to make every second count. I knew they meant well, but the last thing I wanted to be considered was an example of a life lesson learned. I wasn't a plot-line on a soap opera. I wasn't the last few pages of a romance novel. This was my life. And I had lost the father of the baby that was growing inside me. I didn't have the luxury of using this experience to help me in the future. It was happening to me now.

I had been over my memories of the last few weeks of Paul's life a million times since his death. I had to do my best to preserve them permanently for both myself and the baby. Moments that at the time had seemed mundane were now amongst my most precious possessions. I couldn't afford to leave their preservation to chance, so I took control as best I could. Those long hours I had spent in bed with the curtains drawn while my parents sat downstairs worrying weren't about my resting for the baby's sake, as the series of doctors who had poked and prodded had ordered, they were about rehearsing and memorising the last remnants of Paul's life. Time that only we had shared. Moments that without my action would be forgotten forever. So, three days before the funeral on another sleepless night, I picked up a note pad and pen from beside the bed and began

a bit. If you stay she'll feel like she has to talk. If I stay she knows she won't have to say a word.'

'Are you sure?'

'I'm sure. I'll see you inside in a minute.'

Vicky gave Melissa a huge squeeze, exchanged a troubled glance with me and joined the others.

'You ought to go in,' said Melissa quietly. 'I just don't want to be in there with all those people.'

I looked at her and smiled. 'Do you want a fag?'

Melissa

I was confused. Ever since Chris and Vicky had discovered that they were going to be parents again Chris had vowed to give up smoking for good.

'You haven't started again, have you?'

'I haven't got any, mate, I just wanted to know if you wanted one.'

'Do you know how cruel it is to tease an ex-smoker like that?'

'Of course I do. That's why I did it.' Chris shoved his hands deep into his trouser pockets. 'Should we go for a walk?'

'We can't.' I looked over at the queue of people filing into the church. 'You're supposed to be the one representing us all in there.'

Chris looked at his watch. 'It doesn't start 'til eleven and it's twenty-five to now. That gives us plenty of time for a walk around the block.'

'You don't have to do this, you know.'

'Too late. I'm already doing it.'

Chris led me across the tarmacked car park to the road outside the church and turned left towards a busy-looking main road. As we passed by a set of traffic lights in our funeral attire I could see that all the drivers of the various stationary cars were watching us with moderately detached interest.

'I think we're causing quite a stir,' said Chris. 'Random funeral goers heading in the wrong direction.'

'I can't say I care what anyone thinks at the moment.'

'No, I don't suppose you do.'

We spotted the entrance to a park and Chris led me past the chipped cast-iron gates, along a narrow path with holly bushes growing on either side that eventually led to an open field.

'Shall we sit over there?' He pointed to a bench opposite a graffiti-covered fountain.

I nodded and we walked over to it and sat down. We were sharing the park with a man walking a grey terrier, a woman pushing a pram and three teenagers kicking a football. Chris turned round so that he was facing me head on. 'Everyone knows how tough this is for you, Mel.'

I shook my head. 'No they don't, Chris. Believe me when I say they really don't.'

'What makes you so sure?' asked Chris.

'Because no one knows I slept with him, Chris. No one knows that I slept with Paul on the night of Laura's party.'

258

Vicky

I felt as though my head was about to explode.

There wasn't a spare seat in the entire church. It was standing room only. I felt that everyone in the room was eyeing me suspiciously as though I had some kind of twisted ulterior motive for saving the empty seats on either side of me. In the last few minutes alone I had turned away a middle-aged couple, a teenage boy dressed in a band T-shirt and jeans, and now two pretty girls in their twenties were heading towards me at speed. I looked at my watch. The service would be starting soon. If Chris and Melissa didn't turn up immediately it would be too late.

Everyone knew how difficult this was for Melissa. Everyone knew that it must have been tearing her up inside that so much attention and sympathy was being directed towards Hannah with none left over for her. Of course Hannah was carrying Paul's child. Of course they had been living together at the time of Paul's death. But Melissa had been closer to him in spirit than anyone else. Foolishly or not she had dedicated nearly a decade of her life to loving Paul unconditionally. She had been there for him even when he hadn't deserved it. She had been his greatest supporter when everyone around had been telling her that she needed to break free. Surely that sort of love and dedication deserved recognition on this day of all days? Surely the sacrifices she had made entitled her not to be overlooked? I had said as much to Chris when Hannah had first asked him to speak at the funeral but I knew his hands were tied. Grieving pregnant girlfriend of the deceased trumped grieving ex-girlfriend every single time. There was no way round it. Publicly acknowledging Melissa's contribution to Paul's life would be seen as a slight towards Hannah. And even if Hannah didn't think that, her family and friends surely would. They would only see a pregnant woman devoid of all hope. They wouldn't want to understand the simple truth that Paul really had loved Melissa and Melissa had loved Paul.

Melissa

How had it happened — how had I come to sleep with Paul? I'd asked myself the same thing a million times in light of the fact that Billy was by far the best thing in my life. I'm guessing that the key was Paul's first words to me that night when I opened the door and he told me that he wanted to talk about 'our baby that never was'. In that instant everything that had already happened that night was wiped away. All that existed was me and Paul and a secret that I had been keeping for the longest time.

I led Paul to my bedroom so that we wouldn't be disturbed when Susie and her boyfriend returned from their night out. With the door closed we stood and looked at each other and Paul began explaining exactly what had happened with Claudia.

'I was completely out of order earlier, Mel. There's no excuse for it. No excuse at all.'

'So how did it happen then? Were you trying to get at me?'

'No, of course not. This wasn't about you, it was about me. I've had a lot on my mind and I thought that the answer was just to keep on drinking. I hadn't seen Claudia in months, but then she just came out of nowhere and was throwing herself at me at every opportunity.'

'And you just couldn't resist?'

Paul was silent.

'I don't understand why you feel the need to drink so much? Why do you feel the need to act that way?'

'Because of you,' he replied. 'Because of what you said to me the night that we split up. I thought about phoning you a million times that night and a million times every night since but could never think what to say other than that I was sorry . . . which was just too pathetic. I decided that tonight was going to be the night that I would get you to tell me. I decided that tonight would be the night that I found out the truth.'

I sat down on the edge of my bed and told him everything he wanted to know.

'It was about a week after I found out you'd cheated on me that I discovered I was pregnant. My period was late and I kept telling myself that it was probably down to the stress of the split. But eventually I could no longer ignore what had actually happened. I bought a test — I think I might even still have it in a drawer somewhere — and it told me everything I needed to know. The following morning I saw my GP and got

261

him to sign the form I needed to get referred to the clinic. The following week I walked alone to my appointment, arrived at the clinic at just after ten and by half past it was all over.'

I could see he wanted to ask why I hadn't told him, why I hadn't given him the chance to make amends. I could see that he probably even wanted to ask if I had considered even for a second about continuing with the pregnancy. But I knew he wouldn't ask any of these questions out loud. He wasn't allowed. No, that wasn't right exactly. He had disqualified himself . . . that was more accurate . . . he had disqualified himself . . . taken himself out of the running . . . invalidated any rights he might have had under normal circumstances. There could be no questioning of my actions when his own had been so selfish. I had done what I did because I'd felt utterly abandoned. I had done what I did because I knew that I was on my own. Right or wrong didn't come into it when it had been his conduct that had been the catalyst. Any guilt for our loss was his alone.

Holding me in his arms as I cried, Paul reminded me of how, back when we were first together, we used to talk about what it would be like to have kids. How we'd bring them up — righting the wrongs inflicted on us by our mums and dads — while passing on the stuff that we thought they'd done well. We used to try to picture our future kids; how they would look; how they would act; who they would be once the nurturing process was over. Sometimes he believed the fantasy and sometimes he didn't, but deep down he had always felt that one day the fantasy would become reality, even after we'd split up.

'I ruined everything, Mel,' said Paul, unable to quell the tremble in his voice. 'I ruined every last thing we had that was good. How did you stay sane through all that happened? How could you think it was possible for us to remain friends?'

I couldn't see the point of telling him the truth: that I kept him as a friend, that I believed in him and encouraged him to become a better person because of a misplaced belief that one day we might get the opportunity to make right the wrong that had blighted both our lives.

As tear after tear fell in one continuous movement, Paul lifted my chin and gently grazed his lips against my cheek. Before I knew it we were hurriedly undressing each other and I told myself that what we were doing had nothing to do with sex and everything to do with saying our final goodbye. Goodbye to everything we were and everything we'd always hoped to be. It would never happen again. But Paul was the most important person in the world to me and I'd given him up without having the opportunity to savour everything that we had been together.

Afterwards we lay in each other's arms barely breathing for fear of breaking the spell that we had created between us. I felt as though some of the burden that I had carried for so long had been lifted. I felt less weighed down, better equipped to cope with carrying on with life, more able to deal with the problems that would inevitably come my way. We hardly exchanged a word for over an hour. But as it became obvious how little time we had left, conversation seemed to spring out of nowhere. So we talked about the good times, digging up fond memories of the early days. I reminded Paul of the first Christmas day that we had shared after we moved in together. How we had ended up spending all morning in the kitchen preparing the food only to lose interest when it was finally cooked. Leaving everything to go cold in the kitchen we had camped out on the sofa until late in the evening alternating between watching TV and dozing off in each other's arms. Paul reminded me of our first holiday at a cheap out-of-season resort in Kos. It rained constantly, all the resort's bars and clubs were closed and there was only one restaurant open the whole time we were there. Yet our spirits had remained so high and we had had so much fun that Paul confessed it was the best holiday he had ever taken. On and on we had mined our history for the times that had meant the most. All the bad things had distorted our story over time, and all the good times had been almost forgotten. But in the short time allotted to us this imbalance was corrected.

It had been nearly four in the morning when I saw Paul glance anxiously at my bedside clock. Though I wanted for him to stay until morning I had already prepared myself that this couldn't happen. The look of sorrow on his face spared me any sense of rejection. This was simply one more thing outside our control. And so, closing my eyes, I kissed him one last time.

'You should go.'

Paul got dressed in the dark. As he stood by the door I sensed that he wanted to say something but couldn't find the words. Finally he moved towards the bed as though he were about to kiss me goodbye but he stopped, turned and left the room.

Chris

'I didn't know,' was all I could manage to say when Melissa finished telling me about her last night with Paul.

'No one knew,' Melissa replied. 'I didn't dare tell a soul.' She started to cry again. 'I feel so guilty, Chris. Really guilty. I didn't mean it to happen. I just wanted one last goodbye. I didn't think for a second it would end up like this.' She sobbed even harder, hiding her face in her hands.

'You and Paul . . . well, you had a connection, didn't you?' I said trying to calm her down. 'And . . . well, like you say it didn't give you a chance to say goodbye.'

'But that doesn't make it right, does it? Hannah's carrying Paul's kid. I slept with Paul knowing full well what I was doing. What kind of person does that make me?'

I thought about my own recent mistakes: all the lies and deceit I'd perpetuated just to be with Polly. 'It makes you a human being like the rest of us. Nothing more, nothing less. Just human.'

Melissa looked up at me. 'But that doesn't

make it right though, does it?' she said quietly. 'Being human is just the kind of excuse that used to trip off the tip of Paul's tongue whenever he got himself into a tight corner. Well, do you know what? That kind of excuse didn't work for him so I don't see why it should work for me either. Sometimes you can't hide behind excuses. Sometimes you just have to own up to what you've done and accept the consequences.'

With that she started crying again and I pulled her closer to me and listened to the sound of her heart breaking and I realised that she was absolutely right. Sometime you did have to own up to the things you've done. Sometimes the only thing you could do is tell the truth and accept the consequences of your actions.

Vicky

The clicking heels of the two girls in search of seats were getting closer and closer. I made one last scan of the church and saw Chris and Melissa making their way up the central aisle. The sense of relief was overwhelming and I wondered what Chris had said to persuade Melissa to come into the church. As they sat down Chris saw his friend Tony sitting with Polly and Chris's face became ashen, as though he was about to be sick.

The vicar opened the service with the hymn 'He Who Would Valiant Be' which reminded me of my youth — secondary school assemblies on cold, wet Monday mornings. Standing next to

266

my friends. Sharing a hymn book — one between two. Refusing to sing because you're fourteen and what's the point? But secretly mouthing the words anyway because you're not that much of a rebel that you're prepared to get told off for refusing to join in. How could I not have joined in with words as comforting as *'Since, Lord, Thou dost defend us with Thy Spirit, We know we at the end, shall life inherit'*? Sung in unison with the whole room grieving as one it sounded plausible. Like the truth or something near it. And I wished that I believed in the words that I sang. I wished there really was something that carried on once this life was all over, because the thought that this might be it — that one day I might say goodbye to William and Chris as I left to go to the supermarket, or to Mum's or out to get my hair cut and never see either of them again because of something as random and as pointless as a car crash — terrified me. If this was it, if this life was all you got with no second chance to be with the people who mean the most to you, then the only alternative was to cling on to William and Chris with all my strength. Cling on and never let go.

As the hymn came to a close the church fell silent and I turned to look at Chris. His eyes were closed and his breathing was deep and jagged. It must all be getting too much for him.

'Don't worry, sweetheart, everything's going to be all right,' I whispered, taking his hand in mine.

He didn't speak. But his hands were shaking and he was rocking backwards and forwards just like that time in the car. And just like before he let out a groan from deep inside his chest, pulled his hands away from me and furiously rained down a cavalcade of blows against the top of his skull as though he were trying to smash his own brains out. Everyone in the vicinity watched on in bewilderment as Cooper, Melissa and I tried calm him down. He was crying now. Awful, uncontrollable sobs that wracked his entire body. We managed to get him out of the church and I persuaded the others to go back inside. I said I would look after him. When we were alone I knelt at his feet, put my arms around his legs and held on tight. Chris took his hands away from his face and fixed me with a grief-ridden stare. 'I don't know how to say this,' he began. 'You know I love you, don't you? You, William and the baby. You're my life.' He stopped to wipe away the tears that were trickling down his face. 'It kills me to know what I've done. It kills me in a way I can't even tell you.' He bent down to pull me closer to him. I didn't resist because in an odd kind of way that I can't even begin to explain I knew exactly what was coming next.

Cooper

After the first hymn the vicar said a prayer which was followed by a reading — a passage from 1 Corinthians chapter 5. I didn't really listen to any of it though. My mind was elsewhere, wondering if my brother was okay.

I'd never seen Chris like that before. As kids it

had always been me who had been the emotional one while Chris gave the impression of being totally in control. While I had moped around in my bedroom contemplating why yet again my advances towards some unsuspecting girl had been rejected, Chris had a queue of girls desperate to go out with him. Outside the world of girls Chris always came over more confident and assured: applying for jobs for which he was way under-qualified but getting them after winning over the interview panel with his charm; talking to strangers at parties and turning them into friends who last a lifetime; and when Dad died of a heart attack it had been me and Mum who had fallen apart while Chris had held it together — contacting everyone who needed to know, making all the arrangements so that neither Mum nor I had to do a thing. So I'd always assumed that Chris was different. That he didn't feel the things that normal people felt. That he was almost superhuman. From the evidence of the day so far this was far from true. Chris was just an ordinary person who thought he had perfected the art of suppressing his emotions only to be proven wrong by time and circumstance. He was just a guy who had lost his best friend in the most terrible way and today the hurt had been too much for him to bear.

'I'm going to check on Chris and Vicky,' I whispered to Naomi as the vicar closed his bible and announced to the congregation that we would all be singing another hymn. 'You know, make sure they're all right.'

'Couldn't do any harm,' whispered Naomi. 'I

don't think he'll be in any condition to give the eulogy though, do you?'

I shrugged. I looked at the order of service in my hand. After the hymn the Vicar was going to say some introductory words then it was the eulogy. 'I'd better go. I haven't got much time if this whole thing isn't going to turn into a disaster.'

'It won't be a disaster,' said Naomi. 'I'll come with you and help make sure everything's okay.'

The congregation rose as the organist began playing the opening notes of 'Abide With Me', and we made our way to the back of the church. Everyone stared at us curious about our involvement in the earlier commotion. I did my best to keep my eyes fixed on the doors at the back.

Chris and Vicky were nowhere to be seen. I was about to check the toilets when I heard the sound of raised voices and looked through the glass doors of the church to see Chris and Vicky apparently having a violent row. A tearful Vicky was yelling at Chris to let her go while Chris was desperately clinging on to her. Over and over again he kept begging her not to go. Over and over he kept telling her that he was sorry. And while I knew that my brother would never hurt Vicky, the scene was no less disturbing especially given that she was pregnant. I stepped outside and yelled at Chris.

'What do you think you're doing?'

'Just go back inside, Coop,' he yelled. 'This has nothing to do with you. We're fine. Leave us alone, okay.'

'I'm not going anywhere.' I took a few steps closer. 'Whatever's going on there's got to be a better way than this to solve it.'

'You don't understand,' said Chris, real desperation in his voice. 'I've made a mess of everything, Coop. Everything. All I want is for her to listen. All I want is for us to talk.'

'So that you can tell me more lies?' spat Vicky. 'He's been cheating on me, Cooper. Cheating on me while I was at home looking after our child. And with Tony Palmer's girlfriend of all people. See that? He hasn't got a loyal bone in his body. He cheats on me, he cheats on his friends. It wouldn't surprise me in the least if he's cheated on you too some time in the past.' She turned to face Chris. 'You're not worthy of being a father, a friend or even a brother. You're the lowest of the low and I hope everyone learns the truth about you.'

I'd never seen Chris look so cowed. Time felt as though it was standing still. No cars drove past. No people appeared. Naomi, Chris, Vicky and I stood frozen in time. There was silence except for the faint sound of singing from inside the church.

'I never want to see you again,' said Vicky wrenching her arms from his grip. 'I don't want to look at you. I don't want to talk to you ever again.'

'You don't mean that.'

'You don't know me if you think that I don't mean what I'm saying. You don't know me at all.' She held out her hand. 'Give me the car keys now or you will regret it more than you've

271

regretted anything in your life.' Chris held out the car keys and Vicky snatched them from his open hand. 'This is your best friend's funeral, and you turn it into a mockery.'

'I just want the chance to make things right.'

'I don't care what you want,' said Vicky. 'Your wants. Your needs. They don't register with me any more. If you need anything at all from now on talk to a solicitor because I know I will be.'

Vicky walked away but Chris quickly caught up with her. 'What about you and the baby? What about William? I need to see him.' Vicky wrenched herself free again.

I decided that this had gone on long enough and grabbed my brother before he could catch up with her. Chris was taller and three years older than me and the last time we had fought had been the best part of twenty years ago. I'd barely got a single blow in before Chris had tackled me to the ground and punched me so hard in the face that my nose bled. I would have ended up with much worse had Dad not come home early from work and heard the commotion. Belting both of us around the head he managed to separate us before too much damage was done. Still, it was weeks before Chris would even sit in the same room as me and months before we exchanged a single word.

But that was then.

I'd filled out since my teenage years. I was taller, broader and stockier than he had been in his youth. If it came to blows now I was in no doubt which one of us would come off worse.

'Let her go. I mean it, Chris. Just let her go.'

I could see the dilemma play out across Chris's features. The loss of face in backing down to me, his desperate need to keep hold of Vicky, the desire to not have the whole situation spiral out of control.

'Just let her go, Chris,' I spoke, more forcefully this time. 'What if she falls? You'd never forgive yourself. So let her go while you have the chance.'

For a moment I was afraid that I was going to have to hit him but then he stepped away from us both.

'You're right, I shouldn't be like this. I'm sorry.'

He sounded defeated. As if he had nothing left to live for. Naomi put her arm round Vicky.

'Are you okay?'

'I'll be fine,' she replied. 'Things just got out of hand.'

I was unsure what to do next. I looked to Chris in the hope that he might offer some guidance but there was none. It was up to me.

'Go home, Chris. Go home before you make things worse than they already are.'

Hannah

The hymn was coming to a close when I spotted Cooper and Naomi returning to the hall. I looked around for Chris as he was supposed to be giving the eulogy but I couldn't see him anywhere. As Cooper and Naomi took their seats the vicar announced that he was now going to call on Mr Chris Cooper to come forward and share a few thoughts on behalf of all Paul's friends and family. Cooper stood up and made his way to the microphone at the front of the church, seemingly unaware of the murmurs of disquiet around him.

'Hi,' he began. 'I'm not Chris Cooper. I'm Chris Cooper's kid brother, Jamie. People don't call me Jamie though. They call me Cooper. I don't know why. I'm standing here today because my brother can't be here. I think the truth of the matter is that it got too much for him to handle. You see, Chris loved Paul like a brother. And as his actual brother I know exactly what that kind of love feels like and believe me I wouldn't trade it for the world. I'm guessing that if it was me who was supposed to be up here talking to a room full of people about how much I missed Chris . . . well, I doubt whether I'd be able to do it either. Sometimes you can be too close. Sometimes it can be a bit too raw. Love is like that. That's why Paul meant so much to us all. And all of us — his partner Hannah, his mum Eileen, dad John, and brothers Matt and Alex, his extended family back in Telford and the family of friends that he made here in Manchester — we'll all miss him every single day for the rest of our lives.' Cooper looked up from the microphone for the first time. 'Things will never be the same without Paul being here with us and nor should they. We want to miss him. We need to miss him. Because we all know this: the only things you truly miss are those that mean the world to you.'

Melissa

From the moment that Cooper said that about Chris loving Paul like a brother I had found it impossible not to keep the turmoil I was feeling in any more. I wasn't the only one. Sounds of grief were audible all around the church, from both men and women. I had never felt sadness like this before. It felt different. Sharper. More real. And the fact that I was sharing it with so many others made the emotion more intense.

As Cooper returned to his seat the vicar waited a few minutes for people to compose themselves before he stood up to address the congregation again. On behalf of Paul's family he thanked everyone for coming, gave out the address of the cemetery and signalled with a nod to the undertakers standing at the rear of the church to come to the front and remove the casket containing Paul's body. I didn't want to think about him lying in a box. I didn't want that to be the last image in my head so much that I kept my eyes fixed to the ground until I was sure the coffin had gone.

The vicar announced the final hymn, 'Amazing Grace', and as one we all rose and sang. When the vicar asked everyone to remain standing for a final prayer I said my own. I talked internally about how much I missed Paul; how I felt his absence like an ache in my heart that would never be relieved; about my regret at not having told him how much I loved him the last time we had seen each other and finally how much I wished that he was still there to talk to.

As the vicar concluded his prayer with an amen I said a loud amen of my own.

I was so wrapped in thought that I wasn't even aware that the service had finished until Naomi touched my arm. Startled, I shook my head as though trying to clear a fog but it didn't seem to want to go. People were moving around. The collective volume of a hundred separate conversations rose to deafening proportions.

I looked over to Cooper's empty seat and wondered where he could've escaped to so quickly.

'Where's Cooper?'

'Outside,' she explained. 'He said he needed some air. His eulogy was amazing, wasn't it? You could feel the whole church hanging on to everything he said. I think it was incredible for him to step after what happened with Chris and Vicky.'

'Why, what's happened to them? Haven't they come back yet?'

Naomi seemed reluctant to say anything further. 'I don't mean to be rude, Melissa. But it's not really my place to say what's gone on.'

'Vicky's my oldest friend. Just tell me what happened.'

'Maybe you should ask Cooper. He should tell you. Not me.'

I began making my way to the exit to find Cooper. Every few steps I was stopped by people I knew, people who were my friends as well as Paul's. They all said the same thing: how shocked they were by the news, how they couldn't believe he was really gone, how difficult it must be for me given the circumstances. And all I could think was, 'I need to get out of here. I need to make sure Vicky's all right.'

Eventually I made it through the rear doors and outside. Chris, Cooper and Vicky were nowhere to be seen. Standing out of the way of the stream of mourners I pulled out my phone and switched it on, conscious of its inappropriate polyphonic chime as it started up. I dialled Vicky's number but it just rang out several times before switching to her voicemail. I left a short message telling her that I loved her and asking her to ring me back when she had the chance.

I looked up at the midday sky. The grey start to the day had vanished and it was now a beautiful summer's afternoon. The sun felt warm against my skin and for a few moments I enjoyed the sensation but then a huge wave of sadness crashed over me and the tears started to fall once more. The angrier I got with myself for letting go, the more furiously they came until I took a deep breath into my lungs and held on to it with a determination that surprised me. By the time I had no option but to gasp for air, the tears had subsided.

Desperate to conceal all traces of my grief I headed towards the ladies' toilets inside the church lobby to fix my make-up. When I was a few feet away the door opened and out stepped Hannah with a well-dressed woman in her fifties. The resemblance between them was so strong that it could only have been her mother. Hannah seemed lost in a world of her own but then she met my gaze and I saw the same anguish and despair that I felt in my own soul. I wanted to say something that might alleviate her pain. But I couldn't. I stood back and watched as Hannah's mother continued with her tale of some long-forgotten relative as she guided Hannah towards the exit. I hoped Hannah might stop and turn round, might acknowledge my existence, but she didn't. As I stood there with tears of guilt welling up in my eyes, I acknowledged that had I been in Hannah's shoes I would have behaved in exactly the same way.

Three Months Later

Ed and Sharon's
New Year's Eve Party

December 2006

Melissa

For a long time after the funeral I felt as though the 'off' button for my grief had been broken or that a gear somewhere inside me had snapped. All I wanted to do was shut myself off from the world. Things with Billy weren't going well, either. I convinced myself that telling him about sleeping with Paul would hurt him too much to justify easing my conscience. So I tried to get on with the business of being a couple as best I could and for a while things were okay. We went away for a weekend, we spent time with his friends as well as mine and we even managed a trip to Ikea to buy a couple of table lamps. But whether it was my burgeoning sense of guilt or the fact that I felt wrong pretending to be happy when I quite clearly wasn't, I gradually found myself sabotaging everything good that we had. It started out with small arguments but soon progressed to whole days where I would barely say a single thing. We would've probably carried on like that for months because even though I was being horrible to him Billy was always gentle, kind and understanding, explaining away my mood swings by saying that I had been through a lot and that it was completely understandable that I wouldn't be myself for a while.

At the beginning of November, however, in the middle of a row that had started with my refusal to accompany him to a family wedding because of essay deadlines, I'd finally had enough and before I knew what I was doing I told him I'd slept with Paul on the night of Laura's party. His look of hurt is something I'll remember for the rest of my life. His first words as he recovered from the shock of my confession were: 'But I thought you were different'. It was those words that hurt the most. He was right. I'd given him the impression that I was different. I'd let him believe that I was something that I wasn't. But I wasn't different. I wasn't special. I was just like everybody else. I moved out the next day.

As for Ed and Sharon's party that year, none of us made it. Vicky and Chris were going through their separation so the last thing they wanted to do was go to a party; Cooper took up Naomi's offer to spend a few days at her uncle's cottage in Cornwall and as for me, my New Year's Eve was spent looking out of the window of my childhood bedroom watching other people's fireworks while Mum and Dad sat downstairs watching TV. When midnight came around, and rockets and explosions filled the air, I thought of the previous New Year's Eve and how hopeful it had made me feel. Suddenly I missed my friends, I missed what we all had together and I wanted to let them know how much they meant to me. I typed out a group text message on my mobile saying everything I wanted to share. But before I could press 'send' an idea hit me that made me add a final PS — after a year spent going to other people's parties, whatever my circumstances come the summer when the weather was warmer, when we'd all feel better and above all when we'd all be together, I'd finally throw a party of my own.

Seven Months Later

Melissa's Party

July 2007

Melissa

It was Saturday and I was sitting on the sofa in the living room typing out a text message: 'Am throwing a party tonight. Would love for you to come. Feel free to bring Seb and Bri and a bottle! Let me know if you're up for it and I'll send details. Xxx Mel'. The text was to Billy as he'd been on my mind ever since we had run into each other in town a few weeks earlier. It had been midday, on the day after the last exam paper of my degree, and I'd been leaving Costa Coffee near Piccadilly station, enjoying the freedom of life without exams hanging over me when I practically bumped into him. It was the first time that we had seen each other since splitting up and at first I was a bit embarrassed.

'Melissa,' he said, appearing almost equally stunned, 'how are you?'

'I couldn't be better. I finished my exams yesterday.'

'I'd forgotten about your finals otherwise I would have sent you a good luck card or something.'

'There's no need but thanks anyway.'

'How did you get on?'

I shrugged. 'I did my best and that's all you can ask, isn't it?'

'Well, congratulations anyhow. I'm sure you

did brilliantly. Any plans about what you're going to do next?'

'I'm going to work full-time at Blue over the summer to get some money to make a dent in my overdraft but otherwise I have no idea.'

'How about doing a Masters?'

'I think I'm done with education for now,' I laughed. 'I don't know . . . I'll find something.'

I told Billy I was sharing a flat in Chorlton with Laura and filled him in about Vicky, Chris and Cooper too. Billy had just been promoted to senior designer and was back living with Seb and Brian but he was getting tired of living like a student and planned to move on to something better by the end of the summer at the latest. There was no mention of him seeing anyone new and I had nothing to say on that score. Even so, there was something about his manner that made me think that he had moved on and I considered asking about Freya, but then thought better of it. At best he was being nice by not rubbing my nose in it and at worst probably didn't consider it to be any of my business whether he was seeing anyone or not and I couldn't really argue with that.

As the conversation came to an end I kept telling myself to invite him to my party. Explain that it wasn't a date and reassure him that he could bring whoever he wanted. I had a whole speech prepared if he asked what I was celebrating. 'It's sort of an all-purpose party,' I'd say. 'A house-warming party for me and Laura; a belated New Year's Eve for those who hadn't felt like having one back in December; and a last get-together for some of my university friends now that we were about to graduate. Above all it's a moving-on party: a party where everyone will put the past in the past and look forward to a brand-new future.'

I didn't say any of that of course. I tried a couple of times but I couldn't actually get out the words. Partly, I didn't want to come across like some kind of stalker, but mostly I was scared of him turning me down.

In a bid to take control of the situation I looked at my watch and said that I had to go even though I easily had another twenty minutes.

'I'd better be off too,' he said. 'It's not like my lunch is going to buy itself.'

Then with a complete lack of self consciousness, he kissed my cheek. The gesture lasted no more than a few seconds and felt as natural as breathing. Something had changed inside me. A light had been switched on. The coldness I'd felt since Paul's death began to thaw. It was as though I was springing back to life. And I felt the beginning of a sensation that I hadn't experienced for the longest time: hope.

Chris

It was just after half past ten and I was in bed in Cooper's spare room staring at the ceiling and contemplating my life. The thoughts that were my constant companions had done their usual tour of duty around my head one after the other: about the new baby and when it might arrive;

worries about how living apart from William might affect him in the future; excitement at seeing Vicky and William for our afternoon in the park; sadness at knowing that these few precious moments would be over all too soon. But of all the thoughts that went through my mind the main one was always the same: how much I loved Vicky and how much I wanted her back.

Things had been tough since the split, there was no doubt about that. On the night of Paul's funeral, with nowhere else to go, I ended up on Cooper's doorstep. Without making a single comment about what I'd done he invited me in and told me I could stay as long as I wanted. We talked a lot that night, staying up until the early hours. We talked about the funeral and how much we both missed Paul; we talked about the women in our lives and the mistakes that we felt we'd both made; and then finally, as the night sky that we had sat watching through the bay window in the living room began to lighten, we talked about our relationship with each other: stuff from the past when we were kids; long-held misconceptions; secrets shared. The evening was a revelation and changed for the better not only my opinion of Cooper but my relationship with him too.

Over the months that followed, Vicky and I met up regularly. We tried couples' counselling for a while but for every occasion that I felt as though we were close to making a breakthrough there was another when it seemed like things were irrevocably broken. The turning point was Christmas. Now that William was four, Christmas had taken on a new significance. He was getting excited about Father Christmas. He had a role as an angel in his pre-school nativity play. Christmas was no longer just a ritual to be endured but something in which he actively participated and might remember for the rest of his life. Neither Vicky nor I could stand the thought that the first Christmas he could remember would be the one that we spent as a family torn apart. So we both doubled the effort we were putting into making things work and this resulted in my moving back temporarily over the Christmas period.

And now, even though I was back living with Cooper, things were good. Not great. But good. I saw Vicky and William regularly during the week and Saturday and Sunday were always spent as a family. There were times when I felt as though we were on the verge of getting back together again, the baby growing inside Vicky drawing us closer together with each passing day, but still there was something keeping us apart, one indefinable piece of the puzzle missing. I had no idea what it was. But as I climbed out of bed, sorted out my clothes for the day and made my way to the bathroom for a shower I determined that today was going to be the day I found out.

Cooper

I was making Naomi breakfast when I heard the front door slam shut signalling that Chris had left the flat.

'How did he seem today?'

'Okay, I think,' I replied as the eggs frying in the pan in front of me began to spit. 'It's hard to tell with Chris these days. There's a lot of stuff going on with him and Vicky.' I looked at Naomi. 'If you were Vicky do you think you would take him back?'

'I don't know.'

She gave me a comforting half smile and returned to her newspaper. When the eggs were done I slipped them on to two plates already piled up with bacon, beans and white bread. It was Naomi's favourite breakfast and represented one of the things that I really liked about her: her lack of fussiness about food. Unlike Laura she didn't bang on about calories or fat content, cholesterol or the evils of hydrogenated fats.

'Mmm, that smells lovely. I can't tell you how much I love bacon.'

'You don't have to. The drool at the corner of your mouth says it all.'

'Very funny. Do you know, Coop, this is all but perfect apart from . . . '

'A lukewarm mug of tea?' I reached across to the kitchen surface and picked up the waiting mug of tea. 'Here's one I made earlier that was steaming hot and is now . . . '

'Absolutely perfect,' said Naomi taking a sip. She smiled. 'You do know that as long as you're making lukewarm tea and fry-ups like this I am never going to let you out of my clutches?'

'I wouldn't have it any other way.'

* * *

For a relationship that had started as the result of an ill-conceived blind date, I was positively amazed by how well we were getting on. Naomi really understood me. Wanted the same things as I did. We were heading in the same direction. And because all my insecurities seemed to have disappeared, I no longer felt as though I had to play the grown-up all the time. For the first time in my life I was in an equal partnership. All this would have been perfect if Laura had stayed on the other side of the world. The fact that she had been seeing someone else while she had been out there had helped things considerably. Picturing her in the arms of another bloke meant that I could feel justified in hating her. And if I hated her then I couldn't be feeling anything else.

But then Paul had died and it had completely knocked my world off its axis, churning up my insides into one big mess. I hadn't fully understood this until the moment I got Laura's call that she was home some months after the funeral. Just hearing her voice brought everything to the surface. At the time I'd kidded myself that the anger I felt towards Laura was to do with her selfishness. But over time I realised that my anger had nothing to do with Laura's behaviour and everything to do with the fact that, in some way that I couldn't quite pinpoint, I was still in love with her. This moment of self-realisation hurt. It really hurt. Partly because I had always thought that I was better than that — still being in love with an ex long after the two of you are supposed to have moved on is the biggest cliché in the book — and partly because of what this new knowledge might mean for me and Naomi. Could I carry on seeing her knowing how I felt about Laura? Would it simply be a matter of time before Laura and I eventually got back together?

I didn't know the answer nor did I want to know. The best way that I could remain in a state of blissful ignorance was to avoid Laura altogether. My plan had worked up to a point. I hadn't seen her since she had turned up to collect the rest of her things. And in the meantime I had become closer and closer to Naomi, so that I was almost convinced that what I felt for her was bigger and more intense than anything I had ever felt for Laura. But I needed to be sure. And the only way to do that would be to see Laura face to face and talk things through — something that I had been putting off. But now that Melissa's party was finally here there was nowhere left to hide. Unless I wanted to make my peace with Laura in front of all of our friends and my new girlfriend, the only option was to try to see her some time today.

★   ★   ★

'So what are you going to do while I'm in town?' asked Naomi setting her knife and fork down on her empty plate. 'You can't sit here all afternoon on your own. Why don't you join my sister and me? She won't mind, honest, she's your biggest fan.'

'I'm her biggest fan too.'

'So, you'll come then?'

'Thanks, but no thanks. I've got a lot of stuff I've been meaning to do and I think today is the day to get it done.'

Melissa

I was willing my phone to deliver a reply from Billy when Laura came into the room. Her blond hair was tied back in a ponytail and she was wearing a long slouchy grey jumper that I knew for a fact used to be Cooper's, matched with faded blue tracksuit bottoms. This was Laura's official lounging-around-the-flat outfit. It had come out every weekend since we had moved in together and for as long as she wore it you could guarantee she wouldn't be venturing outside.

'So you've done it then? Sent the dreaded text?'

I nodded. 'And I wish I hadn't now. This is torture. I sent it fifty-five minutes ago and he still hasn't replied.'

'Maybe he's taking a nap.'

'Next to his delightfully young, thin and pretty girlfriend.'

Laura laughed. 'I'm telling you he's single.'

'But you don't even know him.'

'I don't need to,' smiled Laura. 'I can just feel it in my water.'

'Well, I guarantee that the predictive skills of your water are off course this time. I know for sure that he's got a girlfriend. I just know it. I mean he was mad about that girl I told you about long before he ever met me.'

'Didn't you say that she wasn't interested in him?'

'But that was ages ago. You know how things change.'

'Okay, so maybe they have hooked up but she probably dumped him and he's been licking his wounds ever since.'

I smiled in spite of myself. I liked the idea of Billy, however unlikely, being single and sort of sad. I liked the idea that I might be the one to cheer him up. I looked over at my phone lying dormant on the table. I just knew that he wasn't going to reply to my text. 'This is ridiculous. I'm thirty-six years old and yet I'm still acting like a lovelorn teenager.' I turned off my phone.

'And when you're eighty-six, and still living in this flat with me you'll be exactly the same,' replied Laura. 'Face the facts, babe, no amount of time or experience is going to change that.'

I detected a slight cloud pass over Laura's face and guessed it had to do with Cooper. Like most warring former couples they both had their grievances and both were too proud to admit to each other that they might be wrong. Laura believed that Cooper had started it with his refusal to speak to her when she called him on her arrival back in the UK. Cooper believed that Laura had inflamed the situation a few days later by refusing to speak to him when he called her at her parents' house in Bristol to make amends. Since then, with the exception of a minor shouting match back in November on the day Laura finally moved her stuff out of the house, they had yet to say a word to each other, civil or otherwise.

'So how are you feeling about tonight?'

'About the prospect of coming face to face with Cooper and his new girlfriend? I'm fine.' She paused. 'Do you think they're right for each other?'

'They seem okay to me.'

'I know that but, you know, do you think they'll go the distance?'

'None of us has got a crystal ball. If I did I'd be looking into it right now trying to see what Billy's up to.'

'You're right. We're far too old for this. I'm going to make myself a coffee, do you want one?'

I declined her offer and she got up and went to the kitchen leaving me to return to the note pad I'd been using to write down a list of the remaining things we needed to do for the party. Only one item had a tick against it: 'Send text message inviting Billy to party.'

'Once I've had breakfast I am completely at your disposal,' Laura called from the kitchen. 'Feel free to order me about any way you like. Any post yet?'

'I heard it drop through the letterbox a while ago but I was too busy willing my phone to do something to go and get it.'

Checking that my Saturday morning ensemble — faded hooded blue sweatshirt combined with red-checked over-sized men's pyjama bottoms and cow-print socks — was okay for a journey on which I might encounter people from the neighbouring flats, I made my way out to the communal hallway.

Lying directly underneath the letterbox was a large heap of post which I sorted into three piles.

The guys upstairs had a few bills and a reminder from the TV licensing people; the trendy couple on the middle floor had bills, bank statements and stack of credit-card applications; Laura and I had a couple of official-looking letters, a gas bill, a promotional offer from Habitat and a handful of letters that had their original address blacked out with marker pen and replaced with our current one.

'Anything good?' asked Laura as I returned to the flat.

'Same old same old really.'

'Anything for you?'

'Just bills, circulars and some stuff that Susie forwarded.' I flicked through my post plucking out anything that wasn't a bill. The first letter in a plain white envelope was from my university asking me if I wanted to sign up for the alumni newsletter. The second letter in a brown envelope was from the police relating to a statement that I had given them back in October when I had spotted a group of kids breaking into a car round the corner from us. They had arrested a number of suspects in relation to the crime and requested that I be available the following Wednesday in order to view them in a police line-up. The third letter was in a white A5-sized envelope and even though Susie had covered over the original address I could still just about make out the handwriting. I didn't recognise it but it looked feminine. I was intrigued. I opened it up and was surprised to find that the only thing inside was a photograph of a smiling baby. A baby girl — fair hair,

298

grey-green eyes and wearing a pale yellow polka-dot sleep suit. I checked inside the envelope again. It was empty. I turned over the photograph and in the same handwriting as on the front of the envelope were the words: Bethany Georgina Bannister. I turned it over again and stared at the baby. There was no doubting her parentage. The shape of the eyes and the chin were unmistakable.

'What is it?' asked Laura, glancing up at me. 'Are you all right?'

I handed her the photograph and her eyes widened just as mine had done. 'Is this from who I think it's from?'

I nodded. 'It's definitely a picture of Paul and Hannah's baby.'

Vicky

It was just after midday when Chris, William and I arrived at Pizza Hut for lunch. The restaurant was heaving with parents and their offspring and the staff appeared rushed off their feet.

'I knew we should have gone somewhere else. It's always busy in here.'

'It'll be fine,' said Chris. 'Anyway, we're here now.'

'But we could be waiting for who knows how long?'

'And what if we do? William had an ice cream not ten minutes ago, you hate pizza and I'm not that hungry anyway.'

Chris was right. It wasn't really as though any

of us were hungry. I wondered what was really bothering me and was inundated with potential answers. There was the fact that I was standing when I wanted to sit down. There was the fact that every day this week I'd woken up feeling nauseous and was having to guzzle Pepto-Bismol like it was going out of fashion. And there was the fact that I was shattered because William had woken me up at twenty to five to ask me where foxes go in the daytime and then refused to go back to sleep.

But what was unsettling me above all else was that despite already having endured the kind of disheartening, misery-inducing and all-over crappy beginning to a day that would normally see me spiralling towards the black clouds of depression, I couldn't help but notice that I was actually happy.

From the moment that Chris arrived and got William ready while I made myself a quick breakfast, I was happy. All the time William was playing monsters with Chris while I got dressed without any interruptions, I was happy. I was happy even though it had been raining when we left and William had insisted on going to the local park rather than Tumble Jungle. And now, as we stood in a crowded pizza restaurant — the kind I had always vowed that I would never set foot in before I had children — waiting for a table that might never materialise I realised that even this hadn't taken the shine off the happiness I felt at being in the company of the two people that I loved the most.

A young girl in her late teens, with tied-back

hair beneath a Pizza Hut baseball cap, came over and smiled. 'Sorry for the wait. We're just preparing a place for you.' One of her colleagues gave her the nod and she led us to our table.

The waitress quickly set out our cutlery and asked us if we wanted anything to drink. We ordered and said we wanted the 'all you can eat' buffet and once we'd got our drinks we stood up to get our food (three slices of ham and pineapple for William, two slices of cheese and tomato and some potato salad for Chris and pasta salad for me).

William picked up a slice of ham and pineapple only marginally smaller than his head and said: 'I love pizza.'

'Really? I'd never have guessed.'

William nodded. 'Do you like pizza, Daddy?'

'I love pizza.'

'Do you love pizza more than you love Mummy?'

I was pleased to see that Chris was wearing the same 'where do these questions come from?' expression on his face as me.

'No, sweetie, I don't love pizza more than I love Mummy,' he said. 'I love Mummy much more.'

It was all I could do not to burst into tears.

Melissa

I walked the few dozen yards into Grange Road and came to a halt outside the house that I had shared with Paul all those years ago. Everything about it was different from how I remembered. The outside woodwork was freshly painted and the front door had changed from dark green to brick red; the once neglected tiny front garden had been tamed and the privet hedge carefully trimmed. What surprised me most, however, was the 'For Sale' board in the front garden with a small 'Sold' sign fixed diagonally across it.

I took a deep breath, rang the doorbell and waited. I heard the sound of footsteps hurriedly making their way across bare floorboards and then Hannah opened the door.

She looked just as pretty as I remembered her. Her hair was tied back in a ponytail and she was wearing a blue striped top and jeans. She didn't look like a woman with a young baby at all. She looked like me when I was her age.

'Hi,' I said, unsure of what I wanted or was going to say. 'I'm really sorry if I've disturbed you, Hannah, and I know this must seem really odd but — '

'Really, Melissa, it's okay. I'm glad you're here. Please come in.'

I followed her through the hall towards the front sitting room. The inside had been freshly decorated too and the sitting room was barely recognisable.

'Looks like you've done a lot of work here.' I took a seat in a red velvet armchair next to the fireplace. 'It looks amazing.'

'Paul did most of it,' replied Hannah, sitting opposite me. 'When I moved in he said it was a good excuse to do all the things he'd always been meaning to.'

'Well, he did a good job. But now you're moving?'

Hannah nodded. 'I thought I'd be all right here on my own. I thought it would be good for Bethany to be here. But . . . there are just too many memories. Everywhere I go. Everywhere I look.' She looked directly at me. 'There are times when I'm sitting here and I look at the clock on the wall and I find myself thinking — just for a fraction of a second — Paul will be home in a while, I'll start cooking supper. And I'm almost up and into the kitchen before I remember that he isn't ever coming home. It's mad, isn't it?'

'No,' I replied, 'it's not mad, Hannah.'

'Do you miss him?' She was unafraid to hold my gaze. I was afraid this was a trick question and my anxiety must have been written all over my face because she added quickly, 'It's okay, I'm not going to jump down your throat or anything. I just want to know that I'm not alone in this, that's all.'

I concentrated on a large knot in the wood of the bare floorboards just in front of her feet.

'No, you're not alone. I miss him every single day, Hannah, and sometimes I don't think it's ever going to stop.'

Cooper

Laura was sitting at a table in the window, a cappuccino in front of her, by the time I arrived at Blue-Bar. She hadn't noticed me so I stood watching her for a few moments as she reached across to the middle of the table to a glass container stuffed with sugar sachets. She picked out a brown one, tore it open and carefully scattered the contents over the top of her cappuccino with a smile on her face that suggested she was taking great pleasure in watching the tiny bronze crystals sink into their liquid surroundings. She must have sensed that she was being watched because she looked up and smiled, so I walked over and after a brief embrace sat down in the seat opposite her.

'I'm really glad that you called,' she said. 'I hated the way that things ended.'

'Me too.'

Laura held out her hand for me to shake. 'Friends?'

'Of course.'

'Good.' She narrowed her eyes in a comically evil fashion, 'Because you don't want me as an enemy! You wouldn't believe the sheer evilness of some of the thoughts I've had about you.'

'Do you know what? The funny thing is I would.'

As I took off my jacket a huge smile broke across Laura's face.

'What?'

'I'm just glad to see that T-shirt you're wearing is still in active service.'

'This old thing? It was the only thing that was clean.'

Laura looked crestfallen. 'I bought you that.'

'I was just joking about the ironing thing. Truth is I automatically reached for it this morning when I was getting ready. Must be my subconscious messing with me, what do you reckon? I notice yours didn't make you wear that Jigsaw top I bought you the Christmas before last.'

'It did but I ignored it. The last thing I need at my age is to begin taking style advice from my subconscious.'

Laura caught the eye of one of the waitresses and beckoned her over. I ordered a large coffee and two blueberry muffins.

'Why do you order two? I won't eat it, you know.'

'So that you won't break bits off mine every five seconds like we both know you will.'

'Guilty as charged but just be aware that even if I do eat this muffin I'll probably still steal some of yours.'

As we waited for our order we caught up with the stories of each other's lives.

'I'm working at H&M in town,' she sighed, 'but only until I've scraped together enough cash to pay off some of the debts that I built up while I was away. Today's my day off.'

'And after that? Is it back to the yoga?'

'I'm actually thinking about going back to college or something. Melissa's been a real inspiration on that front — thanks to her I feel like it's not too late to make a change so maybe I'll do a drama degree or even something completely different like photography.'

'I could really see you being a cool fashion photographer.'

Laura pulled a face. 'I'm not sure I can myself. Plus I doubt whether many of fashion's elite photographers started their careers at the age of thirty-eight which is how old I'll be by the time I've finished my foundation course, managed to find a college that actually might accept me and completed the degree. Maybe I should go back to teaching yoga after all.'

The waitress arrived with my coffee and our muffins and I finally plucked up the courage to ask her the question that I most wanted answered.

'So did you find what you were looking for?'

'How do you mean?'

'On your travels.'

'It wasn't about finding myself,' she said quietly. 'It was about doing something different.'

'With someone different?' I was still holding her gaze. 'I know all about the guy you met while you were out there. And before you ask no one told me. I worked it out. Your whole going around the world thing had nothing to do with finding yourself and everything to do with wanting to get away from me. How do you think that made me feel when I was ready to spend the rest of my life with you?' Much to my own surprise my voice was raised and almost angry. 'I can't believe you thought so little of me and what we had.'

'I did love you, Coop,' replied Laura. 'I did cherish what we had. I just couldn't be sure, that's all. I couldn't be sure whether it was what I really wanted or whether I was choosing it because I was scared to be alone. And I *was* scared to be alone. I've always been scared about being alone. You were right! All my life I've been surrounded by friends and family — people who I know will look after me if life ever gets too tough. That's why I decided to go travelling. I wanted to prove to myself that I could do things on my own. And do you know what? I managed just under a week alone before I couldn't stand it any more. That's why I got together with someone, Coop — because I was just too scared to be on my own. I don't have what it takes to be independent. And even though sometimes being with him made me feel lonelier than ever, at least I wasn't alone. At least there was someone near.'

'And what about the funeral? Why didn't you return anyone's calls? Why was it okay to make everyone have to worry about you when there were other things — real things — that we needed to be focused on instead?'

Laura pushed her cappuccino to one side. 'I feel terrible about that, Coop. I know I should've called. I should've contacted you straight after you left the message telling me Paul had died. But I just couldn't do it. When I read your email I went into complete shock. And I knew if I called you, Vicks, Mel or Chris, then it would become real. Too concrete. But if I stayed where I was . . . if I didn't contact you guys . . . well, then I could pretend it wasn't real. It would just be a sad story happening on the other side of the world which had no bearing on my life. And if that sounds selfish . . . well, I wanted to be selfish. So I ran away. Moved from Thailand to Australia to try and put as much distance as possible between me and this horrible reminder of the seriousness of life.'

Melissa

Throughout all the time that Hannah and I spent talking in her front room she hadn't alluded to the photograph or the reason she had sent it. It didn't matter. All that mattered was that the photograph hadn't been sent in spite; in fact it might have been the opposite — as an olive branch of sorts — the signal of a desire for us to make peace.

We talked a great deal. About things connected with Paul and things beyond him too. Hannah shared with me her plans for the future. With the proceeds of the house sale combined with Paul's life insurance she had decided to buy a house near her parents' home in Worcestershire. She wasn't sure that the move would be permanent but for the time being it seemed to be the best avenue open to her. Sensing the doubt in her voice, I wanted to assure her that her plans made perfect sense but a small child's wail crackled through the baby monitor cutting me off. Hannah explained that Bethany was due her next feed and disappeared only to return the best part of half an hour later with Bethany in her arms.

'And here she is.'

I walked over and peered at the bundle in her arms. Bethany was beautiful. Really beautiful. She looked like Paul and she looked like Hannah and just seeing her so small and so tiny, representing the last remaining part of Paul in the world, made me want to smile and cry at the same time.

'Would you like to hold her?' She passed Bethany to me and I sat back down in the chair and lost myself in her eyes.

I stayed at Hannah's for nearly an hour. Though I was pleased that Hannah and I had made our peace we were never going to be best friends and the last thing I wanted was to overstay my welcome. Just as I was about to make my retreat Hannah took a deep breath and fixed me with her own grey-green eyes.

'Say no if this in any way makes you feel uncomfortable. And I know I have absolutely no right to ask . . . but I was wondering whether you'd been to visit Paul's grave since the funeral . . . and well, if you hadn't . . . I was wondering whether you'd come with me today. I've been meaning to go but I just couldn't seem to find the strength. Mum and Dad offered to go with me a million times but I always found an excuse. But sitting here with you . . . I don't know . . . I feel like I'm ready to see him. Does that make sense?'

'Yes, I've been meaning to go myself but I've been too scared to go on my own.'

'So will you come with me?'

For a moment or two all I could hear was the sound of my heart beating in my chest. 'I will,' I replied. 'Of course I will.'

Cooper

It was fast approaching three o'clock. Naomi would be coming back from her trip to town soon and I wanted to be there. I'd made up my mind to tell her about my meeting with Laura and the reasons behind it.

I began trying to bring things to a close with Laura. 'It's been really nice but I'm going to have to go.'

'Of course. What time are you getting to the party tonight?'

'About eight. It's good that we've been able to do it. It's been tough, hasn't it? Everything has been really tough. And I've been looking forward to this party. To start living again.'

'You're absolutely right. And it's not just you who feels it. You know how usually when you throw a party, the closer it gets the more texts you get from people dropping out? This has been the opposite. All week I've been snowed under with messages from mates promising they'll come. Tonight's going to be special. I know it.'

Melissa

Hannah and I pulled up on the gravel drive of Buxton Road Cemetery. As Hannah climbed out of the car I leaned back to take a peek at Bethany happily gurgling away in her car seat before helping Hannah load her into the pram. Then with me pushing the pram and Hannah holding the bouquet of flowers that we had bought — freesias, stargazer lilies, spray carnations and a large-headed pink rose — we set off on our journey.

It was odd being back at the cemetery. There

had been so many people here at the burial that thankfully I barely saw anything of what was going on. Lost inside the crowd, one of many, I could close my eyes and listen to the sounds around me: snatches of the vicar leading the service, the breeze blowing through the leaves on the trees and the tears of those for whom the day was beginning to take its toll. I'd felt blissfully divorced from the proceedings. I'd felt free. But that was then. And now Hannah and I were standing in front of Paul's headstone.

Hannah turned round and placed my hand on the bouquet so that we could jointly lay the flowers at the foot of Paul's grave.

'We've got to move on,' she said. 'We've both got to let go. And we've got to do it now because we might never find the strength to do it later.'

Cooper

Naomi was not taking the news that I'd spent the afternoon with Laura quite as well as I'd hoped for.

'You did what?' She put down her mug of tea on the kitchen counter.

'I spent the afternoon with Laura.'

'While I was in town with my sister?'

I nodded.

'So what is it you're saying exactly? That she called and asked you to meet up with her?'

I said I wished it had been that simple. 'No, it was me who called her. I wanted the two of us to sort things out before the party tonight.'

'Well, I'm thrilled for you,' snapped Naomi. 'And I sincerely hope the two of you will be happy together.'

She left the room, slamming the door behind her, and by the time that I caught up with her she was about to walk through the front door.

'Naomi,' I yelled. 'Will you just stop for a second?'

'What? So that you can break the news that you're getting back together? I thought you were one of the good ones, Cooper.'

'But I am,' I protested.

'Then you wouldn't have gone to see her behind my back, would you? What was I? Your back-up plan in case she didn't want you back when she finally came home? I always knew that you weren't quite as over her as you made out and now I've got the proof. How could I have been this stupid?'

'Move in with me,' I said quietly.

Naomi stopped and stared.

'What do you mean?'

'I mean exactly what I've just said. I was going to wait until after the party tonight to suggest it but since you've got a gun to my head I'll say it now: come and live with me.' I reached into my pocket and handed her a small velvet box.

Naomi bit her lip. 'I don't understand.'

'Just open it.'

She opened the box and a huge smile spread over her face. 'It's a key.'

'To be precise it's a key to my house. And it's yours for as long as you want it.'

'Are you sure?'

'I've never been more sure of anything.'

'So what was this afternoon all about? Why did you feel the need to keep your meeting with Laura a secret?'

'That was me not wanting you to worry about something that you had absolutely no reason to worry about. But if you want — with the exception of birthdays, Christmas and occasional surprises of a favourable nature — I can promise you that this will be my first and last ever lie of omission. What do you say?'

Naomi just grinned, put the key back in the box and kissed me.

Melissa

It was nearly four by the time Hannah and I arrived back in Chorlton. After helping her inside the house with all Bethany's things I gave the baby one last squeeze before hugging Hannah goodbye.

'Thanks for everything you've done today,' she said.

'It was my pleasure,' I replied. 'It has been good for me . . . so thank *you*.'

I'd neglected to make any mention of the party because it seemed inappropriate but now that I was preparing to leave I wanted to invite her, even though I was sure she wouldn't come.

'Look, Hannah, I'm throwing a party tonight,' I began, as she rocked the baby in her arms, ' . . . nothing special really . . . just a bunch of friends too old to go out clubbing any more

313

getting together for some food and drinks . . . and maybe a little dancing. Anyway, I'd love it . . . if you felt up to it and can find a baby sitter . . . anyway . . . what I'm trying to say is that I'd love it if you'd come and of course feel free to bring any of your friends . . . but obviously I'd completely understand if you didn't want to.'

'It feels like a lifetime since I went out without Bethany,' smiled Hannah, 'and as for drinking and dancing I can't even remember what those are. But if I can get a sitter then yes, I'd love to come.'

✳ ✳ ✳

Feeling relieved that the afternoon had gone so well I headed towards the high street, suddenly realising that there were a million things to do for the party and only a few hours left to do them. As I scanned my list my eyes lingered on the item that I'd crossed off this morning: 'Send Billy a text inviting him to the party.' Reaching into my bag I pulled out my phone and switched it on for the first time since this morning. I'd received seventeen text messages and three voicemail messages but although they were all related to the party none of them was from Billy.

I felt sick. It had been over six hours since I'd sent him the text so he'd obviously received it and decided for whatever reason not to reply. And I began to wonder how I could have been so ridiculously optimistic as to think that he might still be interested after the way that I had treated him. That day when I'd bumped into him in town, more than likely he was just being polite. And now I had invited him to a party and he was probably fully aware that it was *significantly* more than just an invitation to a party, which was why he hadn't replied.

There was little that I could do to save my dignity other than keep my head down and hope that I didn't bump into him again but that didn't stop me altering my course towards his house. I had no idea what I was going to say. And it was unlikely that he would even be in. Something inside me made me want to at least try to see him. At the very least I wanted the opportunity to tell him . . . what exactly? That I'd spent the afternoon with my ex-boyfriend's partner and their baby? That now I'd visited Paul's grave I was ready to move on? That I was sorry for the way I'd behaved when we were together and now I wanted his forgiveness?

It all seemed too ridiculous. Too unreal. The kind of thing that only happened in films. Why should he drop everything to be with me? Was I really such a catch that he would even bother giving me the time of day? I didn't have a single answer to any of the questions that were chipping away at my confidence. All I knew was that I needed to talk to him face to face and whatever would be would be.

It was odd that after all these years my story with Paul had come to such a strange close. From those early days when we'd first met to the moment before things had finally fallen apart, our relationship had been a complete and utter rollercoaster. Being with him had made life seem exciting. Being his friend had been a thrill. But I always knew that love itself wasn't enough. We needed a fresh start, a clean slate, the opportunity to start over as if we were two different people. But we could never be different people. Not with all the baggage and the history between us. We'd spoiled things too much to ever make things right. Our only hope for true happiness would be to find love with someone other than each other.

Outside Billy's house, my heart was thumping so quickly I thought that I might pass out. Here I was, a thirty-six-year-old woman, standing on the doorstep of a man more than ten years my junior hoping beyond hope that he might find it in himself to forgive me and take me back. How had this happened? How had I become this person? I didn't know and I didn't care. Despite every single lie that I had told myself since bumping into Billy my true feelings were finally being outed. I loved Billy. I didn't know whether the age-gap thing was going to be a problem. I didn't know whether he had a girlfriend. I had no idea how he felt about me. But what I did know was this: thinking about Billy made me feel hopeful about the future and if there was a chance that he might take me back then I was prepared to take it.

Concentrating on the second-floor window that I thought belonged to his flat I could see signs of life so made my way up to the front door. I was about to press the buzzer for Billy's flat when I saw a movement through the frosted glass so I knocked on the letterbox several times and took a step back as the front door opened.

It was a couple I'd never seen before. The guy was wearing a green tracksuit top and behind him stood a girl in a grey hooded sweatshirt.

'Hi . . . look, I'm sorry,' I began nervously, 'I'm trying to get hold of my friend Billy. He lives here. One of the flats on the second floor. He's tall and he's got dark hair and I just wondered — '

'Do you mean that guy?' The girl gestured behind me.

I turned round to see Billy standing at the bottom of the path. He was dressed in jeans and the T-shirt that he had been wearing the night we first met. In his left hand were a number of carrier bags and in his right hand was the hand of a girl that I instantly recognised as Freya.

The couple who'd answered the door brushed past me and made their way down the path. Billy stood out of the way to let them past.

'Melissa.' Billy let go of Freya's hand. 'What are you doing here?'

'Nothing,' I replied trying my best to hold it all together. 'I've made a mistake. A really big mistake. And I ought to be going.'

'Hang on a moment.' He fished in his pocket, pulled out his keys and handed them to Freya. She took them and made her way up the path looking straight through me as though I wasn't even there.

Billy and I stood in silence. I couldn't believe that I'd been so stupid. That I'd done such a good job fooling myself that us getting back together might have been possible.

'This is really difficult for me, Mel,' he said quietly. 'I don't know what to say.'

'Then don't say anything,' I replied, trying my best not to cry. 'Just be happy and enjoy every second. Because do you know what? It's the greatest feeling in the world to have your dreams come true. The greatest feeling ever. And if I could wish that kind of happiness on anyone I really couldn't think of anyone I'd rather wish it on than you.'

Vicky

When we arrived home I invited Chris in for a coffee. We all took off our outside clothes and shoes and William announced that he wanted some quiet time, which was his way of saying he wanted to watch TV when he knew that he'd already seen too much that day. As I had a lot on my mind I agreed, arranged him on the sofa, swapped The Wiggles DVD for Balamory, pressed play and then called Chris to follow me into the kitchen.

I began sorting out mugs for the coffee and asked Chris to wash out William's Thomas the Tank Engine beaker and fill it with water while I began searching around in the cupboard for the 'good' coffee rather than using the no-name supermarket stuff sitting on the counter. I finally located it and was about to plunge a spoon through the gold foil covering the mouth of the jar when Chris said my name and I turned round to see him clutching William's soap-sud-laden beaker in his hands.

'You're dripping,' I said, looking down at the pool of suds on the floor.

'I know,' he said flatly. 'What are we doing, Vick?'

'What do you mean? You're washing up and I'm — '

I stopped suddenly as I realised what he was getting at. Chris put the cup down and put his arms round me.

'I know this situation is all my fault,' he began, 'I know it. And I know I've got no right to tell you when or how you should put this in the past. But when we're getting on better than we have done in ages and we both know that the new baby is going to be the best new start that we could ever have imagined, why is it that there's still something that's stopping us from getting past what happened? Something that doesn't seem to be going away.'

'Because there is,' I sighed putting down the coffee jar. 'But it isn't something you don't know about. It's something that's been there right from the start. I love you, Chris. I haven't stopped loving you all this time. And I don't doubt that you love me and that you want it to work as much as I do. And that's why this hurts so much.'

'What?'

'I don't think I can do this, Chris. I don't think I can take you back.'

'But why? I don't understand. I've done everything you asked. What else is there?'

'Trust. I just don't trust you any more and I'm not sure that I know how to. I've really tried but it just won't come.'

'Then stop trying,' said Chris. 'Don't force it. If you don't want us back together until it's there then that's fine by me. I'll wait for you as long as it takes, Vick, whether it's one year or twenty. It doesn't matter. All that matters is that we never give up on each other.'

Melissa

I can't say that it didn't hurt knowing that Billy had moved on. And I can't honestly say that I was pleased that he had found happiness because truthfully I'm not that nice a person. The best I could say was that, in my head at least, I really did want him to have the best life possible because he was one of the most amazing people I've ever met. Maybe one day — in the not too distant future — my heart would feel the same way. In the meantime I decided that the best thing would be to put all thoughts of Billy to the very back of my mind until I could deal with them and instead concentrate on the fact that I had a party to throw.

Getting back to the flat just after five I was relieved to see that Laura had taken it upon herself to get all the shopping. As I helped her unpack she told me about her afternoon with Cooper and in return I told her about Hannah and going to the cemetery and the thing that had just happened with Billy. We both shed a few tears because it was that kind of moment and then Laura said we should consider that a line had been drawn under the mess that had been our lives for so long and from this moment forward things were going to be different. Our first act as the new and improved versions of ourselves should be to proclaim a ban on all relationships until we'd got our acts together. I said I was pretty sure I could hold out until the end of the year but that I had my doubts whether she could even last out until the end of the party!

★　★　★

The party was everything I hoped it would be and more. People started arriving just after eight and by ten o'clock you couldn't have shoe-horned a single extra person into the flat. On the far side of the room by the TV, Cooper was holding court in an animated manner with a bunch of my friends from Blue-Bar while Naomi lingered by his side. In the kitchen behind me a stunning-looking Hannah and some of her friends were laughing and joking with each other, while puffing frantically on Marlboro Lites and knocking back plastic cups of white wine. And in the middle of the room that had been designated as the dance floor, Chris, Vicky and Laura were throwing shapes with dozen of others as though there was no tomorrow.

Working the party in full hostess mode I made sure to talk to as many of our friends as I could physically manage and caught up with all their news. Cathy and Brendan had split up their band but were planning on teaching music at youth clubs, my friend Lewis had managed to secure his first-ever show at a gallery in the city centre and invited me to the opening night, Carl and Louisa told me that their daughter Tamsin had just turned one, and shared the news that Louisa was six weeks pregnant with their second child, Manjeet and Aaron had moved back from London and were getting married; Joel and Rowena had split up and Tina (formerly of Tina and Alan and then later of Tina and Susan) was now back with Alan and was awaiting publication of her first novel.

Minutes before midnight just as the party seemed to be hitting its height Alistair and Baxter — who were once again doing a sterling job of providing a bunch of thirty-somethings with the perfect soundtrack to let their hair down to — segued the music from 'Groove Is In The Heart' to 'Rock'n Roll Star' — and I found myself thinking that this was one of those rare moments in life when everything suddenly comes together and you know without any shadow of a doubt that this, what you're feeling right now, is what it feels like to be happy. What's more you become aware that life won't be like this tomorrow, the day after, or even the day after that, but that makes you appreciate it all the more. As long as you know that every once in a while someone somewhere will get it into their heads to throw a bunch of friends, cheap booze and good music together, you can be sure that no matter what life throws at you everything will be okay in the end.

As 'Rock 'n' Roll Star' came to its victorious conclusion, instead of going straight into another song Alistair and Baxter turned off the music until they had the attention of everyone in the room. They each grabbed a can of Foster's from the side of their decks, opened them in unison and, holding them aloft, yelled across the room 'To absent friends!' and we all raised our bottles and glasses in the air. For a few minutes afterwards no one moved; everyone seemed to be looking to Alistair and Baxter to see what would happen next. Baxter gave me a sly wink and nudged Alistair who reached across to his record box, pulled a twelve-inch single out of its sleeve and laid it gently on the turntable. 'Live Forever' came out of the speakers and, feeling as though I'd finally been set free, I set down the drink in my hand and along with everyone in the room closed my eyes and sang my heart out.

Acknowledgements

Thanks to the following: Sue, Swati and everyone at Hodder (for all their hard work); Simon and all at United Agents (for that thing that they do); Jane B.E. (for being the second best decision I ever made); Richard C and Louise N (for a great idea); the Sunday Night Pub Club (for existing); Vic, Elt, Math, James, Ange and Mike (for the SingStar competitions); the board (for the PLR parties); Jackie, Danny and Nadine (for excelling in loveliness); The McCabester (for always being entertaining); John and Sue (for the kid Kieran); Sharon F (for tip top advice) and finally, Team Gayle in all its many guises. Cheers to you all!

We do hope that you have enjoyed reading this large print book.

Did you know that all of our titles are available for purchase?

We publish a wide range of high quality large print books including:
Romances, Mysteries, Classics
General Fiction
Non Fiction and Westerns

Special interest titles available in large print are:
The Little Oxford Dictionary
Music Book
Song Book
Hymn Book
Service Book

Also available from us courtesy of Oxford University Press:
Young Readers' Dictionary
(large print edition)
Young Readers' Thesaurus
(large print edition)

For further information or a free brochure, please contact us at:
Ulverscroft Large Print Books Ltd.,
The Green, Bradgate Road, Anstey,
Leicester, LE7 7FU, England.
Tel: (00 44) 0116 236 4325
Fax: (00 44) 0116 234 0205

Other titles published by
The House of Ulverscroft:

WISH YOU WERE HERE

Mike Gayle

After ten years together, Charlie Mansell has been dumped by his live-in girlfriend Sarah. All he wants to do is wallow in misery, but mates Andy and Tom have a better idea: a week of sun, sea and souvlaki in Malia — party capital of the Greek islands. But Charlie and his mates aren't eighteen any more. Or even under thirty. And it shows. It isn't the cheap beer, the late nights or even the fast-food that's the problem. It's girls. And life. And most of all . . . each other.

BRAND NEW FRIEND

Mike Gayle

When Rob's girlfriend asks him to leave London and live with her in Manchester, it means leaving behind his best mate in the entire world. Believing that love conquers all and confident that he'll meet new mates, Rob takes the plunge. Six months in, and yet to find even a drinking buddy, Rob realises that making friends in your thirties is not easy, so his girlfriend places an ad in the classifieds. Three excruciatingly embarrassing 'bloke dates' later, he's on the verge of despair . . . until his luck changes. There's just one problem. Apart from knowing less than nothing about football and the vital statistics of supermodels, Rob's new friend has a huge flaw. She's a girl . . .